T0365851

CITADEL OF ICE

Life and death in a glacier fortress during World War I

Robie Macauley and Cameron Macauley

iUniverse books may be ordered through booksellers or by contacting:

iUniverse
1663 Liberty Drive
Bloomington, IN 47403
www.iuniverse.com
844-349-9409

Because of the dynamic nature of the Internet, any web addresses or links contained in this book may have changed since publication and may no longer be valid. The views expressed in this work are solely those of the author and do not necessarily reflect the views of the publisher, and the publisher hereby disclaims any responsibility for them.

Any people depicted in stock imagery provided by Getty Images are models, and such images are being used for illustrative purposes only.
Certain stock imagery © Getty Images.

Map design by the author.
Cover photographs taken by Leo Handl, 1917. Used by permission of Michael Wachtler, Archiv de Bernardin-Wachtler.

ISBN: 978-1-6632-6716-0 (sc)
ISBN: 978-1-6632-6717-7 (hc)
ISBN: 978-1-6632-6718-4 (e)

Library of Congress Control Number: 2024924678

Print information available on the last page.

iUniverse rev. date: 01/15/2025

For Alex and Angela.

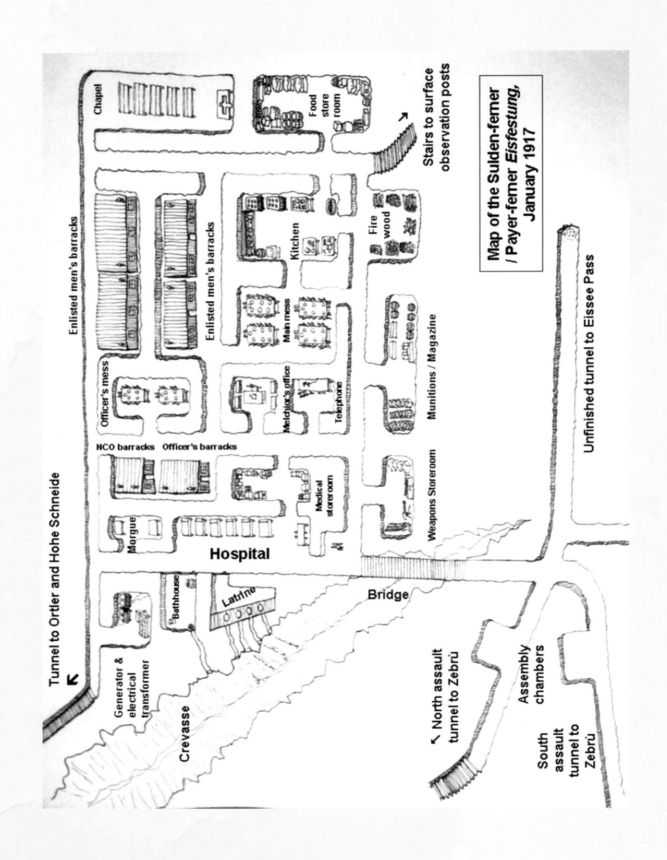

Map of the Sulden-ferner / Payer-ferner *Eisfestung*, January 1917

Tunnel to Ortler and Hohe Schneide

Enlisted men's barracks

Chapel

Food store room

Stairs to surface observation posts

Enlisted men's barracks

Officer's mess

Kitchen

Fire wood

Main mess

NCO barracks   Officer's barracks

Melchior's office

Telephone

Munitions / Magazine

Morgue

Medical storeroom

Hospital

Weapons Storeroom

Generator & electrical transformer

Bathhouse

Latrine

Bridge

Crevasse

North assault tunnel to Zebrù

Assembly chambers

South assault tunnel to Zebrù

Unfinished tunnel to Eissee Pass

iv

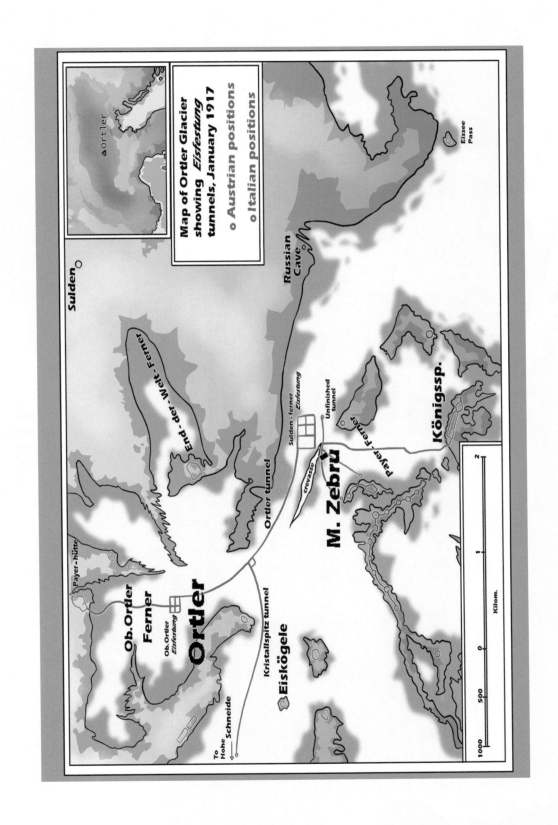

Map of Ortler Glacier showing *Eisfestung* tunnels, January 1917

○ Austrian positions
○ Italian positions

Sulden ○

Ortler

Ob. Ortler Ferner

Payer - hütte

Ob. Ortler
Eisfestung

Kristallspitz tunnel

Eiskögele

To
Hohe — Schneide

End - der - Welt - Ferner

Ortler tunnel

Sulden - ferner
Eisfestung

crevasse

M. Zebru

Unfinished
tunnel

Payer - Ferner

Russian
Cave

Eissee
Pass

Königssp.

1000   500   0   1   2
Kilom.

Contents

ACKNOWLEDGMENTS

My profound gratitude to Pamela Painter for giving me the original manuscript and suggesting that I finish it, and to Harry Stern, Jonah Straus and my dear wife Angela for their comments and suggestions on the text.

Thanks to Amy Crockett for her work on the cover.

Thanks also to my father Robie: my co-author, my inspiration, and my mentor.

—Cameron Macauley

I. Emerging from the Glacier

I am plummeting into darkness, hurled with wrenching force into an endless void, tumbling over and over, anticipating at each instant a bone-shattering impact and with it, the end of all sensation, of joy, and of life itself. But my fall spins on, prolonging my fright until I finally tear through the fabric of the dream to find myself in my sweat-soaked bed, the covers tossed onto the floor.

Sleep has fled in horror, so there is no option but to get up and make coffee.

My cluttered apartment is a cavern of soft shadows, illuminated by the faint pre-dawn horizon peeking in through the window shades. I switch on a desk lamp to add some color without driving away the darkness completely. When I'm not dreaming, the darkness is comforting.

To keep me company, I turn on my television to catch the morning news. It is almost never good, but it is a human voice to replace the long-gone voices of my wife and sons, now in their graves these many years. As the screen wobbles into focus, I see an icy slope on a mountainside. Some men with ice-axes are working at something buried in the snow. Then the camera focuses shakily on a human head protruding from the ice. In my excitement I knock over the sugar bowl while I stare at the television. It is a man I used to know.

The unseen narrator informs me that they are chopping a corpse out of the glacier, an Austrian soldier from World War One (as they refer to it now—for me it will always be *Der Gebirgskrieg,* the Mountain War). He says that the glacier is shrinking in this unseasonably warm summer of 1966, giving up its war treasures one by one.

In the television's silver glow I settle into my easy chair, cradling a coffee cup in my hands. I had had a premonition that I would see him again—I have dreamed of that terrible moment when he let go of the cable and plummeted away, his hands outstretched as if he were celebrating a triumph. In my dream his corpse dwindles to a morbid speck, like a bullet fired into that great quilt of ice wrapping the mountain. I never see the impact; he must have plunged deep into the snow, to lie there perfectly preserved until yesterday: one of the last men of the great Royal and Imperial Austro-Hungarian Army still on the glacier.

The flickering screen shows his frost-encrusted face as they struggle to free him from the ice. On the collar of his uniform I can make out the three stars on an embroidered background (it would be blue and gold, if only I had a color television) that signify his rank as a colonel. His hat is gone of course, as is his hair—the little of it that remained in 1916—but there is still a faint bristle of moustache on his upper lip, and as chunks of snow fall off I recognize his rounded chin. His arms lie at his sides in a typical military stance, and I believe I can make out his clenched fists, still clothed in black leather gloves.

Two swarthy mountaineers are chopping at the ice with picks. They look much like the soldiers the Colonel once commanded—the same rough-hewn, muscular bearing as the *Standschützen* and *Freiwillige Schützen* volunteers who held the South Tyrol against the Italian advance. Now they are hacking at the Colonel's frozen tomb, and if it weren't for their colorful modern-day athletic garb I could imagine that these are his very men, returned from their graves to resurrect him. The blonde one could be my old friend Franz Pichler, the one with the stiff black moustache could be Lieutenant Pauli, who died in an avalanche.

At length they lift him out, his military great-coat stiffened like a tarnished suit of armor, his leather boots gray with rime and age. Even in death the Colonel maintains his dignity, commanding respect from those who have come to relieve him of his duties. They slide him carefully into a black plastic sack, and the camera zooms in as one of the men sweeps the snow off his visage, gently so as not to wake him. There he is: Colonel Stefan Georg von Buchholz, his skin wrinkled like old leather and as pale as wax, his mouth hardened into a frown of concentration, his closed eyelids laced with delicate white crystals. I half expect them to open with a flutter, exposing his brilliant blue eyes as he shakes the snow off his sleeves and looks around him. He would rise solemnly to his feet, expecting his rescuers to snap to attention and salute. Then he would turn to me and say: "The war is over, Captain von Fuchsheim. Prepare to retire in good order."

Abruptly, the TV cuts away to a commercial.

I feel out of breath, confused. Why has the Colonel suddenly re-entered my life? Nothing happens without a reason. I switch off the television and finish my coffee in the half-light of dawn.

Buchholz was a good man, not brilliant and too often manipulated by his superiors and his subordinates, but he cared for his troops, which was a rare virtue during that war. His death was the result of negligence and despair, and once again I mourn him as I did half a century ago. It feels good to have seen him again, to know that he did not vanish but has lingered all these long years so that we could exchange one last salute.

I stand up slowly to open the curtains and unlatch the pane. An apathetic breeze pushes its way into the room. Outside the summer sky over Regensburg is hazy as yesterday's rain evaporates; a torpid sun emerges at the edge of the horizon. My dusty apartment seems perplexed by the light; I rarely open the windows these days, preferring to spend my time dozing in front of the television when I am not engaged in my woodcarving workshop downstairs.

Sitting on a shelf over my desk I have a little sculpture of walnut wood, a bust of a man in an Austrian military uniform. He is bald and the grain of the wood suggests age-spots on his polished pate; lighter streaks confer texture to his moustache and the fringe of hair behind his ears. He has the self-assured expression of a commander who is defending his homeland: his jaw is set with determination. One eyebrow is slightly arched under a creased forehead, as if he might be considering the next step in a military plan in which men would die and victory was by no means certain. His eyes are, of course, walnut-brown, but in real life they would have been the pale blue of the horizon as seen from the peak of a mountain on a bitterly cold winter morning. This is how I remember Colonel Buchholz; I made this sculpture a few years ago and decided not to sell it, although I've had offers.

He gazes down at me and his eyes announce that I have a task, something I must start and finish in the remaining time allotted to me. I sit down at my writing desk, sweep aside the bills and newspapers and pull an ancient notebook off the shelf—my crystallography notes from university, the pages brown at the edges and half of them still blank. Licking my fountain-pen, I lay its point to the paper and begin to write.

I plan to describe here the story of the great Ice Citadel of the Ortler Glacier, a story that I suspect has not been told before, except possibly in some obscure military reports. As I am one of the few men to have survived the last action on the Ortler, and all the others are quite dead by now, the story will die with me if I don't choose to tell it, which would deprive the world of a fine tale of military engineering, courage, and of the tragic deaths of many brave soldiers on both sides. My service took place on, or, so to speak, *in* the glaciers—in caves of pure crystal ice, some of them grander and more beautiful than any cathedral on earth. A war so strange that one never believed it; one lived it but could not prove it existed. Unearthly beauty, like the center of a diamond seen through a microscope, mingled with arctic death in every moment.

It is not just out of pride that I am writing this story; it is to honor the memory of you, Colonel Buchholz. Had we not been forced together by war and separated by rank, I am certain, dear Stefan, that we would have been the best of friends. Therefore I intend to tell the story of our fortress under the glacier, offered to you in the spirit of Bernard de Fontenelle, who remarked. 'I hate war: it ruins conversation.'

II. The High Country

In early June of 1916, I went on leave from the 11ᵗʰ Bavarian Infantry and returned to my home in Regensburg for the first time in almost two years. After the filth and mud of the trenches it seemed decadent and hedonistic to sit in a cushioned train seat wearing clean clothes and have a hot meal served to me on a china plate. Outside the window there was a countryside that had not been shelled, did not smell of corpses, in which people lived in houses and led safe, uncomplicated lives. But I had only to close my eyes to see the landscape of Hell that had become my second home.

In the evening I arrived in Regensburg and the sense of unreality grew even stronger. Here beautiful young women—they were all beautiful, since I had not seen a woman for almost twenty months—promenaded along the train station platform in elegant clothes, twirling silk parasols on their shoulders. In the streets the traffic seemed gentle and impossibly relaxed after the frenetic pace of the front: there were no ambulances barreling past, no staff-cars honking to get through, no frenzied messengers with urgent directives from headquarters. The trees were not splintered skeletons but verdant foliage which rustled pleasantly in the breeze; the air smelled of warm food, coal-fires and soap. There were men in uniform, true, but they strolled about languidly with sacks of fresh bread under their arms.

It occurred to me abruptly that this was *peace*, the hope and desire of people everywhere, natural and effortless. Why was it so difficult to achieve? Ah, but war is the hard part: war takes money and equipment and hundreds of thousands of men on each side. It is a monumental endeavor to create an inferno of explosions and muddy wastes in which the dead lie stinking. And all so that a few men in the corridors of power can congratulate each other: "We won." I pity youths who are deceived into thinking that it is good to die for one's country.

I felt a tingling wave of despair come over me as I walked up the steps to my home—still the same as it had been on that night so long ago when I had run off with my dufflebag on my shoulder. I rang the bell and a tiny, wizened woman answered the door.

"Hello, Mother."

At the sight of me, she burst into tears.

My ten days of leave passed by in a blur of lunches and dinners, afternoons in the park and evenings drinking schnapps and listening to music. I avoided talking about the war as much as I could and took every opportunity to sleep and bathe, as if to make up for months of going unwashed, my eyes heavy with weariness. Although meals were sumptuous by army standards, many items could not be found in shops—spices and smoked meats, cheese and chocolate, coffee and wine were all mere memories. Mother had learned to make a kind of greasy ersatz soap using chicken fat and lye, and people made do in similar ways to compensate for shortages.

At length it was over, and I prepared to return to that living nightmare that was the Western Front.

My last night at home was the occasion of my sister Lisl's engagement party. She had come to an understanding with the intrepid Werner Einecke, my school chum who was also home on leave and who was now a Zeppelin crewmember sailing the skies in one of our giant dirigible airships. No date for the wedding had been set, but Lisl spoke excitedly of reserving the cathedral and, absurdly, whether it would be possible to serve French champagne. Werner regaled us all with stories of soaring high over battles in a massive inflated flying-machine, and how it was the technology of the future.

At midnight, the whole party, quite tipsy and sentimental, went to see me off at the Regensburg station. A trainload of wounded from the Eastern Front had just arrived and we walked among stretchers on the platform, trying not to be affected. It was ghastly: hundreds of pale young men wrapped in bandages, missing arms and legs and eyes, some of them moaning quietly as they waited to be carried away. I noticed a stocky fellow with one leg making his way along on crutches, his trouser-leg pinned up under him. It was my cousin Günter, on his way home to Hausen. I wanted to greet him, but he seemed lost in thought, and I knew it would be too painful to tell him about his brother Fritz, who had been killed in front of me at St. Mihiel. I wondered if his other brother Helmut was still alive. Then I walked past him without a word.

When the train arrived there were tears and embraces. Just then, an officer made his way through the crowd, calling out my name. When he found me, he explained that his headquarters had just received by telegraph some new orders for me. He enjoyed announcing the whole matter as the engagement party gathered round in drunken awe to listen—I was to be posted on detached service, to join the Austrian 14th Army Corps in the Tyrol!

So—I should be taking the train south to Innsbruck, not back to the meatgrinder on the Western Front. A cheer went up from my friends Dieter and Ulrich. Ah, the fresh air of the mountains! Chalets in the high meadows, goatsmilk cheese, fields of edelweiss; alpenstock and lederhosen! Guarding a mountain pass instead of lying in a muddy trench under artillery fire. *Gott sei dank!*[1] My mother clutched me and wept rivers.

It demanded another brandy all round, and so off we went to the station *Schenkstube*[2], a room filled with clanking steins, pungent smoke, and loud jokes as other officers waited for the trains that would take them off to rejoin their regiments. It was two in the morning when the Innsbruck train, amid flowing sideburns of steam, chuffed into the station. My friends and family eased me aboard; everyone got kissed twice more; my mother produced a rivulet of tears she had held in reserve; Werner stowed my gear in the rack and they left me asleep on the compartment seat with a brandy bottle in my arms, like a mother cuddling her baby.

I awoke when we stopped in some station, slept again, woke again. People-noises came into the compartment, subsided, then departed again somewhere south of Munich. I woke up in the blue-gray morning, sat up, rubbed my eyes, and stared at the landscape slipping by. Wait a moment, who was sending me off to the Alps, and why? In the exuberance of yesterday, had Werner and Dieter and Ulrich paid somebody to dress up as an officer with a message? He had given a very convincing performance—and now they were wishing only that they could see my face when I discovered that this was all a *vergebliche Jagd*, a wild goose chase. I shuddered and swore.

I searched about on the seat next to me and found two envelopes. The smaller one, with my name written on it, contained my railway pass and my typewritten orders: "Captain Melchior von Fuchsheim shall on this date proceed by rail via München, Innsbruck, and Bozen to Meran where he will report to Brigade Adjutant Meier at 1st Division headquarters." The other was marked "not to be opened except by Major Wolfgang Meier." So, it hadn't been Ulrich or Dieter, it had been the Imperial German Reichswehr playing tricks on me.

I sweated and breathed out brandy fumes; all through that long afternoon my head ached and my nerves vibrated like a spiderweb in a high wind. We Germans with our little religion of bureaucracy!—when some matter takes form as a set of documents sent through proper channels and ornamented with official signatures, it has become at least an icon, at most a saint's toenail. Invoked by consecrated paper, I was on my way.

I became sober enough to realize that somehow someone in the Austrian Fourteenth Army Corps had requested me and had plucked me out for purposes unknown. But he had failed to determine that I became dizzy when exposed to heights—as proved numerous times on family holidays in the Bayrischer Wald—and that I detested snowstorms and climbing. I would tell all this to Major Meier who, doubtless, would not understand.

I had no charming visions like those of my friends and family. I knew that the Süd-Tirol was not for flatlanders. The Tyroleans were half chamois and the Alpini[3] were half catamount, and these folk fought in the midst of blizzards for the possession of a few acres of snow. Not for me, thank you. As the train panted through the Brenner and began to rock down the long valley to Bozen, I took a little warmth from the brandy bottle to

---

[1] God be thanked!
[2] A bar licensed to sell alcoholic drinks.
[3] Elite mountain warfare soldiers of the Italian Army.

ease the ache. In a while, all these mountains seemed like successive pictures viewed through our stereopticon at home, and I think I came to superimpose one view on the other. Fitful and tremulous, I dozed.

A file of climbers, linked by ropes, inched up a tall, perpendicular face of rock and, inexplicably, I was translated to the head of that column, groping upward to find handholds in the rock. Did I wake or sleep? My lungs labored in the thin air, the cliff became smoother and smoother. And, as I told myself "it is too sheer to climb, too hard to breathe," I took to the air and began the downward plunge. Now, the mountain from which I began to fall was just the mountain at the left of the railway, the one I'd been gazing at for the last few kilometers. I was descending through the air in dazzling sunlight, watching the valley below me become more distinct—the river like a shiny, blue braid, a few scattered red roofs like confetti, and, aha! a tiny train puffing along a thin, black seam.

I raised my head and looked up from the train window to see high above us the body of a man who seemed to be riding the air gracefully in a long dive, a microscopic man at first, then growing and growing by increasing magnification until I could make out his limbs, now the white patch of his face, now the dark hair blowing in the wind, now, more distinctly, his army uniform.

I felt quite fatalistic and not in the least personally affected as I looked down and saw the wagons of the train come closer and closer. Behind the windows, I could see the faces of passengers looking out at me and, although it was still too far to determine, I imagined their looks of curiosity or fear. I would reach the train broadside at, I calculated, a forty-five degree angle from above. I began to take pleasure in noting particular features—the Austrian state railways markings on the side of a wagon, the tight roll of smoke from the engine. Particularly, I noticed the face of a man who was wearing a captain's uniform, staring at me from the window, ruddy-cheeked, tall of forehead, an amused hook to the mouth—in fact myself. I was about to crash through the window and kill him.

I rose from my seat and was drawn to the window by a hydraulic force of astonishment. I must have thrown it violently open because, a moment later, in the actual world, I was leaning out into the thick, cold air that coursed along the side of the train. My heart was pounding and I was gasping uncontrollably. The hurtling body was nowhere to be seen. At my back, I heard someone loudly asking, *"Sind Sie verrucht?"* [4]

I closed the window, begged his pardon, and sat down. How could I answer his question? It was meant for me, it was meant for all of us in 1916. I remembered that once in school I had read the words of Heraclitus, who warns us that the way upward and the way downward in fact follow the same route.

Creaking and hissing, the little engine finally brought us into Meran late at night. I never saw the town. I slept on a cot kindly lent to me by the stationmaster, and in the morning at reveille, I reported to headquarters. Major Meier was not there, but a duty officer took my papers, gave me other papers, and explained that I would not proceed by train but would ride in an army truck going west along the Vintschgau river valley to the Italian Front.

I found the driver warming up our vehicle, a scarred gray supply transport with large tires for negotiating ice and snow. I climbed in and without a word we rumbled out onto the road from Meran towards Trafoi. So, in the chilly gray of the false dawn, my hands clutched around a tin mug of coffee, my eyes half open, I inspected the towering mountains as they stood at attention in their gray and white uniforms.

Curious, I pulled out a map I had purchased in the station and amused myself by trying to identify the peaks around us. They seemed encumbered with oddly inappropriate names: on our right the *Texelgruppe* with the *Kirchbachspitz* and the *Graue*—the Texel group, the Churchbrook peak, and the Gray Slope. On our left, the *Hochwacht* and the *Hasenohr*, which are the Highguard and the Rabbit's Ear, perhaps a confession of an inability to

---

[4] Are you mad?

give words to such majesty and vastness. Up ahead, but invisible yet, stood the high giants' kettles of the Madatsch, the Ortler, and the Martello—where one finds snowfields huger than seas, winds that burn like icy blowtorches, and crystal glaciers that stretch like fallen skies to the far peaks. That is where I was going.

My driver broke the silence: his name was Anton, a *guter gebirgler*[5], as he told me, from a village up above Bozen. He had a face as brown and rugose as an alpine slope and a cigarette hung perpetually from the ledge of his lip, trailing a pungent curl. He was indifferent to my foreign uniform, my strange accent, and my odd destination.

Suddenly, there was a faraway report like a single, deep drumbeat in the air. "Artillery?" I asked, and Anton shook his head gravely. "*Brontidi,*[6] the locals call them," he said. "They're deeper and louder than artillery. No one knows what causes them, but they can create problems." He raised his gloved hand to point through the windscreen. High on the face of what my map named as the Weisskugel, I saw a white glissade begin, chute faster downward, setting up a smoke around itself until the whole face of the mountain became a pale billow.

"*Eine lawine,*"[7] Anton explained. From this distance it seemed like a dusting of powdered sugar, a pretty gesture; there was no hint that avalanches killed people frequently on these mountains.

We lapsed into silence again as the truck rocked along the narrow road and with fascination I watched the cigarette smolder to within a hair's breadth of the lip. Finally, at the last second he spat it out the window and said, "Did you hear what happened last February on the other side?" By "the other side," I take it that he meant east of the River Etsch and the town of Trient.

When I did not answer, he went on, "They sent out a *jäger*[8] battalion from Schwarzenberg, a patrol in force. The first day, some wounded came back. The second day, a storm came up and all communication was cut. Third day, it settled down enough so we sent out patrols. Not a sign of anybody, not a trace, as if the whole lot had stepped off into the gorge. But those boys were real Tyrolers and we knew that wasn't it.

"Well—spring came along. The Italians brought up some guns and began to shell our positions. The sun came out and the weather turned warm. All at once, a couple of Italian shells burst over a big snowfield and an avalanche started—just like that one up there. I was watching with all the other men in our company, and when the avalanche slid down, we saw a strange black army standing there in the sun. Two hundred and sixty men, standing there in a long line, frozen stiff."

"Mm, mm, mm!" I said, wondering how much of this was true. Without my observing how it came to be, another burning stump of tobacco had appeared on his lip.

I'd read something about this war in the German newspapers, but it seemed remote, romantic, unlike a present day war at all—more like a steel engraving of Suvorov and his army retreating over the alps in 1799 in the leatherbound *Famous Commanders* in my father's library. The newspapers assured us that the war was entirely serious, that the valleys of the Etsch, the Adda, and the Val Camonica are the backdoors to Italy. Maps with little curving arrows demonstrated that columns marching down those thin valley creases could threaten to turn the left flank of the Italian defenders and endanger Verona, or even Milan, or so the imaginary generals who direct newspapers enjoyed telling us in the summer of 1915. By 1916, they were speaking of a bitter struggle for the high mountain passes and their correspondents were describing men wounded and dying in the snow to protect the floor of an Austrian valley 3000 meters below.

The most brutal portion of the struggle was carried on in the valley of the Isonzo, a lethargic river that empties into the Adriatic. The Italian *Generalissimo* Luigi Cadorna was determined to smash through the Austrian defensive line and take Trieste and the Dalmatian coastline, but five pitched battles and two hundred thousand casualties later he had succeeded in occupying only a few muddy acres of shell-pocked swampland around the ruined town of Görz. In May of 1916 the Austrians under General von Hötzendorf launched a surprise offensive

---

[5] A native of the mountain region.
[6] Literally, "little thunder": mysterious thunder-like noises sometimes attributed to meteors or geologic phenomena.
[7] An avalanche
[8] Literally "huntsmen"; an elite rifle unit.

in the Dolomites south of Trient to try to regain mountainous territory occupied by the Italians the previous year. After two weeks the Austrians had advanced as far as Asiago and were begging the Germans for additional support, but Germany was struggling with the French and the Russians and had no troops to spare; the Austrians were forced to retreat. Both sides suffered staggering losses: close to three hundred thousand men died in thirteen days.

The rising sun, in ascent over the Sarntaler Alps, gave our valley a pale smile and gilded the uppermost peaks. We passed though neat hamlets of steep-pitched red roofs, whitewashed walls, and one admonishing finger of steeple. We passed Töll, Rabland with a smelly carbide factory, then Plaus. Three veins ran along the green valley floor—our road, the railway line, and the River Etsch. The river might have been a canal, for it flowed tamely between high, stone-faced banks.

All along the roadside, army transport was beginning to come to life and move out. Onward to the Stilfser-Ortler-Sulden front went mule-carts, trucks, and horse-drawn wagons. Their cargos were boxes of shells or cartridges, bales of barbed wire, lumber, or bags of flour. We passed a field kitchen and a blacksmith shop on wheels, a line of cattle, anti-aircraft guns, a searchlight like a giant's monocle mounted on the back of a heavy truck. Returning from the west came empty wagons and now and then an ambulance.

At some time in his life Anton must have observed a tour guide and now it seemed to him obligatory to inform the foreign gentleman about the various points of interest: "Please note ahead and to our right the mighty Kirchbach and Lahnbach peaks, 3091 meters and 3006 meters respectively. *Sehr schöne!*⁹ Approaching the village of Naturns, to our left is Schloss Dornsberg. *Sehr malerisch!*"[10] He pointed up at the castle, assuming that I should be eager to examine the battlements and the belfry through my fieldglasses.

The floor of the valley slowly rises; more toyshop villages—Staben and Tschars, Kastelbell with its ruined towers atop a rocky knoll, and Latsch with some fine orchards. Sturdy women in black with white stockings and white smocks, boys in red vests and kneepants, girls as blond as summer.

All of it perfect if time could have spun its wheel and brought us five years hence, my imagined wife and future two children on holiday with me, riding in a *charabanc* to our hotel on its wooded perch.

It is about fifty kilometers from Meran to Stilfs, and when we reached the upper valley, the pretty Tyrolean world, with its rows of poplars lining the road, its verdant, forested hillrises with their castles bright as birthday cakes in the sunlight, lay behind us. Up here, it was a scene of wrinkled and riven visages of gray rock, immense sweeps of brown scree washed down from above and high spearpoints reigning over all. They were not neatly snowcapped as in paintings but mottled rock-gray and ice-white.

I think Heraclitus was wrong, because looking upward belongs to a different universe from looking down. One looks up from the valley incredulous. It is like staring up at the works of a crazed sculptor who was also something of a genius. In one of his moods, he was fascinated with sharp edges, and one's eyes dwell on heaped cutlery, fantastic scimitars, serrated blades, and gargantuan chisels of stone. Next, he delighted to *trompe l'oeil* and two mountains, actually separated by a wide valley, seem to be part of a single slope when, all at once, a cloud materializes, fills the valley, and drives them apart.

In the dusk after sunset, he cut profiles out of flat slates. He could make a cold, cheerless geometry of rock or, changing the air to blue and gold, produce charming fancies—an array of pastries, a display of porcelain, a scene of giant whitecaps. He could model with sharp shadow, wash surfaces with a ruddy or a creamy warmth, change even the great exposures of black rock to a deep blue. I had yet to see this world from the top, looking down.

After twenty months of seeing only mud and charred trees, this was, to me, a vision from Valhalla. The contrast between this rugged nobility of spires and dizzying heights, and the impoverished world of the muck-filled trenches took my breath away.

At a hamlet called Prad, we left the broad Vintschgau and turned into the narrow cleft that leads southward.

---

⁹ Very beautiful!

[10] Very picturesque!

For the past hour, we had seen little military traffic, but now it crowded the road that runs along the Trafoi brook and we were slowed to a crawl. At the village of Gomagoi, there was one of those small frontier forts the Austrians had built before the war, and a regimental headquarters of the *jägers* now occupied it.

We stopped at the guard post and a sergeant came out and asked for our papers. A bit of a shock for me—the man was lavishly hairy, with brown shoots curling from beneath his cap, a great, moping moustache, bristles thrusting from his nose. He observed my pass suspiciously. The thickets over his eyes drew together, his moustache spread, he sprouted more growth in all directions. Then his right hand ticked in a gesture that was slightly more than muscle twitch, slightly less than salute. I laughed.

He leaned over toward Anton and said in broad Tyrolean, "Up there, don't let him fall into a *Gletscherspalte*."[11] A minute or two on our way, Anton said, "Sorry, sir, but they don't respect Prussians too much hereabouts."

"Really? I thought he was most considerate—worried about my safety and all that."

Anton's cigarette drooped seriously from his mouth. He was deciding that Prussians must be just as stupid as one had always heard. Earlier, I had tried to explain to him that I was not at all Prussian but Bavarian, which was to him a footless distinction, rather like that between a pink-brown pig and a brown-pink pig.

The mass of the Ortler was now to our left, although we could not see the summit. Our truck rattled and growled as we ascended the road in sharp curves and, it seemed to me, Anton was constantly within millimeters of taking us over the edge.

When the village of Trafoi came into view, he said. "Here's where we say goodbye, Captain. Too bad you can't go on with me up to the Stilfser Pass—the view is even better there. It's the highest pass in Europe, you know. That's where the front lines are. The Macaronis sweated a battery of guns up there and they don't mind dropping something on you." It was his most ambitious speech of the journey. The truck chugged to a halt.

Trafoi is a highland meadow, a green tablecloth spread among the grim towers of rock. It has a few houses, a small church, and a hotel called the Schöne Aussicht, now an officers' quarters where I found the man to whom my orders were addressed, *Hauptmann*[12] Franz Pichler.

These mountaineers were all hair! Coming out of the dark doorway, he startled me—hair the color of bright lager falling nearly to his collar, a thin, young, sharp-edged face burnt to a chestnut hue. He did not salute but he gave me a quick smile and a handclasp. A Goth frozen in ice and chiseled out, still young, fifteen hundred years later. His uniform was faded to a grayish white and a big sheath knife swung from a strap around his neck.

"So, Melchior—*Kom, kom!*" He clapped me on the shoulder, all boisterous *kamaradschaft*,[13] and steered me out onto the terrace. He yelled to some other officers to join us, seized a waiter by the sleeve. "*Schnell, schnell,*[14] beer! Beer for everybody. This captain has come all the way from Berlin to inspect the food and drink at the Schöne Aussicht."

When it came he stood, one boot on a chair, and raised his foamy stein for a toast. "Here's to encounters. Here's to the King of Italy!" A dramatic pause and a sly look around as the breeze tugged at his hair. A loud groan from all at the table. "I mean, to the royal arse, and here's to my right foot." Another pause. "I told you this was a toast to encounters!"

---

[11] Crevasse
[12] Captain
[13] Camaraderie
[14] Hurry

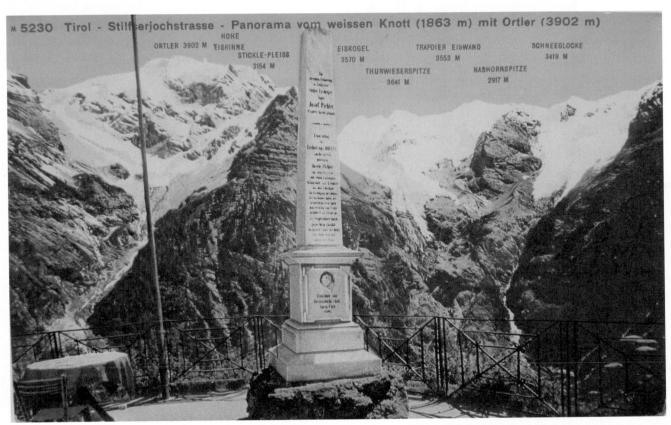

Postcard showing the memorial to Josef Pichler and the Ortler with neighboring peaks.

Barks of laughter and a hearty downing of beer. How young they all were, with their bronzed, smooth faces and their schoolboy jokes. On the Western Front they were not much older, I suppose, but two years of war had given us a grimy, elderly air, the gerontic bearing of the survivor. The tall *Offiziersstellvertreter*[15] with a missing tooth in front was Karl; the crop-headed *Stabs-Wachtmeister*[16] with the horse-trader's eyes was Viktor; the choir-boy *Oberleutnant* was Pauli.

Great platters of cheese, ham, dried Grisons beef, bread, and pickles arrived at the table. The joking turned very local and I was left out of it for a few minutes. Something about a Max who left it behind—but did his wife pick it up? A round of laughter. I began to stare at the sinister majesty of the Ortler and I lost all track of the conversation.

Mountains—I'd never really had to think about them before. They were created by God to give the Swiss and Tyroleans somewhere to yodel from. They were guilty of posing for a hundred thousand bad paintings. They were, as Dr. Johnson remarked, vulgar (what better authority than a mountainous and vulgar man?). Now they were real, very much in front of my eyes and haunting my mind, and not precisely from fear.

From Trafoi, the Ortler is seen through a wide V formed by two black-green pine slopes, and beyond it rise three craggy canines, followed upward by the disbelieving eye to the very glacier itself. The Ortler is a *felsengletscher*, or cliff-glacier, and from here what I could see of it was the huge spill of snow, like foam frozen in the act of overflowing its colossal stone kettle. I gazed at it for a long time.

I suddenly realized that the rest of them had stopped talking and were looking at me. "So, Melchior, what do you think of my grandfather's hill?" Franz asked lightly.

"It has begun to fascinate me in a quite unhealthy way," I said. "Why is it your grandfather's?"

"In fact, he was my great-grandfather." Franz downed half his stein. He had a habit of smiling disconcertingly in the midst of the most ordinary or sober subjects and I found myself, like a fool, smiling back.

"Josef Pichler—or 'Pseirer-Josele' as they called him—took two of his friends and climbed the Ortler for the first time in 1804. The Archduke Johann had offered a prize to the first man to reach the summit, and Pichler and his friends scrambled up to the top easily. But when they returned no one believed them—there had been numerous failed attempts to scale the Ortler before, you see. So Pichler went back up with a flag, which he planted at the top. But by the time he had returned, the wind had carried it off and still no one believed him. Finally he scaled the mountain with a torch which could be seen from the valley at night. Then he got the prize. The whole story is engraved on an obelisk at the Weisse Knott hotel in the Stilfser Pass. So, you see, it is my mountain by inheritance. In memory of *urgrossvater*[17] Josele, you must help me knock the Macaronis off it! He made a chopping gesture with the flat of his hand. It was something of a joke, but it was not a joke as well. A bit of the grainy, gravelly pride of the Tyroler came through. It might be a vast, sterile rockpile, but it was their own vast, sterile rockpile.

For the past minute or two, I had been hearing a distant drone, and now I looked up to see a tiny airplane, like a bug on a pane of glass, high over the peaks. Pauli got the field glasses and we all had a look. There was an amiable argument as to whether it was an Austrian Hansa-Brandenburg as Viktor declared or an Italian Caproni bomber as Karl said. His eyes glued to the lenses, Karl added, "You are merely guessing. The machines are nothing alike. The Hansa-Brandenburg is much smaller. Look, you can see the three vertical tail-fins of the Caproni, that's a certain clue."

"In any case, smile," Franz said, "because he may be taking our picture. You see, Melchior, the positions are so exposed up there that photographs tell us everything. There is no such thing as a secret from the enemy. But, as for bombing, have no fears. The air is tricky and a bomb can easily fall in the wrong place, on one's own lines, in fact." The bug traversed the pane with great deliberation and finally disappeared into a pocket of clouds.

---

[15] Warrant officer

[16] Staff sergeant

[17] Great-grandfather

The air was thin but delicious, like the bouquet of a mountain wine. The sun was warm. The Alpine fervor of these young climbers was catching. My head whirled, I slapped my hand on the table and addressed the company: "Officers and gentlemen, pardon my confusion. It's all very well for Franz to kick King Victor Emmanuel on the backside in order to keep the Macaronis off *grossvati's* mountain, and it's all very well to fly a Hansa-Brandenburg-Caproni over and take pictures of each other so there will be no secrets, but…" My head was floating above the terrace and I didn't seem to have things put together in quite the best order "…but my question is…My question is: What in God's name am I doing here?"

Loud cheers and louder thumping of steins on the slate table, shouts of "What's any of us doing here? *Jawohl!*[18] Let's go home."

I raised my arm and pointed at the glacier. "Gentlemen, I call you to witness that some terrible mistake has been made, and nobody is worried about it except me. Listen, friends, I can't climb a ladder without getting vertigo. All my life, I have avoided roofs, belfries, balconies, belvederes. I am capable of falling from a curb in the city." Dramatic pause. "Now, will you please tell me what I am doing here with you mountain goats?"

Beating time with his stein, Franz led the song:

Dort oben, dort oben an der himmlischen Tür
Und da steht eine arme Seele, schaut traurig herfür.[19]

Franz with a mock frown, gave the table a final thump and turning serious, smiled. "Melchior, tell us. What is your profession?"

"When the war began, I had just completed my university education."

"In Germany, did they say anything about your assignment here?"

"Nothing. As I told you, there are those secret orders to be presented to your *Oberst*[20] Buchholz."

"But do you have a specialty? Something you studied at the university?"

"Even farther off the mark. I was—comrades, don't throw things—at Leeds in England to study under the famous Professor William Henry Bragg, a Nobel laureate in Physics. I was there for four years before I returned to Germany."

They eyed me soberly. It was queer enough to go to university, but travel all the way to England for it?

"Physics? What branch?" I suddenly realized that Franz was not quite the uneducated mountaineer he pretended to be.

"Crystallography."

His smile was thin and he looked intently at me without speaking for a long minute. "I must go," he said. "I'll send my orderly for your gear and he'll show you to your room. I'll take you up to the lines tomorrow." He gave a mock salute and was away.

As I finished my stein of beer, I raised my eyes to the Ortler again. Slowly it came to me—perfectly obvious and perfectly absurd. Up above us there were trillions of crystals belonging to the dihexagonal-dipyramidal division, holosymmetric class, of the hexagonal system. In other words, ice. Which had prompted some military madman to send for me.

The others were now standing up to leave. They clapped me on the shoulders pleasantly and said they'd see me later at mess. I nodded and said yes, yes.

I sat a little while longer thinking befuddled thoughts. The Colonel surely did not want a crystallographer, just as Moses did not take a hydrologist with him to the Red Sea, just as Hannibal required no zoologist for his elephants. I felt more than a little drunk.

---

[18] Yes, sir!
[19] Up there, up there on the celestial door
And there is a poor soul, who looks quite sad.
[20] Colonel

III. My Early Observations of Ice

It astonishes me now to think that I went to war, that I was responsible for men's deaths, and that I spent years as part of the great military apparatus whose raison d'etre was to kill and maim. I am by no means a villain or a war-demon but rather a gentle artist with a gift for vision: I can design a structure instantaneously in my head—be it a building, a sculpture or a molecule—and invent a way of creating it in the real world. I should have studied engineering, obviously, but I found my career through much more theoretical avenues, otherwise I would have been put to work building fortifications. As it was, I had the privilege of designing the Citadel of Ice, during a war which Mother Nature herself abhorred and did her best to obliterate.

In 1890 I was born and christened Melchior von Fuchsheim in Regensburg, an ornate old Bavarian town that straddles the confluence of the mighty Danube where it meets the Regen, graced by an arched medieval stone bridge and crowned by one of the finest Gothic cathedrals in the world, whose twin bell-towers stand proudly like an enormous bishop's mitre in the center of the city.

My parents were comfortably middle-class, well-connected and prosperous and keenly appreciative of music, theater, and the arts. We lived in a spacious and rather creaky 18th-century townhouse on Dechbettenerstrasse between the grassy south bank of the river and Dörnberg Garten, an elegant neighborhood of towering oaks and sleepy walled gardens, butterflies and songbirds. Our house was steeped in the history of generations, with a dark and majestic interior replete with portraits of ancestral von Fuchsheims and bookshelves filled with leatherbound volumes. The tall windows with their crinkly-glass panes were hidden by heavy draperies to keep the intrusive world out. Only the kitchen enjoyed the sunlight, with French windows that the cook Theresa would open to let the morning breeze flush out the stale odors of last night's dinner, as old Hans the gardener carried in bushels of red apples, baskets of sweet peaches and a pot of honey from the hives in the orchard.

My father considered himself a patron of the arts and supported a handful of young artists, some of whom later became successful. One of my early memories is of sitting at a table in a Munich restaurant with my father, my mother and the playwright and poet Hugo von Hofmannsthal, a melancholy young man with unruly hair like hay-stubble in a summer field and eyes the color of pond water. At the time he was still unknown, struggling to get his first play performed—a bizarre piece called "Death and a Fool." He engaged my father in an animated conversation during which he thumped the table with his fist and stated emphatically: "English culture is the ideal setting for the artist!"

But von Hofmannsthal was only a minor part of a much grander memory: an ice-carving was being hewn in the *platz* outside the restaurant; the management had hired an old Romanian man to create it and had for some reason specified that it should be Saint George slaying the dragon, however the sculptor had embellished this order and had depicted the knight battling a glassy serpent in front of a detailed replica of Castle Neuschwanstein complete with spear-point pinnacles, gables, tiny balconies, turrets, tented rooftops and battlements, all painstakingly rendered in ice. It dwarfed the valiant saint and his adversary as the artist shuffled around the gleaming sculpture, perfecting it with a dentist's drill, spun by a spring that he would periodically rewind to make the point whine for a minute as he touched up an arch or a cornice.

He was a hunchback with a face from a Grimm's fairy-tale: hooked nose, deep-set eyes, crowded teeth, and an overhanging brow lying beneath curls of unruly gray hair, but when I approached him, he gave me a wink and a welcoming smile. A cluster of passers-by had paused to admire the sculpture, but the Gypsy—as I suddenly realized he was—paid them no heed, only glanced at me now and again with a sly twinkle in his eye, inviting me to revel in the magnificence of his ice castle. It was snowing lightly and flakes had dusted its sloping rooftops, adding to its exquisite beauty.

I gazed for a long while at that masterpiece before my mother came to pull me inside, insisting that I'd catch cold. That night I dreamt of the frozen palace and its creator with his cryptic smile, and imagined myself as an ice-sculptor too, creating whole landscapes of tiny, precisely-chiseled chateaux.

I was inspired enough to attempt my own creation a few days later when we were returning to Regensburg and had stopped off at my uncle Adolf's farm near the village of Hausen. We arrived late in the chilly evening to a welcome of embraces and laughter from Uncle Adolf with his enormous beard, my stout aunt Karla and my three cousins—stocky Günter, sly Helmut and good-humored Fritz, the youngest—grinning and giggling in front of a roaring fireplace. We boys stayed up until midnight telling stories and jokes, sprawled across a bearskin rug that smelled of woodsmoke and beer.

During the night it snowed heavily. We awoke next day to a bright and clear morning, to see the trees around the farmhouse bowed down with ermine overcoats of snow. Outbuildings were sunk into smooth, sparkling drifts and the river was a dark trickle between rounded white muscles, reflecting the sun with a dazzle that confounded the senses. All this was the delight of my three cousins and after breakfast we began a lively snowball fight. Of the three, Fritz was closest to me in age; he was a handsome youth with an angelic smile and a shock of crimson hair that fell over his eyes. He and I quickly bonded as we found ourselves pelted by wicked projectiles at every turn. Günter had a cruelly accurate aim and Helmut was a tactical genius, ambushing us with snowballs the size of cobblestones and twice as hard.

Thinking quickly, I burrowed into the snow and found that it was the perfect weight and density for tunneling. Soon Fritz and I had managed to hollow out a sturdy shelter under the surface, while our opponents searched for us in vain. We rapidly carved out a bunker with a lookout portal and an escape hatch, all unseen from above. Then, breaking up the snow with my gloves and packing it down under me, I tunneled off to another spot and excavated a second dugout from which we launched a surprise attack on Günter and Helmut. Intrigued by our clever invention, they joined us in enlarging it. We dug passageways and hidden trenches with ramparted parapets and made snow-sentries wielding stick-rifles and snow-cannons, ready to bombard any imprudent attackers. With the naïve genius of children we constructed a redoubt that would have impressed von Hindenburg himself and would have held off a brigade of Italians, until we were called indoors for dinner. Later during my war years, I recalled that pleasant day with secret joy.

I distinguished myself in school and became interested in chemistry and physics, much to my father's elation: he wanted me to study anything except law, which he considered mind-numbingly dull and full of hypocrisy. One of my professors loaned me a book on crystallography and after that there was no quelling my interest in this arcane and highly theoretical science. I chose to attend Leeds University because it was foremost in the world for the study of crystallography, being the home of two of the world's greatest crystallographers, Professor William Henry Bragg and his son William Lawrence Bragg.

Crystallography was a painfully young science at that time—indeed, until the Braggs discovered how to use X-ray diffraction to measure crystals, crystallography was based entirely on rather crude measurements of the angles of crystal faces using a clumsy instrument called a goniometer. The theory behind it was that the structure of the crystal reflects perfectly the shape of the molecules that compose it. How many hours I spent fiddling with that foolish contraption!

Professor Bragg was a great teacher, however, and he made me believe that anything was possible. He gave us the outlines of his research on X-rays that won him the Nobel Prize in 1915. He was fascinated by a thousand questions that probed the atomic configuration of the world around us, and his students were put to work on numerous projects. I spent months analyzing the crystalline properties of clay, to understand better how its flat, plate-like crystals slide against one another, to deform in response to pressure. Later I worked on the crystal substructure of iron, which is altered permanently when exposed to heat and carbon. In my final year, we all worked with X-rays to determine the structure of table salt, which rather disappointingly turned out to be a simple cube. You would have thought it preposterous—all these bright students and renowned professors, gathered around tables analyzing the contents of salt-shakers, but I found it thrilling.

For me, crystallography was a window into the structure of existence—the shape of God's building-blocks from which we and everything around us are composed. Atoms and molecules are arranged within a systematic spatial relationship to form a three-dimensional lattice, therefore the characteristics of a crystal can tell us about the physical properties of the substance it is made from. I believed that comprehending this atomic lattice would grant us insights into the best designs for architecture and machinery to function in harmony with nature—a very simplistic vision of what is now called solid-state physics. I viewed science as an elucidation of God's work, a deconstruction of Heaven and Hell, of eternity and of creation itself.

During this year I became close friends with a Danish student named Rolf Struensee, a talented fellow whose only desire in the world was to follow his father's profession and become a glaciologist. I thought this was ridiculous and said as much—glaciers were insignificant, nothing more than inert slabs of ice. Rolf began to convince me of the importance of glaciers, and over many a tankard of warm English beer he regaled me with stories of the Scandinavian ice-fields, of crevasses, seracs[21] and nunataks[22], of narrow escapes from avalanches, and of the utility of glaciers in maintaining the earth's water balance. He explained how glacial ice retains many of the properties of a liquid as it slides slowly downward off the mountains, yet its weight and rigidity cause it to split and crumble in astonishing ways to create a unique environment. Rolf explained to me that the structure of crystal ice conforms to an orderliness of physical laws that seem, at first sight, to be elegantly simple and predictable, but once you discover that ice behaves simultaneously as both a liquid and a solid, the mystery of it becomes ever more intriguing. I learned more critically useful information during those half-dozen drunken evenings than I did in four years at Leeds, and indeed, during the subsequent decades of my life.

Upon graduation Rolf and I spent the summer hiking across Sweden and Finland, and there I had my first encounter with a true glacier, the Storglaciären, an enormous white tongue of ice lolling between the north and south peaks of Mount Kebnekaise. We scaled the lower areas, where great blocks of ice lay tumbled and dripping among mounds of scree and jagged boulders washed by torrents of ice-melt that appeared mysteriously from underneath the glacier. The warm sun sang a strange harmony with the cold rising up from the ice sheet; overhead birds shot past, while around us stretched a vast whiteness that curled about boulders and pinnacles the way a mother embraces her children.

Rolf waxed lyrical, telling me that inside there were hidden chambers of untold magnificence and that the whole icy mass slid ponderously down into the valley at the rate of about 150 centimeters a year. Rather than grinding abrasively across the land, Rolf told me, glaciers consist of stacked layers of molecules with relatively weak bonds between the layers. His theory was that the weight of thousands of tons of ice causes the upper layers to slide across their relatively slow-moving foundations. The pressure also generates heat, causing the deepest ice to melt, forming a cushion of meltwater that constantly flows out from underneath.

It seemed less impressive to me than the Gypsy's ice-castle, but Rolf was not given to fantasy. I could only guess at what he was trying to describe. After a while we hiked down to the valley to try to find some beer.

But Rolf had provided me with a key piece of information that would one day save my life.

[21] A block or column of ice formed by intersecting crevasses on a glacier.
[22] An exposed rocky projection from beneath a glacier to its surface.

IV. The End of the World

Because I am a soldier of the Fatherland and have taken the oath, and because I am a von Fuchsheim, heir to a long family history of being in the wrong place at the wrong time, I had dimly suspected that one day I would meet death in some embarrassing and highly ridiculous way. But I had never foreseen it in the shape of a telpher.

The telpher—short for the technical term *teleferica*—is a cable construction that carries objects and, may God save us, people into the high reaches. It is rigged from four lines of cable that curve up through the empty air to some invisible landing 700 meters above. We were standing by a little, pitch-roofed hut that sheltered the platform and the machinery. Through the field glasses, I could make out up there another little hut of much the same kind.

The cables are wound around drums, which are turned by electric motors, or occasionally by two men pushing a hand-crank, if the motors aren't operational. Running over each cable are four little wheels, and from the wheels are suspended a shallow iron tray of the general shape and size of an iron coffin, known half-jokingly as "the gondola". When I asked about the perforations in the floor, Franz explained that they were where the blood of the wounded ran out.

We had started out from the Schöne Aussicht Hotel just at daybreak. Franz, cropheaded Viktor and I on little army donkeys, and Franz's batman and another soldier leading two donkeys with our kits. In the chill of the autumn morning we went up the valley to Heilige drei Brünnen—Three Holy Springs—where there is a rustic shed with three crude wooden statues of Christ, Saint Johannes, and the Virgin, from whose breasts spout streams of icy holy water—a device in rather silly bad taste. Beyond it is the telpher station, where the others began to unload our paraphernalia while I looked upward with a shudder. On our right was the nearly-perpendicular wall of the Madatsch and on our left the Ortler, where the thin wire ascended into space.

"*Himmelwärts!*"[23] Franz shouted happily, and he and Viktor seized me by the arms and began to propel me, protesting, toward the telpher car. They refused to listen to a rational alternative. I thought I heard a snicker from the *Gefreiter*[24] who attended the machinery. "In we go!" said Franz. "Nothing to it!" said Viktor. With respectful but firm pressure on my shoulders, I was seated.

"This can't be a serious piece of machinery," I said. At either end were inverted, U-shaped pieces of pipe, rather like the ends of some primitive bedstead. The cable on which the little two-wheeled runners rested was about as thick as my thumb. The latticework sides on our iron tray were no more than eight centimeters high. And everything looked dismayingly home-made.

Franz got in and sat down facing me, our legs overlapping. Behind him in the hut, the lance corporal picked up the field telephone and said into it, "Georg? Georg? *Bereit.*"[25]

I just managed to keep myself from groaning. "Look straight at me," Franz said, giving a slightly-exaggerated rendition of ease and nonchalance. A large rolling-pin ran over my stomach. There was an abrupt jerk and the gondola left the ground with a small scraping sound and began to rise, very slowly and level at first and then on an increasingly steeper tangent, swaying slightly and pulled along by easy tugs on the cable above us.

Fifteen meters above the earth, I opened my eyes and found that I was still alive. It was absurd, and I laughed. Franz laughed with me. "There, you see! It's all right. Your color's coming back. Just keep looking at me and, when you can't stand that any longer, look at the mountainside, but don't look up or down. When you were a *bube*,[26]

---

[23] Skyward!

[24] Private first class

[25] Ready

[26] Lad

didn't you long to ride a flying carpet? So, don't complain. On our magic carpet, we are about to visit the roof of the world. Only one of the romantic tours offered by the *Kaiserlich und Königslich*[27] tourist bureau.

I was feeling slightly better, but I would not be playful. I would not answer his grin by grinning back. I wanted to die with, at least, a look of dignity on my face.

"In fact, Melchior, we lose more men off bicycles and rowboats than we do on the telpher: one accident in 10,000 crossings. Five times that many are killed by burst tires or capsizings!"

Keeping my eyes on a spot in the middle of his forehead, I said, "But there must be some little risk on the telpher. Couldn't one catch a bad cold? Or even scrape an elbow by falling 2,000 meters?"

"Listen, I'll tell you frankly about the few danger spots. First, there's the point where we pass the gondola that's coming down—be cautious then because if there's a sudden gust of wind and the cars collide, one of them plunges to the valley. At the passing-point, bend low and be as motionless as possible."

"Odd. I never had these troubles in a rowboat or on a bicycle."

"Very rarely, we have a motor breakdown and the cars will stop, but it's quite safe if you don't get excited. I once sat up here two hours while the sergeant fussed with repairs."

"And how did you keep yourself from going mad?"

"Oh, I sang. I sang all the songs I could remember at the top of my voice, even hymns from the church."

"Dear God, you did go daft."

He gave a rueful laugh. "I can see that I must be honest with you. Yes, I admit that I fixed on those little wheels. I kept staring and staring at them, imagining that they had slipped a micron or two. I stared at them until my eyes began to roll in my head."

I suddenly heard something, and when I turned, the other telpher car was moving on its cables toward the valley and beginning to pass us now. There was no sudden gale. It rolled serenely by with a low hiss on the cables. Its cargo consisted of several cartons and a damaged Schwarzlose machine gun. Franz had timed his story perfectly so that I would not be aware of this routine crisis until it had passed. Now it appeared obvious to me—Franz must have been a mountain-climber guide in peacetime. He seemed to know a great deal about getting plump, nervous, untrained city dwellers up the side of a big rock and down again without loss.

For some reason, now that we had passed the other gondola without collision, I began to feel rather at ease, and we rode serenely through the gray-blue air on the oily hiss of the wheels. I felt expansive enough to say, "Franz, I know it, you are holding something back. I know that you can't resist forever—so, come on, what is the worst?"

He wagged his head sheepishly from side to side like a guilty boy in the third form. "Ah, my friend, it's useless to try to hide anything from you. It's like trying to tell the Colonel that the Staff Sergeant is indisposed when we all know that the Staff Sergeant drank a whole bottle of brandy all by himself last night and fell into the latrine. No lies on the Ortler, we always say—nothing but the grim truth. So, now I will tell you the truth about the artillery."

"Please, Franz."

"Well, this used to be a civilized place, but now there are too many guns up here. The light ones go up on the telpher, piece by piece, the way almost everything does. The heavy ones—weighing many tons—go up on pulley-rigs and levers or anything that can haul. We've just brought in fifty Russian prisoners of war to haul our cannons up to the Pleisshorn. Once up, they're re-assembled and emplaced. There is a terrible amount of iron on top of these mountains.

"So it happens that some of our telpher lines come within sight and range of the Macaroni guns. Well, it's almost impossible to down the cables by firing at them, but the Italian sportsmen loved to hunt these little birds—" he raised his hands to mime aiming a shotgun—"like potting *die Wachtel*[28] in the blue, pow! pow! But then they stopped. They do not do it any longer."

---

[27] Royal and Imperial

[28] Quail

"Because fundamental Italian courtesy and fair play prevailed?" I asked. I was beginning to feel a slight familiarity with the nothingness. The gentle tugging rhythm did not vary, and I felt refreshed to learn that no one would be shooting at us.

"You are entirely correct," Franz said. "But there is nothing that brings out Latin good manners better than a bit of Teutonic instruction. You see, the Macaronis' supply road is over there on the other side of the glacier. It starts at the town of Bormio and runs east along the Zebrù River valley. We, on our part, are neatly entrenched on the Kristallspitzen, 3,800 meters or so high and overlooking the road. Just to add to the amusement, we sweated a pair of 105mm light field howitzers up there and mounted a powerful telescope, waiting for the day when we'd spot a *Stabsoffiziere*[29] party coming up to inspect the lines.

"And it came—a little line of staff motorcars. Do you know how astonishing the echoes are up here? Two guns can sound like the Battle of the Marne. Four guns can sound like Armageddon. So our gunners fired off and disabled the first car and the last car in the parade. Then we banged away with everything, using just powder charges without projectiles, to make noise but not to hurt anyone. It was the funniest sight of the war, Melchior, all those fat Macaroni generals and colonels waddling and shitting their pants back down to the valley. The Italians have been very polite about the telpher ever since."

Although I was unaware of it yet, we had been approaching the rock wall and the telpher station on its ledge. All at once, I heard the noise of the machinery and, as I glanced backward, the telpher car began to tip at a steeper angle. Franz sank and I rose like a pebble in a slow catapult. Now I could look past Franz's head down into the green-black shadow of the valley. I had one arm hooked around the U-shaped support and with the other hand, I clutched the side. We seemed to have canted up to an angle of some sixty degrees. The pressure kept up. Millimeter by millimeter, I leaned farther forward into the abyss. In another second, like the man in my dream, I would be flying.

It was only after the sudden jerk back to the horizontal and the blessed slide to rest under the cable support that I realized Franz had been talking to me through it all. "Be calm; it's all right; this is quite normal; be calm."

I climbed out, my vision still full of the afterimage of the long fall to death, my legs like India rubber, and my mind humming over and over the name of Madame de Tourneville.

I took a few trial steps into the interior of the shed, the presence of that lady vividly before me. Last night, in the mess, they had got to telling me local lore and mountain tales and, among others, someone had told the story of the De Tournevilles.

It is July of 1876—forty years ago. A newlywed couple is just leaving the inn at Glurns, saying goodbye to the innkeeper at the door. The sun is shining and the day is merry. They are relishing the thought of driving through the mountains, just the two of them, enjoying the grandeur of the Rhaetian Alps, traversing the Stilfser Pass, the highest pass in Europe, which is open to traffic no more than three months of the year. For this adventure, they have hired a trap—on which their trunk and portmanteaux are now being placed—and have rejected a carriage with a driver. Monsieur de Tourneville, a young Frenchman (in my scene, I have given him the ruddy apple color of a Norman country squire and assigned him a suit of light gray, fine, silky material) is proud of his skill with horses and insists on driving himself. They will follow the Trafoi Brünnen Thal and then continue on the winding road up through the pass to the restaurant at Weisse Knott. There they will lunch on the terrace and admire the splendid view of the Ortler. They will read aloud haltingly, the obelisk-inscription to Josef Pichler. (She comes to me as an animated young woman in a light green pastel gown and wearing a brimmed hat to guard her very fair complexion.) She converses in French with hesitations, for she is English. They speak of their plan, which is to press on through the pass to the Swiss Inn at Stilfser Pass and there spend the night. The following day, they will descend into Italy and on to Lake Como. They linger a moment after lunch, holding hands, and he whispers something to her which no one else can hear. After lunch, they depart in the trap. But they will never reach the inn.

---

[29] Staff officer

We can presume that he reins the horse some ten minutes beyond the restaurant. It is a lonely place and the sound of rushing water fills the ravine. He says that he feels the need to stretch his legs, and he helps her down. Together, they peer over the edge and look down into the gorge. Suddenly, he has braced himself and has given a mighty thrust. In her summer gown, she looks like a pale, green leaf fluttering and diminishing toward the rocks below. I knew that there was a scream in the air, but I could not hear it.

Several days later, M. de Tourneville is apprehended by the Italian police as he attempts to board a train at Bergamo. Here the visitation of those two ghosts stops. The question hangs forever unanswered in the air between the two rocky walls—what secret love affair discovered or what fortune to be gained? The vision gave me back only the sunshine, the sudden cruelty, and the green gown falling through the air.

My fear of heights is in essence a fear of falling and the sense of helplessness in anticipation of certain death. I can think of no fate more horrifying.

"Don't worry, everybody flinches a little the first time," Franz said, patting me on the shoulder.

"Did I look as if I was flinching?" I asked. "It was all very fine except for that last part, you know," I said, shivering with relief.

"Then you'll find the next leg equally exciting," said Franz, turning me around and pointing to where still another cable line swooped up to another remote cliff. A boulder dropped into my stomach. "How many more?" I croaked.

"Three to the top," said Franz, "then cross-country." He had picked up the field glasses to watch Viktor and the men down below load the car that had just reached the valley.

On the third span, we left the green world behind. The luxuriant valley ferns had gone, then the bright patches of turf and heather and the white flowers; finally, the firs and pines thinned out and their last outposts receded beneath us. Now, we were among the great, desolate shoulders of the mountains where the snowfields never melt. We were in the *eiswelt*[30] itself.

The final span swung us over the glacier, and we looked down at the white plain from fifteen or twenty meters, seeing the absurd shadow of our car whisking along the surface like a ghost sled and jumping the gape of a crevasse. As we passed over it, we could look into the mouth and see the great fissure that plunged endlessly down, first walled by half-transparent ice of an eerie, pale blue, then descending to deeper blues, like pools of ink, like pure night.   Now gliding above the fantastic glacial plain, Franz pointed a finger and said, "It looks still, doesn't it? But if you think in decades instead of hours, it's in violent motion. It moves a few meters a year, no more, but in the eye of God, it's a torrent."

The motion I knew about, of course, but I had never thought of it as a "torrent." It was a colorless sea full of white wreckage. The ice billows pressed forward, pushed on by kilometers of motionless ice waves behind, and, caught in them, was an array of marvelous flotsam. Monster spires of great strangeness, toppling marble altars to unknown gods, giant statuary transported from another planet, ruined Gothic bridges, the sinking dome of a mosque, some gravestones of titans, all awash in the frozen sea.

We came to a long, smooth surface of snow, then across a corner of moraine—the stony, gray desert at the edge of the glacial sea. Then another icefield. The aerial cable that had started so far away at Drei Brünnen now came to its final anchor at an island of gray rock in the midst of the Ortler glacier. Here, built in 1907, was a tall stone rest house for climbers, called the *Payerhütte*. On the scarp alongside it, sheltered as well as possible from the prevailing wind and the Italian guns, stood several wooden barracks and storage huts the Austrians had erected from lumber hauled laboriously up the side of the mountain, each soldier bearing a board or a beam. It looked like the base camp for the North Pole expedition—entirely appropriate since it was named for Julius Payer, the famous Austrian arctic explorer who had died the year before. Inside the *Hütte*, the impression persisted in the

---

[30] Ice world

looks of the rough stone walls, big fireplace, beamed ceiling, and the skis and climbing equipment everywhere. Payer's magnificent paintings of alpine and arctic scenes were displayed on the walls.

We were given *Ochsenschwanz*[31] soup in the room that served as officer's mess. My kit arrived on the telpher and I was shown my bunk in an annex. A good many officers were coming and going and Franz stopped several of them to introduce me. I watched their eyes and their smiles to see what they might make of this strange arrival—a Bavarian captain by his insigne: I thought I could detect a flicker of astonishment and a suppressed question, but all were punctilious about not asking.

They fell into two Tyrolean types—the tall, bony, Germanic one and the stocky, dark-skinned Italian. But the straw-haired, blue-eyed First Lieutenant would bear the name of Gianni Lizzola and *Subalternoffizier*[32] Baldur von Obersdorf would be short, voluble, and adorned with a curled, black moustache. Among the enlisted men I noticed an odd disparity: they were all either stocky, middle-aged and heavily-bearded or they were youngsters just beginning to grow their first thin moustache.

Their gray-green uniforms were bleached almost white. With their shaggy hair, forage caps instead of helmets, unbuttoned tunics, sheepskin waistcoats or leather jackets, and dark green *lodenmantels*,[33] they looked more like a large, business-like climbing party than an army. The one strict rule of dress—proclaimed by a sign over the door—was that one must take a white cloth cape from the long row of pegs whenever one went onto the glacier.

Franz noted my look of curiosity at the apparently lax military standards. "These men aren't Austrian regulars. Most of them are *Standschützen,* the voluntary homeland defense force made up of men and boys who are too old or too young for active military service. We also have a company of *Freiwillige Schützen* from Kärnten. They have no military training at all, but they are superb marksmen by virtue of having hunted all their lives, and they are excellent climbers on rock and ice. Fifty thousand of them signed up to keep the Macaronis from taking over the Tyrol. They may be amateur soldiers but their loyalty is not in doubt, and they will die to defend this country."

That afternoon, Franz and a sergeant named Krebs took me out for a reconnaissance. I was given a fur cap, a *loden* coat, and a white cape. A soldier helped me fix crampons—special ice spikes—onto my boots and gave me an alpenstock, a staff with a steel spike on the end. We entered a long shed behind the *Hütte* where we requisitioned two sleds. Out of the kennel next door we selected two teams of Esquimau dogs, six barking, furry motors to each sled. The dogs leaped and yelped in joyous anticipation as we harnessed them.

The sleds were rather longer than I had imagined they might be, set on springy runners that slid over the snow like lightning, and there was room behind the driver for two passengers or some supplies. I squatted down on the oblong of hide that formed the floor and, with a whipcrack, a chorus of yelps and a puff of snow, we were off.

Our fine July day had vanished. The sun was hidden; an armada of gray clouds advanced from the northwest; a low fog crept along the glacier in the distance, masking the peaks around us in a gray haze.

"Excellent," Franz yelled over the noise of our progress, "we are getting back to normal. You begin to see us in our native conditions. You see that high ridge over on the right—that's the Kristallspitzen, 3,800 meters. It's the western anchor of our defense in this sector. To the left, where we're heading, is the peak called the Königspitz—do you see that tall crown? It is 3,851 meters, and our machine guns are the trump card up there. Now, in between, the Alpini hold a kind of semi-circular line on the Zebrù glacier. We can't see it from here, but their regimental headquarters is at the middle of the glacier in a climbers' refuge called the Capanna di Milano, which lies out of sight in the shelter of a crag."

A wind had come up from the west and one of my first lessons in coexistence with the glacier was that lively air, mixed with fine particles of ice, which can cut like a rasp. Franz calmly took two pairs of snow goggles from the pocket of his parka and gave me a pair to put on. They were teardrop-shaped aluminum cups with lenses of

---

[31] Oxtail
[32] Subaltern
[33] Overcoats made of milled wool that is both warm and water-resistant.

smoked glass, attached to a leather strap. Through them the world appeared sooty gray. In front of us the line of dogs bravely struggled through the snow. The runners hissed beneath us like a pair of angry snakes, while the breeze drove the mist past us in ghostly tendrils.

"But the most important thing to remember is that there is a Macaroni artillery forward observation post over there on the Payer Joch. The corporal has his field glasses on us. The sergeant is on the field telephone, talking with the captain of a battery back on the reverse slope. Both observers would like to make us respect the Kingdom of Italy and the House of Savoy a little more, and so they are urging the captain to drop a round or two on us arrogant Austrians. Besides that, their life is very boring in the outpost and they hope for a little practice in ranging the guns.

"'For two little sleds, Garibaldi?' says the captain. 'Your brains have frozen. Do you know how much labor it takes to bring each shell up here—by truck, by donkey, by hoist, and by manhandling? A man can carry exactly ten kilograms on his back. And do you realize that the gun barrels are worn from all the firing in the past month? God knows when I'll get my replacements from Brescia. So, Garibaldi, just calm yourself. Go back and have a cup of hot coffee.'" Franz had done this comic turn in an Italian accent and Krebs was doubled up with laughter.

We pushed forward in silence for a minute. Then there was a dull whine, an echoing crump from far off and, about fifty meters to our right, a fountain of ice splinters spurted into the air.

"No, *no,* Garibaldi: You haven't been listening," Franz shouted. He and Krebs cracked whips and we made a long eastward swerve to where we could run along under the shelter of a razorback ridge. Whatever the reason, that was the lone shell the Italians chose to fire in this battle.

It was the beginning of a long afternoon. The sleds took a tortuous route to avoid the crevasses and we finally approached the forbidding king's crown that loomed jaggedly to the south of us. We left the sleds and dogs and entered a zigzag path—really a shallow trench cut into the glassy slope of the glacier. Its ice steps were well-worn because men carrying supplies or ammunition climbed it every day, but I, unencumbered, was gasping after only a few meters. Krebs and Franz moved very slowly and let me rest frequently—and they made no remarks whatsoever. After a minute, I would try to take command of my lungs, nod, dig my staff into the ice, and start again.

We inched our way up the mountainside to a point where the steep slope required us to climb a series of ladders secured to the rock face. I dared look down only once, to nervously view the long drop below, and then the smooth white vista of the glacier stretching into the fog. I concentrated on climbing each ladder, watching Franz above me and Krebs just below. After an eternity we found ourselves nearing the summit, and the ladders were replaced by stairs cut into the rock. A stiff wind tugged at our white capes and tried gamely to yank us off the slope.

At last we came to the entrance of the position, a little niche in the rocks covered by a half-frozen white tarpaulin. Krebs pulled it aside saying, "*Feldwebel*[34] Krebs is here. Where the devil's the sentry to ask me the password? I could be Cadorna himself." He stepped inside and we followed.

From the half-darkness a heavy, bass voice said, "He's taking a piss. In any case, we saw you a half hour ago, Krebs, and however much you may look like a greasy Macaroni general, we knew you weren't Cadorna." A figure in a bulky sheepskin jacket rose from a doss on the ground and came forward. He and Krebs laughed and slapped each other on the shoulders.

As my eyes adapted to the light, I saw a little chamber, hardly high enough to stand straight in. The chief piece of furniture was a Schwarzlose machine gun, its funnel-shaped snout at the firing-port, its belts piled in a box nearby. The men on watch spent most of their time lying flat and scanning the expanse of glacier down below. The place stank of boredom even more strongly than of tobacco and machine oil.

---

[34] Sergeant

Austrian officer at an outpost high above the valley.

Robie Macauley and Cameron Macauley

This was it—the famous Königspitz post that commanded the Sulden-ferner glacier. To the northwest stood the Zebrù, with the Italians dug in along its ridge, mimicking our own position. Just beyond it rose the pillar of the Ortler, towering over its neighbors and sporting a cowl of wind-sculpted snow.

Krebs pointed out the few spots notable in local history. Down there was the jagged row of rock teeth where an Alpini scaling party had been turned back and one of their ropes still dangled from a crag. Over there was an outpost we had had to abandon as too exposed after its three men were found frozen to death one morning. "The cold is as much of an adversary as the Macaronis," added Krebs. "Fingers, toes and ears are routine casualties, and staying warm is a challenge when every log of firewood must be transported from the valley."

We worked our way carefully along a knife blade of ridge to another position that was no more than a canvas-roofed nest in the rocks. Here, an earnest young soldier—under the impression that I was some sort of inspecting officer—explained the Schwarzlose's properties. Clearly, as a water-cooled weapon, it had not been made for this climate. It had to be cared for tenderly, kept warm under a blanket like a pet; or it would jam. Sentries would light a candle underneath it and keep a pot of hot water handy, in case ice started to form on the chassis. The trick every soldier tried to master was to squeeze off a single shot at a single skier. A difficult trick because in one second of pressure on the trigger, the gun would fire seven times.

As the freezing mist blew in and began to obscure the field below, we stepped out to see a line of rifle pits and lookouts that seemed little more than graves. We made our way up footholds chiseled in the rock and down glassy ice paths. At the final lookout—where sentry duty must never last more than thirty minutes—we gazed out over a desolate gray moraine and the ice wilderness beyond it.

"That is called *Das Ende der Welt*," Franz said.

World's End, *Ultima Thule*, *la fine del mondo*, the Pole itself, the lightless depths of an ocean-floor abyss. I think that we go to such places in a fearful determination to touch that ultimate, to brush the void. The Sioux warrior would rush to touch his enemy with his coup stick and, risking his life, turn away. Looking out over the absolute white of the glacier floor, I understood that it is not the moment of touching but the moment of turning away that holds the true fascination. The chance to graze the future and return from it—death visited, viewed, and escaped. And when we each come to our own glacier at the end of the world, will this help us to know how to walk into it?

Seized by an urgent need, I unbuttoned my fly and took aim at a depression below me in the snow. I was startled by Franz's interjection:

"Pardon me, Melchior, but that's not a good place to do that. There's a spot back here that's more suitable."

"Keeping the glacier spotless, are we?" I closed my fly with some annoyance.

"Hardly," replied Franz solemnly. "That spot down here contains the frozen corpses of six men. We're planning to carry them down to the valley tomorrow. There was no other place to put them while they awaited transport."

I was deeply embarrassed. "My apologies," I muttered. Then, out of curiosity: "How did they die?"

Franz shrugged. "An Alpini scaling party ambushed the position at night. In the fighting a grenade went off, killing our three sentries as well as the attackers. We found them the next day. The Italians will be laid to rest in the Italian cemetery in Trafoi—they're probably from this region anyway."

The north wind we faced on the return trip must have come from Hell itself, it attacked us so bitterly. As the drivers maneuvered their dog-teams along a line of telegraph poles half buried in the ice, marking a trail that skirted the crevasses, the gale struck us dead level with a million tiny sawteeth. The dogs strained forward into the boiling white, their ears back against their heads, the wind pummeling their fur like an invisible hammer. Abruptly the sled slewed on a patch of glare ice and most of the dogs went down, yelping and scrambling. Then we straightened and got onto a rougher track, with barks of progress. For an instant, the wind dropped and we saw that the storm had polished the glacier like a floor of glass, but suddenly the gale was at us again, its salted blast from behind and its snow-demons in front.

I do not know how we got home. It seemed a very long, blind time before we skidded at last to a stop and

22

men were shouting and running out of the half-buried shelter to unharness the dogs, who were now caked with snow. The crust of ice that covered my cape broke with a fine crackling when I stood up.

In front of the roaring stone fireplace in the Payerhütte, we dissolved, standing in our underclothes, boiling-hot cups of coffee in our hands, Krebs going round with a brandy bottle to lace every cup generously. Other patrols had come in and boots were being shed, capes thrown off, and skis stowed away. The talk was loud, Krebs was redfaced.

"God in heaven, you've had the initiation now, Captain!" he shouted. "But don't think this outing on a pretty summer day is all there is to it. Beware—the warm breezes will disappear and the *real* Ortler wind will come soon. And the flowers will fade and we shall be up to our eyebrows in white shit. Are you ready for that, friend?" He gave a mock glare and took a deep swig from the bottle.

"On my way up the valley, my driver told me about a patrol caught in a storm last winter—"

"Ah, the famous Schwarzenberg snowmen, yes?"

"I thought of them when we were out there—could such a thing happen again?"

Franz had been doing knee bends and stamping his feet on the flagstone apron in front of the hearth. "Quite seriously, yes. There is no way of carrying on a rational war up here. The cold-madness will infect us all."

There were jeers from around the room: *Dummes Zeug! Albern!*[35]

"Franz and his famous cold madness: I hear there is a doctor in Vienna who blames all insanity on our sexual nature. Franz, have you sent him your theory about cold weather curdling the brain?" The officer who said this was Dr. Schaller, a thin, high-shouldered young man with a medical corps insigne. He had a peaked nose and a small-mouthed, superior smile.

"Scoff, scoff, Heinrich," Franz said, "but in the worst of it last year, how many men did you send down each week because they suffered from shock—twenty? Thirty? And then there is the mass aberration of that patrol."

"Aberration?" asked the *Sanitätsoffizier*,[36] his superior smile gone and a cutting edge to his voice. "That would seem to be something of a slander against good men."

"That patrol was not struck by enemy fire. Nor were the men lying on the ground as if they had been overcome by exhaustion. All of them had been out on even longer patrols in bad weather and had returned. They were upright on their skis and following a designated trail. Yet something made them halt. And something made them wait until they froze to death—all two hundred and sixty of them."

"Franz, you are indecent!" Dr. Schaller said. "If your brains feel cold, *Alter Junge*,[37] please roast your head in the fire."

"Let him talk," said Lizzola. "If we are quite sane—as you all say—why do we stay up here?"

"Quite seriously," said Franz, "consider the fact that the Alpini aren't savages—they're ordinary *bergsteigers*[38] like the rest of us and they used to be our neighbors. It's just as cold and icy on their side of the lines as it is on ours. We all know it is. So, in the early days, we were easy with their prisoners and they with ours. It was just, 'All right, *Compagno*,[39] back to the rear. The war's over for you.'

"But last winter they suddenly stopped taking prisoners, Melchior. In the morning we'd find one of our little two-man or three-man outposts with everybody dead. The Italians had simply bayoneted them all after the post had surrendered. Cold-madness, you see. War and murder have become the same thing. And now our men have done the same in revenge." Franz was very intense. His coppery brown face glistened in the firelight from the protective grease he had not yet washed off. It was enough to make the angels weep, I thought—the moment that is happening all over the world, the earnest young men in bivouacs who come forth with this remarkable

---

[35] Stupid stuff! Foolishness!

[36] Medical officer

[37] Old boy

[38] Mountaineers

[39] Comrade

discovery, "War and murder have become the same thing!" And, tomorrow, they will all take their rifles and go dutifully into the lines, prepared to kill.

Perhaps it was something the others did not want to hear. There was a brief silence, then men began to move around and strike up smaller conversations. There was a bustle in the room.

Still gripped by his message, Franz turned to me. "In the winter, on the glacier, we can't breathe, we can't fight, we can't move. We are in the very grip of the Angel of Death."

Sergeant Krebs, who had overheard, said, "I'll gladly give them the Ortler if they want it so much. The whole Süd-Tirol, for that matter, if they will give us Capri in exchange."

On that poor joke, the talk ended. After eating some bread and a lump of cheese, I went to the barracks to my assigned bunk. It was frigid—the gale had found every crack in the timber wall and the floor was powdered with snow. In the center of the room, a small iron stove glowed dull red and maintained a tropical zone of its own. Removing only my shoes I rolled myself in a cold blanket and lay niched between a tenor snore in the bunk above and a *basso profundo* below.

I lay wondering if I were really here. There was simply no reason on earth why I should have been snatched from the Satanic cruelty of the trenches to this place. Unless it meant that I had been called upon for a specific task. What had I to offer to these men here on the Ortler? I had no knowledge of mountains or dogsleds; I was frightened of altitudes. My experiences in the trenches seemed alien and irrelevant.

But I had learned some things about myself in those long months on the Western Front: I had become a soldier. I had solved problems under fire, had come to know death intimately. Here, too, I would learn what was needed from me, and I would provide it.

V. Philosopher in a Trench

I pause in my writing to stand up and stretch: it is strenuous to record these chapters of my life and even more exhausting to relive them. I have never taken the time to disinter these old memories and to pore over them, and now I find myself burning with powerful emotions—joy, regret, humor and humility—that are born of these remembrances.

My body reminds me of the abuse it suffered during the war years: my shins ache where the bones were shattered, a scar over my left ear tingles, and my feet throb from frostbite that almost required amputation. When Hilda was alive she used to pamper me: it is a blessing to be married to a nurse. Now that she's gone I've allowed everything to deteriorate.

You are of course, anxious to hear about the Ice Citadel. But in order to understand how the Citadel came into being, you must first understand my earliest experiences in the *Grosse Krieg*—the Great War, that forever changed our understanding of how war should be fought. The technology of killing had become so efficient that the old concept of men fighting men was now obsolete.

On August 9th, 1914 the French had marched into Alsace and captured Altkirch and Mulhouse without much of a fight, and now the German Army was arriving in force. This was territory that France had been obliged to hand over to Germany after losing the last war in 1870, and which the French were determined to recapture. Germany was equally determined to trounce France once again by marching back into Paris.

As we prepared to leave for the front, I suddenly found myself second-in-command of the 4th Company and having to manage the thousand different challenges of getting an army into position to invade France, very few of which I could handle competently after only six months of training. I should add that, with the exception of those few senior officers who were veterans of the Franco-Prussian War of 1870 and a handful who had seen service in South Africa, none of the troops in the division had ever been in battle before.

We had spent several hot weeks marching up and down with full knapsacks and carrying our heavy Mauser rifles—which I was spared, as a second lieutenant, but found myself preparing to go into battle armed only with a small six-shot Reichsrevolver and, of all things, a sword. At this point in the war the army still imagined officers leading their troops across grassy plains, waving their blades as they cried encouragement to the men. I privately resolved to mislay the damned thing to avoid having to carry it with me into the field. The Reichsrevolver turned out to be a trusty friend, however, even though it was about thirty years old when my uncle Wolfram gave it to me; he had carried it in China during his service in the Boxer Rebellion. The metal of the barrel and the cylinder was scratched and the wood of the grip was chipped, but it still fired a good clean shot. I was never a marksman but by the end of my training I could take out a beer bottle at 30 meters, at night in the pouring rain.

In early September our commander Prince Rupprecht brought his forces north to prepare for a massive assault on the fortifications around Nancy, and nine hundred replacements were called up to reinforce the 11th Infantry. Our lives suddenly changed as we were loaded onto trains, disembarked into a thunderstorm, then piled into trucks for a cramped, jolting journey through the night. The next day in the afternoon heat we trudged over a bridge that spanned the Seille, feet sore and bellies growling, wondering when we would be allowed to rest. Gone was our comfortable mess with its port wine and brandy, its beer-drinking contests, and its after-dinner *Zwetschgenkuchen*;[40] gone the warm officer's quarters where my clothes were washed and ironed daily; gone the dull but predictable training drills of marching and shooting at targets. Now we slept uncomfortably on low cots, woke before dawn to weak coffee and stale bread, dressed quickly and stuffed our belongings into sacks before marching off, fully laden and our shoulders and backs still aching from the day before.

---

[40] A type of fruit pie popular in Bavaria.

But no sooner had we arrived than we joined the rest of the Sixth Army in a general retreat to Metz. The fortress at Nancy was too well protected by an outlying network of gun emplacements, and the German Army had depleted itself during a full month of incessant combat. We replacements found ourselves with battle-hardened survivors, all of them exhausted, filthy, seething with rage against the French and beset by a morose, cynical humor. Next to us clean-shaven and well-fed innocents, they seemed ghoulish and fearlessly brutal.

In Metz we made camp on the outskirts of town and had little to do but wash clothes, eat and sleep for three days while the generals fretted. The German right flank, which had thrust to within a few kilometers of Paris, had been pushed back in the first battle of the Marne and the Chief of Staff General von Moltke had suffered a nervous collapse. He was replaced on September 12th by General von Falkenhayn, a much more aggressive strategist who had his eye on Verdun, another massive fortress that the Germans would need to capture. Like Nancy, the terrain around it was well-protected by artillery so that a direct assault would cost the German army dearly.

Falkenhayn therefore decided to cut off Verdun's supply routes. He ordered us to advance west between Verdun and Nancy and set up our long-range artillery on Montsec, a high plateau that overlooked the town of St. Mihiel, which was embraced by a curve of the River Meuse and which controlled the main transportation arteries from the south leading into Verdun: the railroad, the road, the river, and the shipping canal were all side-by-side here. With Verdun's supply lines cut, we would prepare to lay siege to it.

If you look at a map of the Western Front in late 1914 you'll see the "salient", shaped much like a thorn in the side of the French. Certain that we would face a vigorous reprisal, Rupprecht stationed his troops along the river on either side of the town. The 11th marched up into a cluster of low hills to the north, where we were ordered to "dig in". At the time, that phrase didn't mean much to those of us who had just completed six months of training on how to move across battlefields, execute outflanking maneuvers and launch bayonet charges.

The 11th was to reinforce a position that had been occupied by the 33rd Reserve for several days, and as we reached the hilltop I remember seeing the jumble of temporary breastworks with their little cloth awnings and piles of trash and offal buzzing with flies alongside the field kitchens. Much of the line was spread out in what had been a wheat field near a ruined farmhouse, with the crop trampled flat underfoot and a meeting area set up for the officers under a spreading oak tree. Here we were occupying high ground overlooking the river, but just across from us the French had placed several batteries of artillery on hills that were about the same height. Our positions, however, were exposed: there were few trees on this side of the river, while the enemy was thoroughly camouflaged by forest. I hoped it would not be long before our howitzers began pounding those French 75mm cannons—from what little I could see through my binoculars, the French guns were well dug in and receiving supply wagons full of shells. Moreover, the French still held the battered Fort de Troyon, a few kilometers to the north on our side of the river and laden with artillery.

I took a quick walk along the lines the 33rd occupied and saw some shallow trenches, many of them mere ditches half-filled with rainwater, their muddy parapets disintegrating. We would have to do better, I thought, and although I had no training whatsoever in military fortifications I was already thinking of ways to develop a protective line from which troops could fire in safety.

As I was returning to our command post, I noticed a young man with close-cropped red hair supervising a work detail: it was my cousin Fritz, who had helped me construct snow-caves so many years before. He had a sergeant's insignia on his collar and evidently belonged to the 10th Infantry Regiment.

"Fritz, it's you!"

Under a smear of dirt and sweat his face lit up with joy. He had grown considerably—I hadn't seen him for fifteen years—and although he was lanky, he looked good in a uniform. He told me that Helmut and Günter were in the same unit: Günter was a *hauptfeldwebel*[41] but Helmut was still a lowly private.

---

[41] Sergeant Major

"He doesn't want to give orders, he just wants to shoot Froggies," said Fritz. "And you're a high-and-mighty *leutnant*,[42] by God! What are you doing up this way?"

"Same as you, Fritz: trying not to get hit by snowballs." I gestured at the ruts the 33rd had carved out of the soil. "Is that your defensive line? They look more like irrigation ditches than trenches."

"They're just meant to lie down in," said Fritz, laughing. "This isn't snow, after all—it's thick French clay, and all we've got to dig with are those little field spades. Besides, we'll be charging downhill in a day or two. No need to build a castle."

"Don't be so sure, cousin," I said. "Those Froggies are very annoyed with us right now. I wouldn't be surprised if they came charging uphill in a day or two." I bent down and took a handful of the soft brown soil, rich in silica. It held the impression of my fingers just like potter's clay. "Have you ever looked at clay under a microscope? It is truly astonishing."

Just as we were talking, there was a fearful howling sound above us and then a deep rumble to the rear of our position. An angry fist of black smoke raised itself behind our lines.

"It's those French 75s," said Fritz. They're still getting their range—they must be new guns with new crews. If they ever learn to shoot properly, we'll be in for some shit." He peered nervously in the direction of the French lines. Another shell roared over us, and I could hear horses screaming in the distance. Then within minutes they began firing in earnest, aiming first for our supply trucks, blowing up our ambulance and our field kitchen. It was their cruel logic of war—they knew it would demoralize troops who were not yet battle-tested, although our men were disciplined enough to stay where they were. After a brief pause, the shells started hitting our lines.

We were caught in the open with no discernible cover, so everyone simply dove into the grass and tried to find a rock or a stump to crawl behind. The machine-gun crews were trying to set up their MG08s, but at this range there was no hope of doing any real damage to the enemy. The noise was terrible, and each explosion showered us with clods of earth and stones; every so often some bodies would fly into the air, followed by the wails of wounded men. One explosion landed right beside me, and with a shock I realized that my tunic and helmet were spattered with blood. Turning my head I found that beside me the ground had been blasted open, leaving a smoking shell-hole. Quickly I crawled into it and began scraping at the soil with my field spade, a miniature shovel that looked like a child's toy, trying to create a hollow in which to hide myself from the fearful pounding. A man's severed hand landed in front of me, with a wedding ring still on the third finger, and behind me I could hear someone weeping and coughing blood. Cautiously I poked my head up over the lip of the crater. In front of me a dozen soldiers lay trembling, their arms shielding their heads. Fritz was with them, his face streaked with clay and blood.

"Over here!" I called, "Into this hole!" They all turned their eyes towards me, those fragile warriors—boys in uniform who were condemned to die, hoping desperately for a reprieve. As one they rose to a crouch, leaving their rifles, leaning forward as they ran, faces bright with relief that some form of shelter had miraculously appeared, although it was no more than a gash in the earth. With a look of gratitude, Fritz sprinted across the field, throwing his arms out like a diver as he launched himself into the hole.

And it was just then that a shell landed right in their midst. I was thrown backwards by the explosion and enveloped in a cascade of earth and blood—the rich smell of French farmland mixed with the heavy sour smell of German flesh. I fell heavily on my back, deafened by the force of the explosion as stones and pieces of the dead rained down, my face and hair matted with muddy gore. After a moment, my ears ringing, I struggled up to the edge again, looking for Fritz. Where the young soldiers had been there was now another smoking shell-crater, surrounded by corpses too badly mangled to be recognized as men.

I lay there stunned and in horror. It was a frightening fact of the war that in one second, a man could be obliterated from the world as easily as a fly or an ant. This alone was barely comprehensible, but the tragedy of it

---

[42] Second lieutenant

was that we were powerless to protect ourselves, and death could happen at any instant. It occurred to me that in God's great, finely-tuned structure, we were as inconsequential and meaningless as the atoms that compose us.

How much longer the bombardment lasted, I don't know. Eventually I was taken to a truck and carried down into the village where an orderly discovered that I was unhurt, except for my hearing loss. I was given a bucket of water to wash my hands and face, and sent back to the field on foot with a few other able-bodied survivors.

We had lost nearly a hundred men on that hilltop, but our orders were to hold the heights for fear that the French would cross the river there. Our commander, Captain Mecklenburg, a stocky 10-year veteran with a great broom of moustache under a turnip nose, was incensed by our humiliating slaughter and determined to hold the position. He ignored my appearance—my hearing had mostly returned, but I was still wearing my bloodstained tunic and had the haggard look of a shipwreck survivor. Still, there was no time for me to dwell on what I had seen: we had work to do.

"We'll set up our position to the northwest of the 33rd, *Leutnant*," he informed me. "Commandeer some digging tools from those farm buildings, and set up secure positions for sentries and machine-guns. Also put in some latrines back here." He indicated two imaginary points along the remains of a stone wall. "Our field kitchen should be over there, and the dressing station just beyond it. Hurry—there will be another barrage soon." In a trice he had outlined our defenses according to some instructions he had read in a military manual years before. I had been delegated to make this vision a reality, and I saluted hesitantly as he strode off to find us another ambulance.

I took a detail of six men and we picked through the rubble of the nearby farm. It still had furniture and personal items inside it, all in some disarray from their owner's sudden flight. We found shovels, picks, hammers and other implements, including a large quantity of burlap sacks for harvesting wheat. Still shaky and tormented by a pounding headache, I ordered the men to salvage wood from the barn and carry it to a position slightly forward of Captain Mecklenburg's imaginary line.

"The ground's been all chewed up by the shelling," objected *Korporal* Diehl. "There won't be a good place to dig in." He was a bricklayer with a waxed moustache and bulging muscles like some carnival strongman.

"On the contrary," I said, "The artillery has done half your work for you. Just use those shell-holes and dig connecting trenches between them." A shell-hole had saved my life; it was natural that we should take advantage of them. The image of Fritz's wild face kept appearing in my mind. If only he had been given another minute, he might have been saved.

The corporal winced at me. "They're far too deep, sir. Most of them go at least two meters down."

"That's what we *want*, Corporal," I replied irritably, struggling to focus on the present. "They should be deep enough so that the men can walk upright. Fill those sacks with earth and build a step so they can see over the top. Put some planks on the ground so they won't be standing in the mud. Go on, Corporal, it will be worth the extra work." He shrugged and shook his head, thinking no doubt that I'd had my brains knocked loose. But I was already formulating a plan.

In the end we stripped the farm bare, taking boards and beams and cutting saplings to weave wicker fences to keep the trench walls from collapsing in the rain. Under the floorboards of the barn we found a root-cellar full of old potatoes. It was a sad reminder of someone's life, now destroyed by our clumsy war—but it gave me an idea.

The shell-holes made ideal machine-gun nests and with the depth of the trench at two meters, men could walk back and forth without having to crouch. By the third day we had dug fifty meters of trench with a firm sandbag firing-step and two machine-gun emplacements protected with reinforced packed-earth walls. I worked alongside my men, dismantling the barn and shoveling into the fragrant loam—it was good to have something physical to do to help me forget about Fritz. The soldiers were plainly baffled by my notion of trenches, however: at that time no one was building anything so elaborate.

Once we had created a line of defense, I had the men hollow out a space deep under the surface, supporting the sod roof with boards to create an underground shelter. This was also a novelty, although within months every

German regiment would be digging out identical shelters and reinforcing them with cement. My only thought was to create a place where we could all escape those murderous bombs.

Captain Mecklenburg was impressed: "You've built a minor fortress here, Fuchsheim," he observed, poking his head into the dugout, which I had furnished with a table and stools looted from the farm. We had put benches along the walls and even a drain in the floor, anticipating the rain. The company was proud of its work and brought their friends from other units to have a look. I myself felt the pride of a child on the beach who has made a clever sand-castle: I knew this was all temporary and would be washed away under the tide of war, but for now it was an achievement. I only wished that Fritz was here to see our trenches and bunkers, built in the same style as our childhood snow caves.

At dawn the next day the Frogs opened up with another brutal bombardment, throwing us out of our uncomfortable beds under showers of flying earth. A single shell wiped out our supply cache and obliterated a week's worth of rations; another one narrowly missed me as I exited the latrine at full tilt, splattering excrement across my back and sending our carefully-painted latrine sign spinning off into no-man's-land. But with the dugouts and the depth of the trenches themselves, we suffered fewer casualties and were even able to launch return fire with snipers and machine-guns from covered saps that the French artillery spotters hadn't noticed. The men appeared confident and more energetic now that they felt less vulnerable.

When the shelling ended, we were called to a regimental staff meeting. Colonel von Tannenbaum applauded our efforts, although no credit was given to the lowly second lieutenant who had initiated the design. "We've got orders to defend our positions with every means at our disposal," the Colonel told us. "The 4th Company has got the right idea: I want everyone to follow their example. Make deep, wide trenches with flooring and sunken machine-gun nests. We're bringing in cartloads of barbed wire to put in front so the enemy can't approach stealthily at night. And put in a second line of trenches back there, for the cooks and the hospital staff. I'll see that you get picks and shovels and lumber." Captain Mecklenburg beamed with pride, and even though I hadn't been named, I felt satisfied that my work had saved some lives.

And so our trench network began. During the next few weeks we created several lines of trenches, dugouts, and fortified positions that were the pride of the German Army. To avoid the shelling we dug deep into the soft land and built our dugouts under protective layers of earth, rocks and tree-trunks. Eventually some engineers were called in to do the job properly, and I was promoted to *Oberleutnant*,[43] taking responsibility for more mundane things such as communications and requisitioning supplies. The French bombardments had less and less effect as time went by.

In order to keep us guessing, the French mounted several charges and pinned us down with an occasional barrage. At one point, after an especially heavy artillery bombardment, several companies from the French 40th Infantry Division crossed the river on rafts and started up the hill towards us. By now we were well-ensconced in covered positions all along the line, and the shelling had failed to knock them out. It was simple enough for us to rake the attackers with a storm of machine-gun fire, dropping dozens of them in their tracks and sending the survivors dashing back to the river where they dropped their rifles and plunged into the water, leaving their comrades dead or dying on the slope.

Trenches based on my design became the standard from the Flemish coastline to the Swiss border, and although I can hardly take credit for inventing all of it, it was quite an innovation in the early months of the war. The men in 4th Company remembered my brainstorm, and in the late summer months of 1915 they began putting up signs naming each section of the trench: Berlinstrasse, Goethestrasse, Beethovenstrasse, Kaiserwilhelmstrasse, and so on. So I was pleasantly surprised one morning to turn a corner and find a hand-painted plaque informing me that I was in "Fuchsheimstrasse". It was still there, I heard, when the Americans overran the position three years later.

---

[43] First Lieutenant

I remember this all with a twinge of nostalgia, for it was a filthy, nerve-wrenching business, ever hateful and perfused with the stench of the dead, although it was before the use of poison gas had become common and long before the first tanks appeared. After that our clever little burrows could not protect us. But in mid-1916 there was still hope that by originality and cunning we could solve the puzzle of the war and win it. My own contribution was far more humane.

Colonel von Tannenbaum did not forget my work, either. One chilly afternoon in May of 1916, Captain Mecklenburg was shot through the eye by a sniper (he had foolishly gone to hunt mushrooms in the field in front of our trenches) and I was called into the Colonel's *hangstellung*.[44] He had a rather elegant one at the bottom of a concrete staircase, sunk deep into the earth to protect him from mortar shells, with bookshelves and a private lavatory—a far cry from that root-cellar.

When I entered he was sitting at his writing desk. "*Oberleutnant* von Fuchsheim, good evening. Do come in, and pop another log into the stove, won't you?"

I obeyed the order, and the room became comfortably warm. I stood at attention in front of his desk, admiring the photographs of his family on the paneled oak wall: his wife, three sisters and his daughter, all of them very lovely. I noted two cases of *Kirschwasser* stacked in the corner under a phonograph covered with a cloth. On the bookshelf were leatherbound editions of Hoffmann, Kant and von Grimmelshausen.

"I'm going to give you a battlefield commission, Fuchsheim. You've done an excellent job here. It's been a miserable existence here on this line, but a few men like yourself have made it tolerable. Your trench design has saved many lives since we've been here and has confounded the enemy's attempts to take our position. You have no engineering background, eh? Well, you've plainly got more natural ingenuity than some that do."

"Thank you, sir. Just serving my country, sir."

"Well, you may well find yourself serving it somewhere else. They have a need for you up at Vimy. I'll be sorry to lose you, of course, but they're desperately short of experienced officers these days. I understand that the Sixth Army has taken over fifty percent casualties in the past two months."

This gave me a moment of vertigo. Was my reward for good service to be sent to my doom, then?

"See the quartermaster about having your paybook updated, and we'll wait for your transfer papers to come through. You might want to take some home leave, eh, *Hauptmann*? Now would be a good time."

All I could do was gulp and nod.

I left his dugout feeling weak and nauseated. The sun had set, painting a maroon glow on the horizon, ornamenting a deep violet night sky spangled with a vast banner of stars. I stared out into space, wondering where we go when we die—do we really just float off into the ether? In the tranquility of that night it seemed a pleasant destiny, one that I was trying to ready myself for. Let it be quick, I thought, and not a slow death in a hospital somewhere, wrapped in bloody bandages, succumbing to gangrene or sepsis. It seemed too much to ask to be allowed to live through all this and go home again in one piece.

I had ten days of leave in Regensburg before returning to the front, and it seemed to me that I would use those days to bid farewell to all of it. I had seen men prepare themselves for death, just before a suicidal charge into a machine-gun nest, and having accepted their fate, they were at peace and could focus on the task at hand.

But nothing could have prepared me to be catapulted to the very top of the world. Fritz, wherever he was, would have loved it.

[44] Bunker

VI. My Mission

There were no bugles in this camp. We were wakened by a soldier opening the door and clanking one of those unlovely bells the Tyroleans tie onto their goats and cows. The stove was long dead and the temperature inside the barracks was bitter. I donned my boots and coat and walked outside to let the sun wash over my face in the still, bright morning. I went for a stroll along the edge of the camp, where the mountainside fell away beneath us towards the valley. I had slept in lapses, waking to gasp for breath, then dozing for a time. It was usual, they had told me; everyone adapted to the thin air before long.

At breakfast in the mess I sat between Viktor and Franz. With our coffee we were served *grüne würstl*[45] with platters of eggs and bowls of fresh strawberries. I had to gape for a moment, and Franz chuckled. "We don't subsist entirely on army rations," he said, helping himself to a generous portion. "Our men receive regular donations from their families, officers as well as the enlisted. We get clothing, furniture and food—fresh fare from the valley when summer has been kind. In the dead of winter, though, it's canned food and griddle-cakes until you're ready to shoot yourself."

When we had finished Franz said, "You are requested to report to the Colonel. He has been over at the Stilfser positions for three days and he came back only this morning. I'll go along because he wants to see me, too."

I expressed my anticipation. In fact, it was genuine—it would be the opportunity to clear up the mystery about my orders. I asked what sort of a man the Colonel was. I got, of course, what I deserved—the public, officers'-mess version.

"A capital fellow and a shrewd officer," said Viktor in his beefiest way. The old man was a colonel in the Landwehr[46] reserve, with active service in the Bosnian mobilization of 1909. In civil life, he was a company director in Innsbruck. His interest was botany, and he spent his summers mountain-climbing and collecting rare plants. Worked hard for the regiment. I sensed that they didn't like him.

In the flesh, *Oberst* Buchholz turned out to look very much like the average army colonel of 1916—that is, an over-age lieutenant in a colonel's uniform. He was balding, pink-faced and fussy. His cerulean eyes did not meet ours but seemed to veer off and explore the upper corners of the room. He had a habit of bringing his hands chest high, thumb and forefinger together, as if he were holding a baton and about to strike up the band. We had reported to him at eight o'clock in the little stonewalled office that contained his cot, his clothes on pegs, his tactical maps on the wall, his desk, and a small stove. The sun came in through a small dormer window and a chill draft curled around our feet.

He acknowledged me briskly and we sat down. With his elbows on the desk, he stared over his poised hands. "Now that we are fortunate enough to have you here, Captain, I hope that you have begun to form an opinion about solving our problem. You may ask me any questions, either in general or particular. You will find that I like men who ask many questions. I hold that it does not show ignorance, but progress."

"Sir, my question is this: what is the problem?" I hoped that showed progress to him. To me, it showed considerable ignorance.

He blinked; his gaze came down from the ceiling to fix on me, the hands sank to his desk—no Radetsky march for the present. "Ah, but your headquarters in Bavaria received my request—forwarded on from Vienna. It outlined the technical problem and specified the kind of officer we need. You have not read it?"

"No, sir. It has not been shown to me."

His hands crept up to the conducting position and he leaned forward to look at me harder. "You *are* an engineer and also one of those crystal scientists, aren't you?"

---

[45] Boiled Vienna sausage
[46] Austrian National Guard

The truth had a number of boring reservations and qualifications, in particular that I had no training in engineering. The near-truth was simple. "Yes, sir," I said, choosing the latter.

He gave me a yellow-toothed smile as if he had, by using the Socratic Method, brought a backward student around to recognize an important fact.

"Very well then, nothing lost. Put on your cap and coat; we're going outside."

As we followed the Colonel out the door, Franz nudged me and whispered, "Viktor told you he's a shrewd one." I took that as a comment on Viktor.

"He hasn't been shrewd enough to explain why I'm here." I whispered back.

Outside, the morning business of the camp was in full stir. The telpher car was coming in loaded with billets of wood for the stoves. A ski patrol was just starting out across a snowy slope, their white cloaks and hoods giving them a strikingly medieval look. Dr. Schaller and two medical orderlies were standing by a pair of patients on stretchers who were about to make the long telpher journey down to the valley. Some artillerymen were loading a squat little Krupp 75mm mountain gun onto a sledge. With its high shield, short barrel, and long trail, it looked like a caricature of some of the bigger Krupp pieces we'd had on the Western Front.

The Colonel led us down the slope to an enormous wall of ice, the edge of the Ortler Glacier. It nestled against the side of the mountain like a monstrous slab of cheese, glistening in the sun. As we drew closer we could feel a breath of wintry air sluicing off it. The Colonel stopped in front of a white tarpaulin about three meters square covering some kind of hole in the ice. He threw the canvas back with an impatient gesture and said. "Come on, come along."

We walked down a ramp into a crude tunnel. It was a rough oval about two meters high and it seemed to extend about ten meters beneath the glacier. The Colonel took a kerosene lamp from a spike driven into the ice wall, lighted it, and walked into the tunnel. At the end of the rough passage, there was a larger opening. The Colonel held the lantern up. We could see a chaos of ice rubble in heaps, jagged fissures above and on the sides—with one crack that even seemed to penetrate to daylight—and all shapes of fragments and shards hanging precariously from the top.

The Colonel muttered something to himself and let us stare for a minute. Then he led the way back, re-covered the hole with the canvas, and, shortly, we were again facing him from across his desk. He nodded significantly at me and said, "Well, Captain?"

"It is a mistake to use explosives if you want to make any kind of symmetrical opening in ice," I said and stopped. If he liked to proceed enigmatically, I should reciprocate.

The hands posed again and began to tremble slightly. "You have seized the situation at a glance, Captain," he said. The hands gave an unconscious sidewise curvet, and he glanced down in surprise. He put them firmly flat on the desk. "Please continue about ice and explosives."

For the past ten minutes, I had been gathering notes for the performance I could foresee. I must lecture in a style that even our great Professor Bragg would approve. I stood up and the Colonel gazed at me as though he were a university student and I were posed behind an imaginary lectern. I have always wished I could be an eminent professor and frighten large rooms full of young people.

"Ice, you must understand, is a solid crystalline substance formed of crinkled planes composed of tessellating hexagonal rings," I began in my most pompous voice. "In the very beginning, the glacier was formed by snowfall—century after century of snowfall with one layer over another. The first snow becomes compacted and granular, forming first the *névé*, then the *firn* of the glacier. That is, the bits of lace you see on the windowpane are changed into granules when the tiny points melt. These granules aggregate, as we say, around a core and grow into a grain that can be quite small or can be as large as a walnut. And, of course, the whole mass is heavily compacted by the growing weight from above." I frowned at him in an Olympian manner and his eyebrows twitched back. Out of the corner of my eye I noticed Franz trying to hide a smile.

I was beginning to build up momentum: "Thus, glacier ice is a huge mass of interlocked crystalline granules with the principal crystalline axes in different directions. One of the most important aspects of crystals is the matter of cleavage—" I was gathering speed and force "—because there are certain plane directions where minimal cohesion exists and along which the crystal can be most easily split, or cleaved. To be specific, ice crystals cleave in three directions parallel to the faces of the primitive rhombohedron—"

"Very well," the Colonel interrupted. "And so it is wrong to try to blow it up?"

"It is quite wrong, Colonel Buchholz."

"Ah." Silence.

Then—"You have not yet met *Leutnant Ingenieur*[47] Pockengruber. He went down on the telpher to get different kinds of explosives to experiment with. He will be back in a few days. I have a feeling that he will receive your observations with skepticism."

"Colonel, I am guessing that you are trying to create a useful storeroom under the glacier. You wish it to be symmetrical, or roughly so. The nature of ice is such that explosives would fracture the ice far beyond the point at which they are applied. You would end up weakening the material, leading to crumbling of the ceiling and walls. Moreover, explosives release toxic gases which have no means of dissipating under the glacier. Finally, they are costly and will not accomplish the work any faster than chopping away at the ice with hammers and picks."

The Colonel changed the subject by ordering coffee. He did this by simply raising his head and bawling, "Rudi!" There was no sign from the orderly room that he had been heard. The Colonel stood up and, taking a pencil from his desk, called my attention to the map on the wall behind him. It was the Mass Stab 1:75,000 issued by the Austrian Military and Geographical Institute; I had studied one like it on an office wall in Meran. As he was about to speak, a very young and harassed-looking orderly came in with a tin tray on which there were three steaming cups of coffee.

The Colonel took a sip and then aimed his pencil at an irregular line of little red-and-white flags that opposed a line of little green-and-white flags. "Here is the danger, Captain. Here is potential disaster." The right hand, holding the pencil, was tempted into a tiny flourish, perhaps in the direction of the violins. "Here, to the west is the Braulio River Valley and there is the Stilfser Pass, just at the corner where Austria, Italy, and Switzerland meet. The battle lines, as you see, run eastward to our positions there on the Kristallspitzen. Now, beyond is the Zebrù, the highest Italian position, and beside it our lookout on the Königspitz, topping everything else." He stared at the map a moment, then put his hand to his head and sat down slowly.

"But this is really not a line at all. It is a series of wretched outposts. You have seen some of them, I believe. Let me tell you, Captain, you cannot imagine what those nests are like in the winter. The howling blizzards persist for days. Our men are cut off from food, medicine, and relief. They live on tinned beef and drink melted snow. I have seen blind men, men with frozen arms or legs that had to be amputated. Madmen, too. Sometimes a soldier will grow so desperate that he will run out onto the glacier to die. The statistics for mental cases are so alarming that Fourteenth Army headquarters has kept them secret. Last January I lost a dozen men each week to cold, avalanches and madness. We are too exposed and stretched too thin, and I think the Italians know it. Their aircraft have thoroughly investigated our positions."

I had misjudged him as a slightly-comic bandmaster. He was a man of sensibility; there was a note of true sorrow and anger in his voice when he spoke of these horrors. "Captain, in this command we have about 1,500 men and most of them work fourteen hours a day just to keep a scanty picket line in being. Now we face another winter. How we shall survive it I do not know." His eyes looked empty; for the first time, I noticed the tic of a nerve under his left eye.

On the Western Front, we were learning to recognize it as *"eine Nervenerschütterung im Krieg"*[48]—the shell shock that comes not from bursting shells alone. I had seen the Austrian troops billeted in their drafty shacks,

---

[47] Lieutenant Engineer

[48] A nervous shock from war

eating strawberries and drinking beer, but I had not seen beneath their forced gaiety that they faced death every day, and that many of them would die. I had imagined that, somehow, the line would hold—but perhaps it would not. Perhaps we would all die, and the Tyrol would become our cemetery. The Colonel obviously felt the strain as if the whole weight of the mountain was poised above his head.

"So, Captain, now that you comprehend the situation, what do you recommend?" He stood in front of the wall map, the pencil held lightly in his fingers, poised as if to guide a young musician through a difficult piece by Mahler. His eyes rested on me, the Bavarian prodigy who would help him unravel this complex orchestration of troops and guns and horrific cold and howling snowstorms, of a tragic operatic struggle against the Italian invaders who wanted to kill him and all his men. I stood straight as a pikestaff, trying to look capable, but my mind was suddenly overcome by the insistent thought that I was unqualified to help—that the lives of these men could not depend on me: I was an imposter, a charlatan, a simple infantry lieutenant dressed in a captain's uniform.

"Well, Captain?" The Colonel tapped his pencil impatiently. Franz put down his coffee cup and waited for me to say something ingenious.

I shook my head vigorously enough to rattle my brains, and fixed my eyes on the floor. "It's quite a problem, sir. Give me some time to think it over."

The Colonel tossed his pencil onto the table and stared past me, vexed. "Very well, then, you're dismissed." He stood with his hands clenched at his sides as I left.

Outside a bitter wind was pushing in from the north and the frigid air slapped my face like a spurned lover. Granite-boulder clouds slid overhead and the rock escarpment above us made hoarse breathing sounds as the breeze pummeled it. The camp around us was busy with men hauling supplies, but everyone was cold and ruddy-faced.

I walked back to the ice-cave and stepped behind the tarpaulin to look at it again. It was a simple grotto punched in the glacier's side, the ice seamed in gray and brown layers where yesteryear's snows had settled and hardened. The floor was strewn with rubble from the blasts, and some of the ice chunks were black from the explosions.

What was expected of me here? To build storerooms for sacks of dried vegetables and boxes of cartridges? It seemed even more mundane than my duties at St. Mihiel, where we had been under fire. But here the men could hardly conduct a war from underneath the glacier—ice would not provide the kind of protection that mud and clay had given us from the French. Idly, I ran my hand along the rough wall, trying to picture a war at this altitude, with the same trenches and dugouts we had had in France—absurd!

But then a vision from my childhood appeared—the little snow fortress Fritz and I had built on that wonderful winter day. Was it really so strange to imagine shelters in the ice with passageways and lookout posts? No, it could be done. But was I the one to do it? My experience at St. Mihiel was appropriate, except that our true enemy here was Mother Nature herself: she detested this war, she hated our murderous cruelty and had resolved to chase us away or end our hostilities with frost, avalanches and biting cold.

The glacier was our obvious refuge, I saw now—the Colonel simply hadn't the imagination to see how it could be used. I suddenly felt a quickening of my heart, my skin tingling—I could build a refuge for these men, too, one that neither blizzards nor bullets could penetrate, hidden from spying biplanes. And for a few chilling seconds I saw Fritz's bloodied face in front of me, his eyes wide, his hands waving as he ran towards me.

I hurried back to the Colonel's hut and rapped on the door. Inside the fireplace was crackling but the walls exuded the coldness of death; Franz was gone. The Colonel eyed me in silence.

I spoke confidently. "Colonel, I have the solution: you wanted ice chambers to use as re-supply depots, no? Well, why not include ice tunnels for communications and ice barracks for the troops? An ice hospital, an ice kitchen, perhaps even an ice salient for a surprise attack! You need never go out on the glacier in bad weather again! We shall build a city, an Ortler *Eisfestung*[49] in the underground of the glacier! Supplies, ammunition, fuel, building materials for the forts, reinforcements—all will flow unhampered directly to the front, all will be concealed from both observation and attack."

He looked at me a bit stunned, then shook his head slowly. "But this sounds very grandiose. We had thought of a few storage caves, but as for men actually working inside the ice…I don't know. It will be bitterly cold."

"Hardly. In the middle zone of the glacier, the temperature will never drop below the freezing point of ice—it would stay at slightly below zero on the Celsius scale, perhaps around thirty degrees Fahrenheit. I think your blizzards are colder?"

"Much. But tell me, Captain, how you can burrow through iron-hard ice if Pockengruber can't blast through it?" He was staring at the wall map, the colorful maze of ridges and peaks upon which his army was pinioned.

"Simply chop out the passages with ice axes and pickaxes. Crystal ice is relatively fragile and strong crews will give you tunnels sooner than you might expect. You look skeptical, Colonel, but you haven't tried it yet. I believe you will be impressed with how easy it can be. At any one time you have hundreds of men with nothing much to do, if they aren't on sentry-duty or manning the telpher or on ski patrols. A team of diggers can penetrate ten meters a day in the ice. But the glacier will assist us: in the ice there are thousands of crevasses, fissures and natural caves that we can put to use. And we can dig without the Italians even guessing what we're up to!"

The Colonel puffed out his cheeks and grimaced, but his azure eyes were twinkling with approval. "It would provide an opportunity for us to establish new positions," he admitted, speaking slowly. He retrieved his pencil and tapped his wall map with it. "Look here. The Ortler ice-field is divided into three parts: The Oberer Ortler-ferner on the northwest face, which is the thickest ice, but also farthest from the enemy lines. There we could store food and put barracks for men who are in reserve, and the hospital. On the east face is End-der-Welt-ferner, deep ice into which we should place some outposts and tunnels. On the south face is the Sulden-ferner, very thick ice which extends south, parallel with enemy territory. That is where you should concentrate your first efforts, *Hauptmann*. I'd like supply chambers here and here, and a communications tunnel leading past Mt. Zebrù to the Königspitz—there's a thick slab of ice that you can tunnel up into, almost to the summit. It will be a good place for a re-supply depot and a rest-and-shelter chamber for the front line men. We must explore the possibility of digging tunnels between the Madatsch and the Geisterspitz, and to the Kristallspitzen as well." The tic had stopped. His face had a dark flush. The infection of hope was beginning to set in. "Rudi!" he suddenly yelled. "Find Major Stutz and send him in."

"One caution, Colonel. All that I have said is feasible. But we must take into consideration that the glacier is a beast with a life of its own. It is going to resist us in certain ways."

He put the pencil down. "Resist, how?" The Colonel was now in my power. He dwelt on every word I spoke.

"Think of the glacier as something like a river in slow-motion—at least, that is the nearest comparison in nature. It flows at the rate of a few meters a year and it has a current that's a bit faster in midstream than it is along the shores. On a curved stretch of riverbank, it will even creep up the side; it has eddies and maelstroms. On the other hand, it is pure, hard crystal. What I am saying, Colonel, is that we have a moving, changing phenomenon to deal with. Differences in the speed and direction of movement cause great crevasses to open in the summer and, as the ice river moves, some will close and others will widen. Tunnels can be pinched and all our plans altered by a distortion of the ice."

"But how can we deal with it?"

"We'll need to take some measurements, then dig into areas with the fewest fractures. We can put markers on the walls to observe changes in position. Periodically we'll need to widen corridors and rebuild bridges. It is not insurmountable, Colonel."

Major Stutz entered. He did not knock or salute, nor did he click his heels in front of the Colonel's desk;

[49] Ice fortress

he simply bobbed his head curtly and sat down. Now, I had observed that military dress and military manners had suffered many changes in these altitudes, and I no longer expected formality. But Stutz's looks were a contradiction. He had a neat haircut, with a center part that ran all the way to the back, like that of a guardsman in Vienna. His unfaded tunic was properly buttoned; his regulation boots were shiny. I do not know what this said to the Colonel. To me, it said, 'I treat my commander with the contempt he deserves; I treat my army with the respect l owe it.'

He had a lean, long face and deep eyes like firing slits—I never saw the color of his eyes. When he spoke, his voice was rough and hoarse, and he seemed self-conscious about his observations. It struck me that the Colonel found him hard to endure and that was why he had not been invited to the first part of the discussion.

Buchholz began by saying, "As you know, Stutz, our casualty figures here last winter were quite unacceptable—"

Stutz interrupted: "At 14th Army headquarters, where it is safe and warm—"

"Whatever the reason, it is a fact. Please do not concern yourself with the living conditions at Army headquarters. Now, I was saying that..." He went on to produce a very long, complicated sentence, a wonder of grammar, which suggested that the general staff, having interested itself in our problem, had enlisted the leading German scientific minds in a mighty effort to find a solution. He did not precisely say that I was a leading German scientific mind, but he implied it strongly. Then he began to explain the ice-fortress plan as if it were the result of elaborate studies and scientific testing. He referred familiarly to crevasses, the firn, and the tessellating hexagonal shape of ice crystals. He pointed out on the map his scheme for the new installations.

The Major, not overawed, waited to the end. Then he said, "You'd actually have men sleep under the ice? That's unhealthy and dangerous."

"The esquimaux sleep that way all their lives," said the Colonel.

"Because it's the only way they know how to sleep. In the middle of the night, what if a big *schlussbrach*, a big fracture, opens up right under you and drops you a kilometer down? An entire company could be lost and never heard from again."

"It won't."

"Sir?"

"It will not," said the Colonel, "We have the assurances of *Ingenieur Doktor* von Fuchsheim about that; so, no more of your nightmares, Klaus. Now for assignments, and the quicker we begin, the better."

For a man who had been on the verge of despair, the Colonel made a remarkable recovery. Stutz must at once telephone down to Trafoi and get working parties and digging tools up here as soon as possible. We had to make immediate inquiry to find out who, among our own men, had swung a pick in a mine. The Sulden-ferner *Minenstollen*[50] would be cut on a south-southeast bearing, the Oberer Ortler-ferner *Minenstollen* northwest, and both were to be undertaken simultaneously. Major Stutz would take charge of the Sulden-ferner party, Franz the Oberer Ortler-ferner, and Lieutenant Lizzola the storeroom excavations. I would be in charge over all and my orders were to be obeyed without exception. He gave the Major a look at this point and repeated, "Without exception."

They all watched and waited as I studied the chart. Fortunately for me, the Ortler map had been kept up to date with an accurate notation of newly-discovered crevasses. This was to prevent patrols or supply parties from falling through the thin crusts of snow that often concealed them. Having given my scientific lecture, I must now produce my operational directive. I felt like the Captain of Köpenick, an imposter in a uniform.

I purloined a sheet of paper from the Colonel's desk and drew a quick sketch, remembering the design of the dugouts we had constructed near St. Mihiel. First, I explained, I wanted sloping approach shafts at about a 30-degree angle to penetrate beneath the upper, or dorsal, layer of the field to bring us to the center layer, where the temperature is constant. "Take care to put ridges in the floor to prevent slippage—stairs are convenient but with

---

[50] Mine tunnels

constant foot-traffic, our crampons will wear them down. Then we should proceed on a dead level until the point calculated for the upward approach to the surface. Later, when we have time, we can breach the surface in certain spots and put in observation posts using periscopes." As for crevasses, the Sulden-ferner had no transversal faults and only one major longitudinal one. The worst of them would be the marginal crevasses near the mountainsides, for the center seemed to be relatively solid ice. I announced that I would make a quick survey of the ground and would then prepare maps and cross-section sketches for each tunnel-chief.

The Colonel stood up abruptly and the conference was over. He was like a man who had just been injected with some powerful nerve-stimulant. He controlled his hands until we were going out the door. I looked back and saw him turn triumphantly towards the wall map. His hands leapt into position as if to lead a quickstep.

"I had not realized that you were a glaciologist," Franz said respectfully as we took a brief stroll before lunch.

I refrained from telling him that I had not realized it myself until two hours ago. The truth was that I owed much of my apparent expertise on glaciers to my friend Rolf Struensee, who had once told me in some detail of an expedition to Greenland he had gone on with his father. But I remembered that to glaciologists I might not be a glaciologist, but to the Colonel I was the world's leading example—until a real one should appear.

"Yes, Franz," I said solemnly, "though I should imagine that conditions here are a bit different from those of the Humboldt glacier in northwest Greenland. I shall accept this as a good opportunity to increase my knowledge." I had just discovered that becoming an important scientist makes one quite pompous. I was enjoying that.

VII. The Ice Citadel

Thus began the construction of Ice-fortress Ortler and I became its chief fantast, its architect, its King Ludwig, with an edifice more unbelievable than Neuschwanstein.

I had more than one occasion to recall the wondrous sculpture of that old Gypsy as I penetrated the glacier, creating my own ice-marvel in reverse: tunnels, corridors, galleries and state-rooms hollowed out of the glacier's cyanotic interior.

The Colonel had not at all exaggerated the desperation of his circumstances. When the battle for the alpine summits began in 1915, both armies had at first avoided the icy expanses of the glaciers, clinging to the bare stone ridges wherever possible. Gradually, as the war went on, patrols with crampons on their feet began to venture out onto the glacial seas. Skis and dogsleds, which had been recently introduced from Scandinavia, became the principal means of transport over a terrain not negotiable by horses or motorized vehicles.

In April of 1916 the Italians had attacked during a snowstorm and had captured the crest of the Adamello glacier. In May and June, our great offensive south of Trient had briefly occupied Asiago and had fallen back. About this time—without my knowledge—an Austrian Lieutenant named Leo Handl had been attempting to reach an outpost with a group of men and came under enemy machine-gun fire. Spotting a crevasse in the snow, the quick-witted officer anchored a rope and led his men down into the silent underworld of the glacier. By luck, they landed on a sturdy ice bridge and made their way beneath the surface beyond the Italian position to a spot where they could tunnel up through the firn and reach their destination. Handl was elated, and having been trained as an engineer (unlike me) he immediately began developing plans for exploiting the glacier. He discovered what glaciologists already knew—that the great berg was not solid but, in the lower depths, where immense pressures cause melting and motion, there were channels and caves in the ice.

The Alpini and Bersaglieri[51] regiments were excellent mountaineers, showing their greatest skill on rock while we, eventually, had the superiority on ice. They seemed to have unlimited labor to build their telphers, raise heavy guns to mountain positions, and to carry out re-supply. Many times, in my encounters with the Colonel, I was told how the swarming Italian troops could crush our fragile line, which would lead to a domination of the Trafoi and Sulden valleys—and then the Vintschgau and the road to Meran would be open to them. All Austrian forces west of Meran would be cut off and forced to surrender.

The Colonel's first thought had been merely to blast some storerooms out of the ice with a few sticks of dynamite. Whatever would not suffer from the cold could be put there. Knowing little about the effect of explosives on ice, however, he did have some misgivings. He therefore sat himself down and wrote a voluminous request to Meran headquarters, the first part of which requested a sapper trained to lay charges. (Pockengruber had arrived a few weeks thereafter.) The second, and much longer, part of the request (eventually, I saw the whole packet, which ran to some twenty-two handwritten pages and contained a number of misspellings) asked for the presence of "an expert on ice-fields." Because he did not have a dictionary and because he was unfamiliar with this rather arcane branch of science, he did not realize that he desired a glaciologist. In a quaint and prolix style, the Colonel described a kind of hippogriff cross-breed between a civil engineer and a crystallographer. He did not know that he might get, in the bargain, a frustrated ice-sculptor as well.

I imagine this multi-layered document coming to rest, like an unwelcome country cousin, in the office of a harassed adjutant in division headquarters in Meran. He glances at it, finds that it presents a very dense problem enveloped in much rhetoric and questionable spelling. Do not, however, underestimate the mental resources of the Austrian Army! He writes a meaningless but officious endorsement and sends it on to Army headquarters in Innsbruck. Eventually, it is directed to the desk of an overburdened captain, who looks at it and reads a few pages

---

[51] Italian elite light infantry.

(All this because some chap wants to blow a hole in the ice? Holy Ghost!) adds a page of authoritative jargon, and speeds it to liaison in Munich, aware that the Germans are well-known to produce experts on any abnormal subject. The rest is mystery. We shall never know what clerkly Darwin discovered me, because I was on leave and in process of re-assignment, my records must have fallen to him to deal with—and with what joy he must have matched the lunatic Austrian's request with the papers of a crystallographer with some distinction in digging trenches. The fact that I had no formal training in engineering was conveniently ignored.

All would have been much simpler if only someone in the line of addressees had managed to apply the word "glaciologist" to the problem. There were numbers of well-qualified Austrians to fit this description, including Eduard Brückner, author of the estimable *Die Alpen im Eiszeitalter*.[52] Several of them did eventually visit the Ortler.

——— ⨯⨯⨯ ———

The tunnel building began with efforts to rectify the ragged results of Pockengruber's dynamite. I assigned one crew the task of clearing and extending the ramp at an angle of thirty degrees, and I put another crew to work reinforcing the entrance to this adit with timber sides and a ceiling. Ice was a considerably different material to work with than the clayey soil of eastern France, but in some ways easier. When treated with respect, by which I mean through judicious sculpting rather than brute explosions, it is more predictable than mud and somewhat safer.

The Colonel could not keep himself away from our work, and he came nearly every hour to inspect our progress. I found that, unintentionally, I was now giving him orders, which he accepted eagerly. I asked for a man with surveying experience to be designated to assist me; I demanded that all soldiers not assigned to the tunnel work be barred from the area; I required that the ice shards from the excavation be carted off as unobtrusively as possible, and spread out, not piled, on some part of the glacier where they would blend in with the surrounding ice.

The Colonel was delighted. All quite unconsciously, he would stand to attention while taking his orders and then bustle off to see that they were carried out. Soon he was surreptitiously seeking my approval, though I kept up the pretense that he was directing me. We had rather long, dull talks about the tactical situation. It was the only time that he grew poetic and used figures of speech. Once, he told me that we were exposed "like beetles on a frozen pond." Another time, we were "like ants on a sugar-cake." Sometime later, when we had been talking of something else, I suddenly said, "Up here, we could be described as fleas caught on a looking-glass." A bit malicious of me. He nodded vigorously and exclaimed, "I couldn't have said it better myself!" Nonetheless I found myself warming to him. He worried like a mother hen over the lives of his troops, and suffered deeply when they suffered. He fought regular battles with his superiors in Meran and Bozen over extra supplies of food, clothing and firewood. He lived in dread of the day that he should have to order his men into battle against unfavorable odds: he knew of the battles on other fronts where men died by the thousands. His command had taken a toll on his nerves, and he had grown increasingly desperate until I arrived. Now I sensed that he also craved glory, and would jump at the chance to push the Italians off the glacier.

——— ⨯⨯⨯ ———

I chose a day at the beginning of the second week to take my new assistant, *Zugsführer*[53] Erich Pulvermacher, on a survey expedition of the Sulden-ferner. Erich was a long-headed, grave young man who had learned his surveying at a *technische hochschule*[54] and his respectful silences during a stint of service as a footman in a noble

---

[52] The Alps in the Ice Age
[53] Lance corporal
[54] A technical academy

household in Vienna. He was a good man and full of gratitude at being relieved of his monotonous duty attending the telpher station. When I told him to carry out something, he paused for just a moment or two as his mind ticked—not quite audibly—through his options to the soundest one. After my experiences on the Western Front with many different sorts of *unteroffiziere*,[55] this almost brought tears to my eyes, because it is very German to admire efficiency but not very German to possess it. Thus, in this world, we have a reputation for effectiveness only because God in his mercy has placed us here among Italians, Russians, and Spaniards.

Erich and I set out just after sunrise in what one calls in the mountains a *dichte, feuchte Nebel*,[56] or a Scotch mist, very typical of this region. The peaks around us were vanishing specters and the snow itself seemed to take on a grayish cast. The air smelled like wet laundry.

Our dogsled-driver-and-guide was a surly private from the village of Sulden who was supposed to know the ice landscape well enough to keep us out of trouble. At first, I was pessimistic about the visibility but I was assured that it would clear and so I had Erich load the dogsled with a theodolite and its tripod, a sextant, some chain, flags, and a field book while we, with our steel-tipped staves, marched behind. I wanted to survey the Sulden-ferner glacier to the southeast of the Ortler where the Colonel wanted a lengthy tunnel to go all the way to the base of the Königspitz.

At about eight o'clock, the mist began to thin as predicted, and we had a sun like a big, pale Maria Theresa thaler in the sky, which was ideal for my purposes because I wished for enough cover to prevent the Italian lookout on Monte Zebrù from realizing what we were doing and yet enough line-of-sight to allow us to work. We crunched across the firn on the glacier's back with the Ortler behind us and the Italian post on Mount Zebrù to our right. In front of us to the south lay the broken majesty of the Sulden-ferner, blocks and hummocks of ice glistening in the weak sunlight. The summer had melted most of the snow off the slopes but some of it clung to shadowed depressions in the rock like plaster in the fingerprints of a great sculptor who had modeled this landscape and was still making changes, shaping and finishing and implementing sudden, inspired revisions. Ice is a perfect medium for grandeur, but you must understand it and use the right tools. I was determined to discover how the glacier lived, how it resided here in this valley, and create within it a haven for men to take refuge. The shape of it was forming in my imagination.

Everything went well the first part of the day, and my plans began to take form swiftly. I could almost visualize my under-ice communication system, a modest imitation of the Berlin *untergrundbahn*,[57] with supplies and fresh troops moving briskly toward the front on sledges in one track while tired soldiers, wounded, and equipment in need of overhaul moved to the rear on another. Electric lighting would need to be installed and certain items would need to be kept handy in niches chopped into corridor walls: axes and shovels in case of cave-ins, kerosene lanterns and first-aid kits. Also some sort of alarm system would be needed in the event of an enemy infiltration. My mind whirled with new ideas and plans.

As I had suspected, the central area of the Sulden-ferner glacier presented no very nasty problems insofar as I could judge from the surface. The three or four marginal crevasses varied from a meter to ten meters in width at the top, but I wanted to have a look at the great longitudinal crevasse with which we had to deal. At one point, it ran rather close to the Zebrù, but I proposed to examine it farther out, some two thirds of the way from the camp at Payerhütte.

By late in the afternoon, we had finished surveying the route right up to the lip of this great schism. As we came close, I felt in myself a pleasant anticipation that I could not explain. And when I looked down into the gulf, I experienced a feeling of joyful intoxication that was even stranger. Here, close up, was that descent that had so fascinated me in my fleeting glimpse from the telpher car. I wondered how deep into the ice such a monstrous

[55] Non-commissioned officers
[56] A dense, damp fog
[57] Underground railroad

fissure would penetrate—if it went as far as bedrock then we would have a measurement of the depth of the ice, which would be helpful in planning construction. But beyond that, I felt a profound thrill at the thought of entering this mysterious ice-canyon, to discover what wonders the interior of the glacier offered. I told Erich that I must get a look at the inside. He shook his head doubtfully but said nothing.

I had the two men drive pitons (eyeleted steel spikes) into the surface and told Erich to tie the end of the heavy rope around his body and keep the lighter signal rope in his hand: two quick yanks would mean I wanted to descend further, three quick yanks would mean to stop. When stopped, another quick yank would mean 'pull me up!' Then I made a kind of sling for myself and, ice axe in hand, had them lower me down the wall. The sun had changed from a pale, silver thaler to a rich, golden guinea riding above the Swiss Ober Engadin and the whole ice world was hued with that wonderful, decadent, faded gilt one sees on the picture frames in old palaces. I felt half-enchanted as I floated into the crusted maw.

Palace indeed!—one for which even my rather baroque imaginings were unprepared. As Erich and the soldier lowered me, the colors transformed themselves from that gold-washed alabaster to an icy blue struggling to emerge from a translucent prison; Erich paid out the line and I descended haltingly. I made myself swing in a slow circle to take in the fantasy around me.

Like a thief entering through the broken ceiling of a Pleistocene Winter Palace, built by an insane Romanov dynasty at the beginning of the world, I slid gently down. Past the huge buttresses of the vault and then into the flamboyant Gothic wilderness of the ceiling—glistening pinnacles, great twists of *cornicelli*, strange garlands of hoarfrost, spear-point finials, gross capitals overflowing with flora, and wide swags of transparent ice.

It made even Ludwig II's Herrenchiemsee look prim and puritanical. I could not help thinking of our late monarch, *der Märchenkönig,*[58] as I came to rest on a ledge some fifteen meters below the surface—and how he would have been mad with envy of the chandeliers among which I now stood. In his island palace, where he spent exactly nine days each year, he had a crystal hall of mirrors with enough huge lustres to burn 2,500 candles at a time. I remember my grandfather describing the nights when our king would sit for hours gazing at the tear-drop glitter around him and, whenever one of the lustres had to be brought down so that its candles could be replenished, he would clap his hands like a child. I felt like clapping mine now. The boy who was dismayed at a tall flight of stairs, who shuddered to go even with his father over the iron walkway that spanned the railway tracks, was spellbound, lost in euphoria in the black night beneath the ice.

I walked along the ledge for a few meters, signaling Erich to bring the line along until I saw a chance for another clear drop. Below me the light faded into an indigo shadow illuminated by a sparkle of ice-dust from the surface. As I started to descend again, Erich shouted something I could not understand, and I simply called up, "Don't worry, I'll be careful."

Four or five meters below the ledge, the walls curved back and I was now like a tiny clapper in the wide bell of the crevasse. Above me the sides looked dazzling white, but here in the shadows, the clear, pale blues had turned to a deep fathom aquamarine and all the spectacle of ornament receded. My lunatic palace had been transformed into a vista of the ocean depths. I listened for a trickling sound of water and thought I heard it—ice-melt from the surface flowing through channels in the ice and downhill to the valley. Except for that distant and intermittent trickle, the world was in absolute silence; I was in the midst of superb, lonely profundity, I was drawn to it; I was in love with it; I was drunk with it. Just to demonstrate to myself, I found a piece of ice the size of a plum that had stuck to my sleeve and dropped it into the emptiness. I listened for a long time but I could not hear it strike.

My original notion in coming down had been to note the approximate place where our shaft would breach the crevasse wall and to decide on the best method of bridging. I had been occupied by such questions as how to cut the bridgehead into the opposing wall, whether or not we could suspend the bridge from anchors driven into the crevasse walls above. I needed to calculate how much material the bridge would demand and how much weight it

---

[58] The fairy-tale king

would bear. Those questions had receded. I jerked twice on the signal cord to tell them to lower me still farther. Far beneath me lay solid earth that had not seen the light of day for centuries, but I knew our rope was not long enough to let me catch a glimpse of it. My mind was becoming clear and purified in this world of absolutes. It was as if I were surrounded by and breathing some strange ozone that lifted all my senses, and I had the chance to see art never yet beheld, and entertain ideas never thought before. I was beginning to hear a faraway, airy music.

The rope jerked suddenly taut. I found myself being hauled up with a violent and powerful pull and, twisting in the air, I watched the light turn from black to blue to diamond again and all the eerie ceiling-work I had so dwelt on now spun before my eyes. I raised my head and squinted against the glare and called out, but there was no answer.

When I was about twelve meters from the top, there was a loud noise up there, the kind of thump made by a heavy boot driven into a football, and the ice wall beside me trembled and shook off some bright splinters. From above there came a shower of ice-pebbles. The pull on the rope stopped, slackened, and I suddenly fell a meter or more before I jerked to a stop. There I swung with no answer to my calls.

I reached out with my ice axe—an instrument rather like a short-handled pickaxe—in an attempt to hook onto a projection. I came close, but I failed by a hand-span and the rope slipped downward a few centimeters more before it stopped again. I hung there and studied the wall minutely, trying to map an escape route up its surface—the ledge where my right boot would land, the niche, one meter to the left where the other toe could find lodging, the handhold six feet above, and then the slab where there was no handhold. I surveyed all this calmly and all seemed to fall into place. Like a child on a swing, I began to kick my legs in a slow rhythm to bring me close enough to catch on.

I was gripped by a strange state of imperviousness, an illusion that there was no danger and that I would not fail to make the right moves. In this deluded condition, when luck so distorts all the laws of probability, fortresses can be stormed, fortunes can be made on the racecourse, and women of incredible pride, beauty, and selfishness can be brought to bed. My axe sank in just the right place and held firm. My boot found the one possible foothold and it was secure. I looped the rope and swung like an acrobat onto the projection above; I was more agile than any chamois.

My plotted way led up over a large, ovoid shape, like half an alabaster egg, through a pack of gargoyles sprouting out of the wall, then in a reverse zigzag across a bow-window of ice where there were some handholds at the top but where footholds must be chopped before I could proceed. My muscles at first rebelled, but twenty months of digging trenches had kept me fit, and I was inspired by my luck in spotting handholds and perches.

In a half hour's time, I gathered some notion of how real climbers must behave, how painstaking and precise make-ready is followed by smooth, quick action. In my state of mystery and élan, it came to me that human failure is usually a compound of impatient preparing and halting execution—and I felt as if in some way the ice had bestowed upon me superior strength and foresight. I was soon climbing so effortlessly that it seemed a shame to reach the surface. As I ascended into the wind I took a last nostalgic look at the dreamlike world below. The walls of the crevasse converged into a depth of blue like no color on earth: rich and cruelly perfect, a darkness that could harbor both love and evil, murder and kindness, frozen solid and entombed forever in clandestine imprisonment until the end of time.

Sounds of mourning were the first voices I heard as I came over the rim of the crevasse. The shell had struck near enough to the dogsled to kill several of the dogs and to wound others, and there was a mutter of whining and yelping. Using the axe, I pulled myself cautiously forward and immediately lay still just beyond the edge. Though the team had been hurt and there were furry bodies lying in wide bloodstains on the ice, the sled seemed to be intact. At first, I did not see either of the men; then I noticed one body huddled just beyond the sled and the other lying across my rope at the point where it was anchored.

I thought back to Franz's mock-psychology lesson in trying to predict the thoughts of the Italian artillery observer. Now, I had to do just that in earnest, to try to look through his field glasses and listen to his mind.

I did not move. Perhaps he had missed my emergence. He was satisfied that the one or two rounds had immobilized our sled, but he was waiting for the possible appearance of other Austrians in the patrol. If he saw any movement, he would order another round. But—as Franz had noted—artillery shells were like treasures here and any unnecessary firing went on a man's report.

To my great advantage, the sun had now dropped very low over the Swiss peaks and the shadows on the glacier were growing long and deceptive. In my eyes at least, the light had changed from a gilt to a melancholy urine-yellow.

The Italian *tenente*[59] was talking on the telephone to his headquarters at the Rifugio. He was requesting that a patrol be sent out. Since the hit, he said, there had been no activity around the sled (I hoped this was what he was reporting) and the small Austrian party seemed to have been casualties. The purpose of the patrol would be to examine the sled for any papers or instruments that might reveal why the Austrians were reconnoitering the crevasse. All this I imagined.

If my imagination was reliable, I would have a grace of about ten or twelve minutes to do what I had to do. In the meantime, I stayed motionless, crouched, my face lowered, still feeling myself under the eye of that guardian angel who had kept me alive on the Western Front.

The observer who had called down the shellfire must, by now, have been replaced at his post by his companion. It is almost impossible to stare fixedly for a half hour at a few motionless spots on a glacier. The new observer would know the terrain as well as the other, but the relationships of objects were changing as the shadows stretched and blackened. Would he realize, for instance, that the shadow of one small ice hummock now had lengthened to a point close to the crevasse and had, in fact, merged with a much smaller shadow? Under cover of the hummock, I was able to sit up and move my arms to get the blood in circulation again.

Then the phoebic magician who had been playing tricks on us with his silver thaler changed to a gold piece, at last showed us a tarnished copper pfennig before he made it vanish behind the mountaintops. It was now half dark, and I moved quickly up to the sled.

The morose young driver was dead from a hole punched through his throat by a shell fragment. Erich was still breathing, though unconscious, and as I could find no evidence of blood or wounds I assumed that he had been hit in the head and had a concussion. When he was struck, he must have fallen across the line that had been wound around his waist at his end and attached to me at the other—and this is what had saved me. My weight had pulled him a few meters along the crust until he had lodged against an ice projection.

Now I had to make a scheme of action very effectively and very fast—the knife and field glasses to begin with. I found binoculars on the sled, the strap knotted around a hook in the frame so that the case would not swing. On Erich's belt I found a big sheath knife and it then took perhaps two minutes to cut the rope and load him onto the sled. I tossed all of our surveying instruments out onto the snow, knowing that the extra weight would only slow me down. Either we'd recover them later or the Macaronis could have them.

---

[59] Lieutenant

Dogsleds carrying supplies across the glacier.

My plan now called for cutting free the dead and wounded dogs and harnessing the sound ones. It took perhaps another four minutes to prove that impossible. Some of the dogs snarled at me and showed their teeth when I came too near. It was clear that they trusted no sledmaster but their grim pilot, who now lay beside the sled in his own congealed blood. Moreover, the dead, crippled, and unhurt were so closely mingled that it would take daylight and time to sort them out. I simply cut whatever traces I could reach and hoped that I had freed the living.

The hardest part would be to try to find my way back to our lines but, because we had been surveying, I had a much keener sense of that than one might ordinarily. I fashioned an impromptu harness for myself, got myself into it, and plotted a course homeward by the luminous dial of our compass. With the binoculars I took a quick look in the direction of the Italian lines. The patrol materialized at the right end of my sweep. They were mostly hidden by a snow ridge, but I could see their capuchin heads bobbing irregularly as they skied towards me from the south end of the glacier.

I was by no means an impressive dog team. The sled, however, with only Erich aboard, glided along behind me quite easily. I leaned forward, dug in with my crampons, and tried to manage a brisk trot. I had to settle for a kind of loping walk. Keeping to this pace, I got some two hundred meters along and onto the reverse side of an extensive swell in the crust before I permitted myself to fall down, gasping, for a rest and for another look through my excellent Zeiss glasses.

The Italian patrol had come into view, spread out in an extended line and approaching the scene of our disaster. The men were moving quite cautiously now, perhaps aware that something had altered on the small stage. My advantages were two: the fall of dark—for a few minutes, the light over the glacier had seemed dyed with a melodramatic Tyrian purple before it slipped into gray—and the fact that immediately close to the crevasse the ice was rough and uneven, and therefore difficult for skiers.

As I watched, the patrol split. A party of four or five had taken off their skis and were approaching the bodies on the ice. The other dozen or more stayed wide, remaining on the powdery crust and continuing to move in my direction. They had unshouldered their rifles and their heads were swiveling as they kept watch. In their white hoods and dark snow-goggles they looked like an alien race.

I tried to rise and I knew that I had to think again. My ribs and my knees ached and my lope across the ice to this spot had been exhausting. Could I continue to haul Erich across the glacier and risk being spotted? I shook Erich but he remained limp and unresponsive, a thin snore issuing from his open mouth. I took another glance at the nearest pair of Alpini through my glasses and they looked remarkably close, though blurred in the darkness as their white capes fluttered in the wind.

Suddenly, I heard a low snuffle behind me and a footstep on the snow crust.

I said, "*Non sparare! Mi arrendermi!*"[60] I thought there must be only one of them, he had approached so silently. I might still have a chance. I didn't know how well he could see me because the twilight, by this time, had been replaced by a kind of hazy moonlight. I raised my hands above my head, slowly rose to my feet, and turned around.

He was about seven meters away, his tongue hanging out, his tail wagging, and a happy expression on his face. He seemed not to understand a word of Italian; in fact, he seemed to be applying for work. His name was General Franz Conrad von Hötzendorf—Conrad to his friends. He was still wearing his harness, and with shaky hands I quickly hitched him to the sled. Erich moaned a little and his eyes opened once. He still did not show any signs of bleeding, and I knew he would survive.

Conrad was accustomed to pulling heavy loads, and with me pushing the sled he was able to keep up a good pace. Like any general worth his salt, he knew where our lines lay; what is more, he knew the best way to get to them in the darkness. I tried to keep the little ridge between us and the Italians as long as possible and, when at

---

[60] Don't shoot! I surrender!

last we had to emerge onto the unbroken plain, I felt that we had left them well behind. They would undoubtedly reason that a search patrol would be out for us and that any further advance might be dangerous.

The search patrol did find us within half an hour. Within an hour, Erich was being tended to by Dr. Schaller and I was sitting before a bright fire with a steaming cup of coffee and a small glass of brandy. When dinner was served I made sure to put a length of sausage aside for Conrad.

The next day, another patrol recovered the surveying instruments (which the Italian patrol evidently didn't want) and the soldier's body. Seven unwounded dogs had all made their way home in the night. Erich was groggy and unhappy about the loss of the other dogs, for whom he had great affection, and swore that he would seek vengeance on the artillery crew atop Mount Zebrù. Not a word about the slain private, nor much in the way of thanks to me for saving his life. All in a day's work, I suppose.

* * *

In early August I learned the full meaning of the Biblical words, "a howling wilderness" when the first real storm of autumn struck the Ortler. The driving sheets of white I might have expected, but the screaming wind was like the sounds in some vast madhouse. To the simple cold of the body was added a frigidity of the soul. Perhaps some element of it was an atavistic shudder bequeathed to us from our ancestors, the first European men, as, season by season, they watched their hunting grounds being covered by a great shroud of ice, and they retreated southward. And when they listened at night to the wind from the north, they heard the same sounds that I was hearing now and they knew that there was an almighty god up there, Deity of Cold Death, Sovereign of the Snows, Lord of Blizzards. And they knew that he was insane.

This was, nevertheless, the best of times to proceed with our work. I had almost the entire reserve force at my command, more eager workers than I could use at first. In the ice chambers and tunnels that were now beginning to take form, the air was no colder than that of the barracks and the men who were working with axes were stripped to their gray army shirts and trousers and, even at that, were perspiring.

The officers had organized the men into teams with former miners to make up the cadres. I watched Lieutenant Lizzola's team chopping away, by the light of carbide headlamps, with great enthusiasm and good humor. They were joking about their *"Drang nach Südpol"*[61] and conferring the *Eisbeinorden*.[62] I had ordered the tunnels cut about four meters wide and two meters high, which allowed enough room for two axemen to work at the same time. It also provided sufficient width for two-way traffic. Close behind the hewers, there were men with shovels and wheeled carts to carry off the broken ice and, still farther back, another team with chisels and hatchets. Their task was to smooth the tunnel floor to a somewhat uniform level and to cut any dangerous projections from the walls. I insisted that the ceiling of the tunnels be arched, to reduce drippage and the chance of loose ice dropping onto people's heads. I also had them cut grooves into either side of the floor, to carry off any meltwater like gutters on a city street. I knew that with human traffic the temperature would often rise and water would start to accumulate. The shifts were thirty minutes and, as men came off theirs, they were given hot coffee or chocolate.

It could have been a scene painted by Georges de la Tour—strapping torsos, muscular arms, sweat on bronzed faces, glittering shards from the axe, all in deep chiaroscuro from the unearthly carbide glare, reminding me of a quote from Job 38:

---

[61] Drive to the South Pole

[62] A pun: "Eisbein" is a pickled ham hock; "eis-bein" means also "icy leg". The "Eisbeinorden" is a fictitious military medal, "The Icy Leg Award."

*Have you entered the storehouses of the snow
or seen the storehouses of the hail,
which I reserve for times of trouble,
for days of war and battle?*

*From whose womb comes the ice?
Who gives birth to the frost from the heavens
when the waters become hard as stone,
when the surface of the deep is frozen?*[63]

The sounds of chopping and hacking and of the ice splinters clinking on the floor reverberated down the long corridors unceasingly. For me it was the noise of progress, of creation—I strolled alone in the tunnels, listening, sometimes switching my lamp off to relish the darkness. The cold emanated from the ice walls around me, but as time passed I grew accustomed to it and left my great-coat on my bunk. My boots made a reassuring thump on the ice-floor, or an odd clunk when I was wearing crampons, and a man's voice could be heard clearly a hundred meters distant. With his mellow baritone, Staff Sergeant Viktor and his Tyrolean soldiers sang to pass the time, and the ghostly music was audible even at the Payerhütte entrance.

I sensed a change of spirit among the men. The Austrian troops—I was beginning to think of them as "us"—had been living and fighting on that knife-edge of existence, scraped raw by the cold, abused by the wind. Whereas before they had seemed like prisoners resigned to make the best of a cruel incarceration, now they were filled with purposeful energy, striking at the ice with vigor. For so many months this glacier had kept them pinned to a frozen wall while the Italians took shots at them. Every so often a fist of snow would pummel them from above, or a hurricane-force blizzard would force them to spend days in their drafty, stink-ridden barracks, when sentries in their outposts would perish, enveloped by the whiteness until they lost hope and died. We had invented a way of escaping this fate, we had created shelter and a haven in which to remain strong, we had deceived that wicked god of ice by hollowing out a sanctuary in the soft underbelly of the very glacier itself: we had devised—I thought, in my euphoria—an instrument of victory.

The Colonel came to visit us just as the first large chamber—the mess hall—was being finished. Men were taking down the ladders after the last touches on the vaulted ceiling were done. He beamed like a Greek at his first sight of the wooden horse and, to the evident disgust of Major Stutz, who stood in the background, paid me several compliments.

"It proceeds faster than I should have dreamed!" he mused, admiring the high ceiling, designed to allow the smoke from our lanterns to dissipate. "So much for Pockengruber and his fireworks. Unfortunately, however, our messages seem not to have reached him and he arrives as soon as the storm is over and the telpher operates again."

"Let him come," I said. "I need the explosives and experts to place them."

"You do? But why?" The Colonel stared indignantly at me and my fickleness.

"Dynamite must be placed along the tunnels to explode and seal them if the enemy gets loose down here. We'll use wire to let it off from a distance."

It had not occurred to him that the enemy could be so treacherous. "Ah, yes, I see. I see. Well, I shall explain everything to Pockengruber, never fear." The Colonel admired everything that met his eyes. He was charmed with the shaft now reaching up towards the Königspitz. Carrying his ice-staff at port, he trotted down the tunnel as if he were leading an assault. He was pleased with the wall-niches that held kerosene lanterns; he laughed like a boy to see the shining chips fly under the axe-blows; and he was overjoyed at the morale of the teams he found hacking away at the tunnel faces.

[63] Holy Bible, New International Version®, NIV® Copyright ©1973, 1978, 1984, 2011 by Biblica, Inc.® Used by permission.

This ample supply of labor led me to new refinements. I had guardrooms cut and installed an office where I put a requisitioned field telephone with wire strung along the corridor walls to the pitheads. I had offshoot tunnels made, one to the mess hall and one to a latrine with ingeniously-devised ice tubes that carried our waste into a hidden pit below. The mess chamber was fitted with storage rooms and was even heated, at a low temperature, by an oil stove with a pipe that carried smoke up to the surface.

As the tunnels stretched father and farther beneath the glacial surface, I put a team to work constructing my railway system. One side of each tunnel was reserved for its track. The carpenters built a number of long, low sledges mounted on steel skis. Using spare telpher equipment, the sledges were drawn by cable through the tunnels, following narrow channels cut in the floor. At intervals along the tunnel-length, there would be winch stations where cables would wind onto or unwind from a drum. At the end of the fortnight, we were able to put the first leg of the Payerhütte-to-Königspitz line into operation. Loads of canned sausage went from surface to the mess kitchen effortlessly, in minutes. The return trip carried a mound of ice chips for disposal along the north face, where the Italians would not see it. I felt a thrill of pride as I watched the first sledges being hauled back to the adit, the same pride I had felt in the trenches, but somehow this seemed greater and more daring.

The ice proved to be a firm but trustworthy medium in which to create a dwelling. The glacier was composed of strata, layers of compressed snow from past winters, visible on the walls like the coarse woodgrain of a massive fallen oak into which we, tiny human termites, were boring incessantly. The lighter strata came from snows that had fallen in the dead of winter; the darker strata were the snows of spring or autumn that had been exposed to the sun and had hardened, raked by wind bearing dead leaves or dust from the valley. With practice we found that we could cut the ice along certain fracture lines and pry whole blocks from the wall, saving us time and effort. These blocks were used to construct stairs or sentry-posts near the tunnel entrances.

The white ice near the surface of the glacier had a decidedly different quality from the depths: it was more porous and riddled with tiny air-pockets, while farther down the weight of the glacier seemed to have obliterated these bubbles, forming ice with a bluish tinge that was much denser, smooth and hard as glass. Although this ice required more effort to dig into, it was trustworthy material in which to work, unlikely to collapse on top of us.

We found it necessary to bore holes to the surface for ventilation, as the oxygen was sparse in the deeper tunnels and was polluted by our carbide lamps and kerosene lanterns. Therefore I sent away to Trafoi for a drilling rig used to dig wells, and stealthily—so as not to inform the Italians what we were up to—we bored regular breathing-holes up to the air.

Indeed, the air inside the Citadel was the one source of discomfort that we had difficulty adjusting to. Unlike earth or even rock, the ice did not absorb fumes and smoke, and when combined with the extreme humidity, the atmosphere was malodorous and suffocating. Soot from our kerosene lanterns and the carbide lamps floated lazily around us and accumulated on our faces and hands, giving every man the appearance of a chimney-sweep. Most of the men habitually smoked pungent Turkish tobacco in long-stemmed Ulmer pipes, or if they were working, cigarettes rolled from newspaper which gave off an acrid reek and added to the smother. We realized the effect the fetid atmosphere was having on us when we enjoyed an opportunity to go up to Payerhütte and breathe fresh air once again. Drilling regular ventilation shafts helped somewhat, though they tended to clog up in snowstorms.

Our skill improved with each passing week and the soldiers themselves learned how to tunnel into the ice more efficiently. I added a series of connecting corridors and large barracks galleries, where the men erected wooden huts which were easier to heat and seemed less ominous to them. We noticed when bedding down at night in the depths of the glacier that the ice emitted a deep, groaning rumble, the sound of the glacial torrent as it flowed gradually down towards the valley. Lying in the darkness, one could feel the vast pressure of thousands of tons of frozen water shifting uneasily around us as though we were in the gut of some dormant behemoth that moaned in its sleep. We regularly had to revise passages that had gradually become too narrow, walls that had cracked open, or doorways that grew too low. We had indeed penetrated a great prostrate leviathan, sprawled across the mountainside and slithering ponderously downhill.

Nonetheless, I felt that the glacier did not begrudge our efforts: our tunnels and galleries were all temporary, would all be absorbed quietly into the ice within a few years. We had inflicted no great harm and all would be forgiven, just as our snow-tunnels at Hausen had vanished and the grass would soon cover my trenchworks at St. Mihiel. All this work was for one brief moment in time, one niggling human conflict that God himself barely acknowledged.

One morning the team I was supervising in the midsection of the Sulden-ferner stumbled on a clump of human remains. They were evidently the corpses of two persons who had been caught in an avalanche, frozen and desiccated with time like a pair of Egyptian mummies. We extracted them from the ice, marveling at their hair and eyes, still perfectly preserved, the climber's boots of a bygone era, and the mottled but fleshy hands clasped together in a final grip of companionship at the moment of death. In the pocket of one quilted climbing-jacket we found a small New Testament, its pages still dry and legible. In the pocket of the reinforced trousers there was a curved briar pipe, cracked with age but still stuffed with tobacco.

One of our cooks, a dour ancient with a voluminous beard, remembered that two climbers had been lost near the summit of the Ortler in 1875. I calculated that in 41 years the ice had carried their remains nearly three kilometers. We wrapped them up carefully in flour-sacks with an explanatory note and sent them by sledge up to the Payerhütte, to be loaded onto the telpher and returned at last to their families in the valley.

The weather continued to be fiercely cold into September and the telpher was interrupted every few days as ice accumulated on the cables, preventing the cars from passing along them smoothly. Fortunately we had filled several of our new supply-rooms with flour, lard and canned meats, but those men who had passed a winter in these heights turned pensive, sucking on their pipes and staring solemnly into the stove.

In early October we completed the living and storage area at the base of the mountain. The Colonel's original grotto behind the Payerhütte had now become several kilometers of tunnels and galleries under the Oberer Ortler-ferner on the northwest face of the Ortler. A second network of tunnels penetrated beneath the Sulden-ferner, carrying men and materiel south to our hidden front lines. In the upper ice we had excavated corridors connected to lookout posts which used crude periscopes made of wooden tubes containing mirrors (a similar design was in use in the trenches so that men wouldn't have to expose their heads). These posts allowed us to observe Italian ski patrols and other movement along the Zebrú ridge. Rope ladders in vertical tunnels led down to the main level, a series of galleries laid out in an orderly grid and connected by passageways. There was an officers' quarters and mess opposite a row of barracks for the NCOs and enlisted men, each housing between 25 and 70 men. A large hallway with a high arched ceiling served as the main mess, bounded on either side by storerooms for provisions and firewood. My office now sat beside the central telephone room—each section of the Ice Citadel had a telephone—and Dr. Schaller's hospital, with a room to serve as a morgue for corpses awaiting transport to the valley. On their own initiative the men added a chapel with a large cross hewn from the ice, which delighted our *feldkurat*,[64] Father Weiss. The next area of the grid had a munitions storeroom and a magazine for explosives and artillery shells, separated by thick ice walls in case of explosion, and a room for our little kerosene generator which furnished electric lighting throughout the Citadel. The west corridor ended in a narrow crevasse into which we tossed our trash, and there were latrines here too.

Unmeasured time slipped past me. It was an era of obsession. Our daily progress was such that it surpassed the Colonel's most ambitious hopes, and yet there was always more to do, another tunnel, another gallery. I left the work areas only to sleep and for ablutions in the icy bathwater that we were all accustomed to. The cooks brought me food and I ate it standing up. At night I might be so tired that, propped in front of the fireplace, elbow on the mantel, a glass of brandy in my hand and a big bellow of drinking song rising around me, I would fall asleep. At midnight, Franz would lead me away and give me a push in the direction of my bunk.

I dreamed of being lost in a maze of thundering cataracts with water as hard as iron.

---

[64] Army chaplain

VIII. Race beneath the Ice

In mid-October the Colonel abruptly called for a conference with the four officers directing the tunnel work. He had installed himself in a spacious new office under the Oberer Ortler-ferner ice, not far from the entrance at the Payerhütte. Here it was warmer and quieter, and he had put in a floor, paneled walls and a ceiling to keep the dripping ice-melt off his desk. Even as we were sitting down, he began to talk impatiently. "The Italians have occupied our position on the Hohe Schneide. Five days ago they overran our machine-gun post under fire and forced our men to withdraw to the Geisterspitz. We lost two killed and nine missing, probably captured. And three Schwarzlose guns, of course." He raised his face and I noticed that his eyes seemed bloodshot enough to bleed. On his jaw were black islands that the razor had skipped over.

It was clearly a shock—since I'd arrived in July there had not been any enemy action to compare with this. An occasional pot-shot from their cannons, an odd sniper, but no frontal assaults. The Italians were growing bold. The officers in the room shifted uneasily in their seats: building the Ice Citadel had taken their minds off our true reason for being here: to kill and be killed.

"This has grave implications for our security," the Colonel went on. "If the Italians are able to place artillery on the Hohe Schneide they would be in a position to take our outposts on the Geisterspitz, and the Naglerspitz. Possibly even the Kristallspitzen." With his pencil, he touched the little red-and-white flags on the map. "Then they would be able to operate freely all along the Zebrù Valley. We must retake that position as soon as possible!" His fist slammed the wall map at the location of Hohe Schneide.

Major Stutz spoke up. "Are you gentlemen aware of the weather? Ah, I thought not, snug in your ice caves." The Colonel let out a sigh of irritation: the weather was going to present the greatest obstacle.

"So, I shall tell you about the weather. It has not been just the usual savage affair; it has been sheer horror for the past four days. Neither we nor the Italians are capable of military action under these conditions. By which I mean that our erstwhile opponents are not going to be hauling artillery pieces up to Hohe Schneide for now. Even when the wind dies down, we've had an accumulation of close to three meters of snow, which will complicate travel and increase the risk of avalanches."

"Thank you, Major!" The Colonel interrupted impatiently. "Nonetheless, I want a fully-armed ski unit prepared to go out as soon as the weather breaks. We should reinforce the three closest outposts with men and ammunition—as well as food and firewood, which they surely need."

"Even in ideal conditions it will be a bloody sacrifice to take the Hohe Schneide from the north face, Colonel," Franz pointed out. "Plus we all know our soldiers are not stormtroopers—they are untrained Standschützen and most of them have never charged a machine-gun nest. Especially not uphill on the ice. The Italians will murder hundreds of them before we retake that peak." Franz knew that the Colonel's concern for his men would keep him from ordering such a disastrous assault.

"Perhaps an attack at night?" suggested Lizzola. "Or we could get a plane to fly up from Trafoi and bomb them."

"Excuse me, sir, if I may? I have a much better idea." I stood up like a schoolboy to announce my plan, knowing that it was the best possibility. "Between the Naglerspitz and Hohe Schneide lies the Vedretta di Vitelli, about 1800 meters of thick ice. It will not be difficult to push a new passageway through the area without being detected, and breach the surface just under their noses. A handful of men armed with grenades could take the position in minutes."

The Colonel's jaw muscles flexed: he was pleased, but struggling to contain himself. "Almost two kilometers of digging. How long will it take?"

"At ten meters a day, it would normally take about six months. But we have become experts in ice-tunneling by now, and the passage need not be as large and detailed as the ones we are digging under the Sulden-ferner.

This will be merely a passageway to transport our men up to the ridge. Plus the ice is not completely solid—we can take advantage of crevasses and fissures to speed our progress. My guess is that we could do it in six weeks. We could start immediately while the weather keeps the Italians from sending up reinforcements."

Stutz coughed. "And what makes you think we will arrive undetected? Are the Italians so deaf that they won't hear our chopping until we're under their feet? Colonel, this is suicide! We'll provide the enemy with a passage directly to our Naglerspitz outpost!"

"Hear him out, Major," the Colonel replied calmly. "How do you propose to plan for contingencies, von Fuchsheim?"

"Men will be stationed inside the tunnel in case all does not go as planned. We can always detonate charges to collapse it, if need be."

Major Stutz grimaced but said nothing. I unrolled my chart of the sector and laid it out. "There is one difficulty. Because that portion of the glacier is sliced up with crevasses, we must bridge a crevasse here, and again, here. But building even simple bridges takes time and resources. Perhaps another week for that, Colonel. If I find some men with titan blood, perhaps less."

I indicated an irregular brown dot on the map. "As one approaches the north face of the peak there is a *flyggberg*, as it is known in Swedish—I don't believe there is a German word for it. It is a rock formation around which the glacier is moving. We must veer our tunnel southeast here, and cross a major crevasse—our ski patrols refer to it as the Great Crevasse. We will then continue to tunnel uphill and emerge at this spot, just outside the perimeter of the outpost. The ice will be too thin for us to dig any further. From there we will launch our assault. Fifty days to finish; with a superhuman effort, forty."

"Klaus?" the Colonel raised his eyebrows in Major Stutz's direction. The Major had been twitching and blinking throughout the conversation.

"We should abandon the idea of attacking through tunnels and launch an assault on the surface at once," he said in his hoarse voice, "Fifty men in a dash with the dogsleds. The Italians won't even have sentries outside in this weather. We'd be over the parapet and on top of them before they know it." Stutz was seeking glory, I mused. An old-style charge into machine-gun fire, with someone waving a sword, no doubt.

"And what if the Italians do have a sentry? That would ruin our scheme." Lizzola had spoken impulsively and he stopped short. "Sorry, sir," he said to Stutz, but he did not look very sorry.

"Remember, Major, it is eleven on the Beaufort Scale, out there," the Colonel said. "Gusts over a hundred kilometers an hour. It is white Hell." He bent his head and stared at my chart of the glacier for a long time while we sat in uneasy silence.

"So," he said wearily, "Tell us how you propose to bridge the crevasses, Fuchsheim. The bridges must be quickly erected and be sturdy enough to get our men and equipment across. Anything that falls into a crevasse is gone forever."

Again, they were all looking at me, but I had considered this problem carefully and had concocted a plan that was pure mad genius. "Sir, I have a notion which I've refrained from mentioning…" As I talked, my bizarre plan began to lose some of its starkness, and I heard myself making the idea seem on the edge of the possible. I charged past difficulties, I went from one dizzy step to another, I improvised technical niceties, made imaginative leaps. It all began to take on a thin color of reality, and I became more and more eloquent. With a final bound, I sprang toward the solid ground.

The Colonel seemed to draw inspiration from my barely plausible idea. "Aha!" he exclaimed, "I understand now. The bridges won't be bridges at all, technically speaking. But they will permit us to achieve our goal. Capital!"

He called for Sergeant Krebs and we made a list of the supplies necessary and the duties of each section. I thought we should have at least a dozen sappers. We had, in fact, a half-dozen, but the Colonel said that for this, one mountain man was worth two sappers. As it was, we did not have supplies in the quantities I thought necessary, but we would have to make do.

Later, while we were having a glass of beer in the mess, Franz said to me warmly, "Melchior, you are a genius!"

"Yes, at telling a tale from Hoffmann."

"Rather more *In the Hall of the Mountain King*, I should say. When you talk of ice or venturing on ice, your eyes glow. One can see that you are carried away."

"Nonsense; I was trying to calm old Buchholz. The truth is that our chances are one in three."

"Let's say they're even. I would never bet against you when you take on that berserk look."

I reflected on the justice of what he had said. I had indeed come to be a little mad. When I was dangling alone on the rope inside the crevasse, I had felt no fear or sense of danger. And out on the empty glacier alone, lost in the dark, being followed by the enemy, I had felt nothing but a strong sense of winning. I felt it now even in the presence of my rational terror.

Our first obstacle was to get our 30-man team and its equipment to the starting-point, which was to be the glacier on the south slope of the Grosse Naglerspitz. This required us to descend into the valley and travel a dozen kilometers to the west, then ascend the Nagler with our equipment on our backs. In the valley the weather was somewhat milder, but an enormous quantity of snow had fallen and hundreds of Russian prisoners of war had been brought in to keep the roads clear. The army was kind enough to transport us by truck to the Stilfser Pass, where we spent the night in a chilly barracks on the Swiss border. The next day we traveled by dogsled, skirting the base of Mount Scorluzzo before proceeding uphill on foot in the driving snow, laden with heavy packs. By nightfall we had reached the Naglerspitz outpost, a collection of huts blanketed by ivory drifts and garrisoned with a dozen hardy Standschützen guards.

We initiated the new tunnel here, through an enormous slab of ice that had been pushed up the side of the mountain, allowing us to put a stairway down to about six meters below the surface. Any deeper and we would have to dig through the dense blue ice; any closer to the top and our carbide headlamps would be seen shining through the ice at night. The men were enthusiastic about this new project once it was explained that we were going to kick Garibaldi's fat arse off our mountaintop, and working in teams of four at two-hour shifts we pushed onward twenty-four hours a day.

Because this tunnel was merely meant to carry our assault force in secret under the ice, we had no need to make the tunnel spacious and precise like the corridors of the Ice Citadel. It had to be tall enough for a man to stand up straight and wide enough for him to carry his rifle comfortably. Within the first few days we encountered three small crevasses that could be exploited as passageways for a hundred meters, and we found ourselves making good time towards "the Rock," as the men called the looming *flyggberg*. It was a bald knob of granite that had been smoothed by centuries of passing ice. The surface that faced us was cracked and pitted; the other side was covered with huge blocks that had split off the glacier. It provided cover from the Italians' line of sight and here we located a wide ventilation shaft, as the air in the tunnel was growing difficult to breathe.

On November 1st we had almost reached the Great Crevasse. This was the point at which my great spin of the wheel, my great bet began. I spent two days with the sappers and with Alois Thöni, the jovial, mustachioed armorer. In the workshop, they were laboring to finish—with much head-shaking—the odd contraption I had sketched for them. The armorer did his best, however to make the device practical and to build it well. The sappers rehearsed their coming action, as well as they could, in a large ice chamber that had been built as a guard-room.

On the 4th Franz telephoned me from the pithead to report that he could discern a faint light through the ice wall ahead. At that news, I called for the armorer and had the sappers load everything on sleds. We made our way forward by the light of our headlamps and the occasional lanterns positioned along the gallery. I walked at a quickstep at the head of the column and at the rear came Viktor; I heard his *Alpenyodel* tone from time to time saying *"Geschwindschritt Geschwindschritt!"*[65]

When we were about a hundred meters away, we began to make out the aquamarine light from the end of the gallery. It grew brighter as we neared and the scene we came upon was shadowy to the fore and lighted brilliantly from the back. The dark figures of the men shoveling broken ice through the large portal, outlined against the pale glare, made me think of Dante in the lowest circle of Hell, preparing to climb up the Devil's back. As Franz and I approached, the men broke through the ice into the crevasse itself.

The sudden breach let in a powerfully cold breath of air, and we stood awestruck on the precipice, looking into an azure abyss. Far off we could hear the howl of the storm.

Franz was full of nervous electricity. He seized my arm and led me to the edge saying, "We're days ahead of schedule, Melchior!" Pointing upward, he added, "Look at what we're escaping."

As before, I saw the soaring walls of ice but, instead of a ragged strip of blue sky at the top, there was a churning tempest of cloudy white. From it descended a fall of fine snow and the whole great rift echoed with a primitive wail that rose and fell like the war-music of the kobolds.[66] For a moment or two, we all stopped and listened, petrified by the sound.

Then, gripped again by the thought of the next attempt, I turned and began to give orders. Franz stayed, but I had his men file back through the tunnel to the rear. The sappers brought the equipment-laden sleds up to the platform where we stood. Alois stepped forward and produced from its wrappings the outlandish weapon they had made for me.

"It looks like harpoon-gun of some sort," Franz said in astonishment.

"And so it is," I answered, showing him how the meter-long steel harpoon fitted into the barrel of the gun. It had a steel-alloy head with a barbed cruciate point and its shaft attached to a light, strong line. The barrel was fashioned from a captured Hotchkiss gun that had somehow ended up in Trafoi, with a bipod to hold it steady. Propulsion was achieved by powder charges taken from 42mm rounds. I positioned the gun on the ledge and loaded the cartridge, stood behind it and put my shoulder to the stock.

"Thar she blows!" I shouted. "The first harpoon in the first whale hunt the Ortler has ever seen!" I pulled the trigger.

There was an earsplitting blast and I flew backward and would have cracked my skull on the ice if Alois and Viktor had not caught me; the steel lance shot the gap of some ten meters and buried itself in the ice wall. From the shaft trailed a rope that we anchored with a piton to the ice wall on our side of the crevasse.

In another minute, we had positioned the gun again and repeated the process. Then the sapper sergeant hooked his harness to the two lines and went hand-over-hand to the other side, where he anchored a much heavier rope to a piton between the first two lines. This third rope was actually two ropes bound together and gave a reasonably sound footing—at least for a mountain goat. These three lines were our "bridge". Each of the men had a chest-harness that they hooked to the two overhead lines that I had fired into the wall. Walking tightrope on the third rope, they traversed the Great Crevasse with little difficulty. It was not a bridge, technically speaking, as the Colonel had pointed out, but with it we were able to cross the crevasse within minutes.

On the opposite wall of the Great Crevasse we began cutting into the ice to continue our tunnel. Balanced on the rope bridge, Viktor chopped out a perch with a small axe as ice chunks and powder fell into the chasm. When my turn came to cross over, I gazed with fascination into the gulf below. Snowflakes swirled around me and wafted gently into the darkness; the sound of running water was clearly audible. I yearned for an opportunity to lower myself into those frozen depths, to look upon a place no man had visited.

Within an hour we found ourselves facing yet another crevasse—this one invisible from the surface due to

---

[65] Quick march!
[66] Gnomes in Germanic mythology, believed to inhabit caves and mines.

the snow, but just as daunting. We discovered that our most vexatious problem was to site the harpoon gun in the correct position to strike the opposite wall at just the right angle and the right spot to anchor the next leg. Given the guns' stout recoil, the slightest miscalculation would send it tumbling into the gulf. As we progressed, we made certain that gunner and harpoon gun were both held firmly in place.

The sappers were magnificent. Their very names inspired confidence: Cornelius Schopf, Gustav Pastore, Maximilian Thoma, Simon Platzer—and even a Johann and Hermann Ortler—all first-class mountaineers. Once the harpoon lines were in position, they were swarming ahead, fixing support lines from pitons a few meters higher on the ice walls and bringing forward the heavier ropes that formed our road. And, after the slow work of tunneling, each new crevasse seemed like a visit to another reality, another plane of existence composed of sheer walls of ice decorated with fantastic stalactites and encrusted with ice-crystal flowers. Franz stared in wonder and remarked that it looked like a monstrance—a holy reliquary inscribed with elaborate designs and symbols. Indeed, the hollow echoes and shifting darkness reminded me of some long-closed tomb.

Austrian troops inspect a crevasse inside the glacier.

The days passed in a fury of precision. I pushed forward with the harpoon gun team—two men to carry the heavy gun and a succession of runners to replenish our supply of rope. The crevasses were separated by walls sometimes only a few meters thick, so tunneling occupied as much of our time as setting up the bridges. We took great risks on the ice walls, but they were shrewdly-judged risks and the few men who slipped were saved and retrieved. If one piton gave way, someone had always thought to insure it with a second. I worked without time for ideas or sensations, locked in my circular madness of firing the barbed spears into the ice, advancing over the swaying ropes, hollowing out a new platform, then tunneling forward to the next crevasse. I was aware of the wind's howl only at the times when I found it hard to hear a shouted request, and I was conscious of the snowy mist only when it made sightings difficult. I was sensible of my own fatigue and hard usage only when my shoulder became too sore to endure the recoil and I had to call for Erich to take over as harpoon gunner.

Then, very suddenly, I was alone and motionless once more and able to gaze round at the fantastic circumstances. The storm on the surface had died away, for now our crack of vision into the upper world showed a fading, purplish light. The windy voice had left off. My vertical world was passing into nighttime silence.

I was sitting on an ice ledge with Erich, Krebs and Viktor asleep in their sleeping bags behind me. Thanks to a runner from the mess, we had just had our fill of hearty beef soup, heated on a small spirit stove. By the light of a lantern, I was studying my chart of the glacier and trying to calculate our progress towards the Hohe Schneide. I estimated that we must continue some 50 meters more. If the oft-displayed proposition about God being with us was correct, we should reach our goal tomorrow, in less than five weeks after we had begun.

For the first time in days, I was able to look around me, and I felt a marvelous peace. I was a mad Ludwig again, perched on my ledge in the perpendicular crystal palace, my spot of lantern yellow amid the diamond glints from the high escarpments, demented by the sheer pleasure of being in this pure and dangerous world.

I fell asleep; I was wakened almost instantly by Erich, who was heating breakfast coffee on the spirit stove. A broad tapestry of sunlight hung high on the opposite wall and, although the snow had stopped, the wind had risen again and the *dudelsack*[67] wails had returned.

The crevasse where we had spent the night was quite small and only about thirty meters deep. I prepared for the whaler's last shot. Once the harpoon had reached its mark, we set up our final rope-bridge and began digging into the white, porous ice of the glacier surface. I realized that the Italians could possibly hear our digging sounds and hoped that the report of my harpoon gun had been mistaken for one of those mysterious *brontidi*.

As the men chopped upwards towards the light, I dropped back and consulted with Erich. "The assault team is in place, sir. They're bringing up sacks of grenades right now. We have twenty volunteers to rush the outpost, sir, and another six men positioned in the tunnel to collapse it with explosives if things go wrong."

"Excellent, Corporal. Who is leading the attack?"

"Captain Pichler, sir."

Franz had volunteered! Suddenly I was shaken with terror—Franz was my one truly close friend in this place, and I could not bear the thought of him being injured or killed. Suddenly a vivid replay of that horror-scene from St. Mihiel dominated my sight, except that instead of Fritz, it was Franz's bloody face straining to reach me through the hail of battle. I must have stumbled because Erich seized my elbow.

"Are you ill, sir?"

"Just tired, Corporal. Very well, come and get me when the team is ready. I'll go supervise the completion of the tunnel. Tell everyone to be as quiet as possible—we are only a few meters from the outpost." With any luck the Italians would be busy making a hot breakfast with much banging of pots and pans and would not concern themselves with hacking sounds from beneath the ice.

The digging team had carefully worked their way upward to the snow-pack that covered the glacier—where the tunnel ended we could see sunlight filtering through an oval patch of thin crust. Listening carefully, I could

---

[67] Bagpipe

hear men's voices beyond it: someone coughing, someone whistling a tune, someone cursing: "*Mannaggia!*"[68] The weather had at last given way and sun had bestowed a pleasant morning on our foes. Somewhere overhead the wind rasped across the mountain's edge.

I was just about to return down the tunnel to check on the assault team when I heard footsteps crunching through the snow above us. The men on the digging team froze and we all looked up at a man's shadow which had fallen across the wafer of light that was to be our exit. The shadow paused for a long moment and we held our breath.

There was a spattering sound and on the thin ice above us we could see a spot growing in size, a spreading blot the color of lemon sherbet. We crouched paralyzed in fear, each of us appealing strenuously to the Almighty that we not be discovered. At length the last dribble of urine ended and the soldier called out to someone else, "*Io ci sarà presto!*"[69] We breathed a collective sigh of relief as we heard him start to walk away.

Just then the roof came crashing down, bringing with it one very startled Italian Alpino in a cascade of ice powder. He was a young man—hardly more than an adolescent—wearing a bulky overcoat and a wool cap. We were so stunned that nobody moved—we just stared at the man and he gaped back at us. Then he let out a shout and fumbled for his bayonet that hung in a sheath from his belt.

Strange to say, we were unarmed except that I still wore my little Reichsrevolver in a holster. And it is even stranger to say that in my entire two and a half years in the German Army I had never knowingly killed a man. I had fired into crowds of Frenchmen and I had hurled grenades, but in all that time I had never seen a man fall as a result.

Now was a moment for action, and the four other men were in the tunnel behind me, so it would have to be *my* action. The Italian was bellowing his head off as he drew his bayonet, no doubt alerting the entire outpost, so I simply picked up a shovel and clapped him over the head with it. His soft wool forage cap did nothing to save him, and he slumped over still clutching his blade.

At the other end of the tunnel I could see Franz running towards us with a bulging sack in his hand. Behind him the volunteers were jogging single-file, rifles in hand.

---

[68] Damn it!

[69] "I'll be there in a minute!"

Austrian scouts on the glacier surface.

"Here, grenades! Throw them!" he shouted, and thrust the bag into my hands. Then in a single motion he had hoisted himself upwards through the hole in the firn.

We followed after him and found ourselves at the very top of the world. All around us lay the magnificent sunlit grandeur of the Alps—a scene of such glory and astonishing beauty that for a few seconds I forgot that I was going into battle. Directly in front of us was a sandbag wall, just barely visible under a heavy cap of snow, and beyond it I could see Italian soldiers with rifles running in our direction. As my comrades emerged from the tunnel, I opened the sack and handed a stick-grenade to each of them. On Franz's signal, we yanked the little strings that protruded from the wooden handles and flung them over the wall. There was a staccato series of bangs followed by screams of pain, then the Austrians pushed the snow off the wall and began firing into the outpost. Two more well-placed hand grenades did the job, and we were masters of the position. We had re-conquered Hohe Schneide.

One by one the sappers and the diggers came up out of the tunnel to see our handiwork. We had killed nineteen Italians, including a lieutenant and a captain, and the fellow I had hit on the head was taken prisoner once he regained consciousness. In the outpost's only shelter we found a warm breakfast on the stove, but I had no appetite after seeing the bloody bodies strewn across the ground. The men quickly arranged the corpses outside the perimeter and covered them with snow. We checked the machine-guns and found them in good order, well-supplied with belts. After that we had only to wait for reinforcements.

The sun was poking its way through a drifting rubble of clouds, splashing the landscape below with light. The Zebrù valley lay before us under a vast blanket of snow, with the frozen Zebrù River just barely visible between ranks of white-clad pines. To the north we could see our outposts on the Nagler and the Geister, and far beyond them, Mount Scorluzzo and the Swiss frontier.

We had cut and beaten a way though the great berg; we had strung a precarious spider path across a dozen gorges. Franz stood beside me on the parapet, taking deep breaths of fresh air. "Let's have a drink to the sunshine," he said, producing a silver brandy flask.

"*Prost!*" I said and took a great swig. By this time, the others had finished inspecting the outpost and were standing around us. He passed the bottle and—*Prost! Prost! Prost!*—it soon came back empty.

Just at that moment, one of the sappers behind me announced, "The sleds are coming—look!"

I turned. Ten or more of them were approaching rapidly over the ice from the north. The leading sled bore a little Austrian flag and, borrowing some field glasses, I made out Colonel Buchholz standing behind the driver. Major Stutz, with the expression of a pallbearer, was in the sled behind.

One of my ancestors—my namesake, in fact—served as a soldier in the Thirty Years' War and, surviving to become a wicked old man, left us his memoirs. I read them as a boy and found them by turns repellent, tedious, and enlightening. At one point, he describes his success as a patrol leader (although he seems to have captured far more farmers' pigs and cattle than enemy troops) and he attributes it to a pair of clever inventions. The first invention had to do with shoes. He devised a shoe, to be worn by his men, with the heel in front and the toe behind. And, with that, his troopers had their horses shod backwards as well. The second invention was a kind of earhorn, or amplifying instrument, with which he could pick up sounds from a great distance.

Then he confesses that he was "so eager for honor and glory that it kept me awake at night" and that, in the end, "I became so godless that there was no roguery which would not do, and I became disliked and envied by all."

Cunning contrivances and delusions of glory—can they be the congenital errors of the von Fuchsheim blood? Even after our victory at Hohe Schneide, I still felt unqualified to do the job that I was doing. My clever plans had succeeded, my cunning invention had solved an otherwise insurmountable problem, but could a trained engineer have done it better? Was I risking men's lives by uninformed guesswork? I lived in fear that my disguise would be seen through, that my false beard would be pulled off and my lies stripped naked.

I was not at all comforted to find that the Colonel believed in me wholeheartedly. The day after I returned to the Payerhütte, I was summoned to his office.

"Captain, our plan was an outstanding success," he said briskly, taking on the style of all commanders who, having failed to devise a scheme of their own, feel the need to take credit for the work of their subordinates. "The ice tunnels I suggested are, by and large, a practical advantage, but the rope-walk across the crevasses was a brilliant idea. We have established a strong position here and devised a new strategy with which to win the war. I suspect that a commendation will be forthcoming from headquarters in Meran." I gathered that he meant that the commendation would be for him, not for me. Very well. He looked very fresh this morning, his eyes clear, his shaving neat, and no acrobatics from his hands.

"Perhaps we should consider it a valuable training exercise," I said, "with some technical findings of interest. I am not sure that such a feat could be easily repeated. Besides, the Italians will surely stumble on the idea of locating their lines under the glacier—it is a logical maneuver."

"You may consider it so," he answered, "but our Italian adversaries are very limited in adopting innovations. Nonetheless, I think now we should take the initiative and use an ice-tunnel assault to break through the Italian lines. I will propose exactly that to headquarters next week when I present my report to them in person. I will request a substantial reinforcement—perhaps a full regiment of professional troops, not Standschützen—to launch an under-ice offensive to the west, towards Bormio. We will establish a fortified *eisfestung* position in the glacier on the north face of the Kristallkamm. Supply lines will extend between glaciers, here." He poked triumphantly at the map. "The Italians will be taken by surprise, just as they were at Hohe Schneide, and we will be in a good position to push onward to the south."

I was astonished by this burst of ambition. Four months ago the Colonel's primary goal was to keep his men from freezing to death or going mad. Now he was planning to invade Italy. It was not that his plan was impossible—it hinged on the same implausibility as my crevasse-bridge plan—but the time and effort involved were immense and unrealistic. At the same time, I wanted to share in his flush of pride, his lust for glory—I just did not want to be responsible for putting men's lives in danger.

"A magnificent proposition, Colonel. We should start surveying the glaciers to the west in order to calculate the manpower required. We'll need to order supplies and equipment before we can start." I said this with as much enthusiasm as I could muster.

He leaned back in his chair with a grin and chuckled. "Cautious Captain von Fuchsheim. We will accomplish nothing if we are not bold. This may very well be the turning-point of the entire war, don't you see? I won't have you dragging your feet now. Push ahead and I will see to the supplies and the manpower." He paused. His cobalt eyes had gone back to their old peregrinating habits on the wall above my head.

"Also, I must inform you that I will be going to Meran for the next two weeks to report on our progress here," he said, "During my absence, Major Stutz will assume command. You will continue to devise the engineering plans, subject to his supervision, until I return."

This was an unexpected blow. First to demand that I press forward boldly, then to put me under the supervision of the one man in the Austro-Hungarian Army who was most likely to interfere with my work. However, Stutz was second-in-command and there was no alternative. Privately I resolved to tell him as little as possible. For two weeks, many things could go unreported.

What concerned me more was the prospect of extending and enlarging the Ice Citadel. The Colonel had mentioned bringing in a full regiment—several thousand men. They would require a large amount of space, every meter of which had to hewn from the living ice. I was dismayed by the prodigious effort this would entail, but at the same time I was thrilled. The glacier was a virgin block of crystal and I was the hunchbacked Gypsy who would sculpt a fortress out of it. It was not only that it had never been done before; much more than that, it was because of something that had intoxicated me during that first moment in the crevasse. I had a distinct sense of destiny awaiting me somewhere in the mysterious frozen underseas. I had an appointment to keep, a revelation to attain, a transformation to undergo.

Please remember that I am not, by any means, a romantic. I am a prosaic Bavarian from a family blessed with all the most stolid virtues. I never was prepared to lose my life for a cause. But now—and I could hear my conniving, hard-handed, narrow-eyed ancestors laughing from their tombs—I was enamored with an element I could scarcely comprehend.

———— ❈❈❈ ————

After dinner that night, I went to the Colonel's office and knocked at the door. But it was not the Colonel's voice that answered "Enter!" When I went in, Major Klaus Stutz, with his cast-iron face and his obscure eyes, was sitting under the lamplight in the Colonel's chair. He waited ten seconds longer than a gentleman would before asking me to sit down.

"Yes, Captain?"

Speaking with Stutz was like conversing with a Morse telegraph key.

"It is nearly December, Major, I wanted to inquire if my request for Christmas leave has been granted." I was tired, I needed a prolonged rest.

"Hmm," he said and began to ruffle through some papers in a folder marked *Urlaub*.[70] The careless way in which he did this gave me to suspect that he already knew the answer. "Ah, here." He stopped at one sheet and squinted down through the text.

"No, Captain, there is nothing to tell you. Your request has been forwarded through liaison to your General Headquarters at Munich, to be transmitted to your regiment." Dash-dot. Dash-dash-dash.[71]

"Good Lord, Major! Do you mean that a simple request for a week's leave can't be granted here? How ludicrous to send it on an 800-kilometer journey." I was trying to stay calm, hoping that Stutz would see the foolishness of this. "As for my regiment, they have no reason to care if I go to the moon on Christmas leave. We shall have their reply next summer!" Mindful of military discipline, I added: "Sir."

The Major was unmoved. "I cannot guess when it will arrive. As for the Colonel's views, I know that he is concerned about our troop strength, that is to say, our inadequate numbers in case of an attack."

"Major Stutz, I am not 'troop strength.' I am an engineer who has his assignment, which is to build the *eisfestung*. I have done more than that, as you well know, and I—"

Stutz interrupted me with a bark: "Captain! I believe we both know that you are not an engineer. You have no background in engineering and have been operating here under false pretenses."

I was too surprised to speak. So at last my identity was revealed. Stutz gave me a slight smile.

"Amazing what one can dig up with a telephone and a friend in military logistics. But I am not going to expose your deception to the Colonel because it is clear that you know what you're doing."

Aha, I thought, it's because this is something the Colonel would not want to hear and Stutz wished to avoid antagonizing him any further.

"Nonetheless," the Major continued, "You have been given far too much responsibility for someone whose entire background consists of a degree in crystallography."

"Sir, I built a defensive line in St. Mihiel that withstood a major French offensive. The Ice Citadel is closely modeled after that experience. It is true that I have no engineering degree, but what I do know, I have learned under fire."

"Perhaps," said Stutz, sitting back in his chair in the same way the Colonel did, "But in twenty months under

---

[70] Leave
[71] Morse code for "no"

fire you received no awards or commendations. A battlefield commission doesn't count—they were promoting men to compensate for heavy losses. And in the end, you were transferred. Why? Because, Fuchsheim, you are insubordinate, by which I mean that you do not submit to authority the way a military officer should. But for the moment, you *will* submit to my authority. Or I will see to it that you face a court-martial for impersonating an engineer."

Blackmail. It was consistent with Stutz's character to do a thing like this. He had observed, as had Franz, the light that came into my eyes when I began proposing plans for the Ice Citadel or the assault on Hohe Schneide. He knew that I would become his slave rather than leave the *eisfestung* before it was complete. But his assumptions about my past wounded me deeply. My eyes traveled to his chest and I noted that he was wearing the Ehren-Denkmünz für Tapferkeit, the Medal of Courage. It was on display for my benefit alone—soldiers did not wear their medals except on special occasions.

"Now Captain, we must prepare to extend our under-ice positions to the west. You and that assistant of yours—Corporal Pulvermacher—will go to Hohe Schneide tomorrow to inspect the outpost. We've installed a telpher line from the Naglerspitz, to keep them well-supplied against any new Italian attacks. Then I want you to survey the Vedretta di Monte Cristallo as far west as you can go—it's a kilometer or two at the most. Map crevasses and any other features. When the Colonel returns, we will begin construction."

I stood, clicked my heels in the best imitation-Prussian style, about-faced and went out, anger roaring in my ears.

The first person I met in the big common-room was Franz, who saw at once that I was troubled. He clapped me on the back, sat me down, and had two steins of beer fetched for us.

"Ah, with my second-sight, I can see it is Stutz," he said. "Here, drink this. Don't talk; and try not to think about it for three minutes."

At the end of three minutes, Franz had me in such good humor that I could report the interview calmly. "I'm ready to wager that the Colonel simply turned your request for leave over to Stutz—and that is the explanation," he said. Then he went on to persuade me that the Colonel wasn't really such a bad old donkey. Worry made him unreasonable. On the other hand, he was generally fair-minded enough, and if the case were put to him again, he would undoubtedly relent. The Colonel, it was widely believed, considered Stutz seven kinds of an ass.

Eventually, I was quite mollified. Even if the Colonel did strut like a crow and talk like a rule-book, he still deferred to me in many instances and took my opinion over Stutz's. Ah, well, I should await his return.

To tell the truth, Christmas at home was not all joy and plum pudding. My mother would be so full of tender worries that she would drive Hans and Theresa giddy with orders to pamper me. Suddenly, something would remind her of how I might be killed, and the tears would begin to spout. My sister would talk of nothing but the fascinating thoughts, whims, preferences, sentiments, habits, looks, foibles, and tastes of the saintly Werner Einecke until I began to hate him *in absentia*. (Actually, he was not a half-bad chap; we had been in school together for five or six years and I knew him better than Lisl did.) My uncle Wolfram, who never let one forget that he was one of the first German captains to steam into Kiaochow Bay in 1897, would advise me *in extenso* about how the war must be conducted: "You're in the midst of it, old boy—you can't see the big picture. Outflanking them through the Alps is the only viable strategy, just like Hannibal, you see." In the background, my two aunts would twitter on about how *truly* difficult it was to buy soap, decent meat, sweets, or whatever, with all the shortages.

The one person that I wished to see was Anna.

I headed to my bunk to prepare for my journey back to Hohe Schneide. A courier had just arrived from the valley with mail, and there was, indeed, a letter from Anna.

IX. Melting the Ice-Maiden

Dear Anna: she was the reason I had joined the army, after all.

When I returned from England to Bavaria in the autumn of 1913, I found myself readjusting to Bavarian culture with a mixture of discomfort and joy. I missed my university classmates and my professors, missed the grand cauldron of knowledge that we had lived in, the long hours in the laboratory and the library—all of that was over now. But I had a new appreciation for the zealous joy of German life, the festivals and raucous singing, the hearty meals of sauerbraten and *Weisswuascht*[72] with mustard and pretzels. And above all, the buxom and very friendly Bavarian girls. Ah, those sweet girls! Here I was graced with a university education and yet sadly naïve about the mysteries of girls.

My sister Lisl was having her eighteenth birthday party and had invited all of the most beautiful young women in Regensburg, or so it seemed. My parents were probably thinking about my marriage prospects and they insisted that I attend, even though I felt it was somewhat beneath me (in my new identity as a university graduate). Our dim Gothic refuge of a home had been transformed by paper streamers, bright new electric lights, and colored bunting into a shrine of celebration, with the phonograph blaring waltzes and minuets (my father eschewed jazz which was all the rage among young people in those days) and our gardener Hans and our cook Theresa dressed comically in the festive garb of royal servants. Every effort was made to keep the young ladies occupied with an abundance of food and drink, and as the sole young man present at the party I was overwhelmed with the sights and smells of all that beauty and femininity. Nonetheless, I soon found myself deeply and rather painfully attracted to Lisl's good friend Anna von Murnau.

Anna came from one of Regensburg's truly aristocratic families and made a point of parading her family's wealth and superiority. Blessed with hair the color of spun gold, eyes like stolen sapphires and lips as red as a saint's blood, she bestowed her exquisite smile sparingly but with great effect. Even my father, who was by no means a lecher, fawned and blushed under her gaze.

I moved through the crowd to get a closer look. Anna was telling Lisl about a ball-gown the Princess Elisabeth of Luxembourg had worn. Melting with inner terror, I contrived to get her to look at me by offering her a plate of chocolate bonbons, but she was engrossed in Lisl's giggling nonsense. When my mother summoned us all to sing as Lisl cut the cake, I tried to get Anna to accept a cup of spiced cider, which she waved disdainfully aside.

But her attempts to ignore me only made me think she was secretly delighted, and so I stepped courageously in front of her and said, "I don't think we've met, I'm—"

"I'm *sure* of it," she replied, stepping past me to accept a slice of cake on a plate.

"My name's Melchior!" I blurted out, doing my best to stay in front of her.

"I don't doubt it," she said coldly, looking for a chair to sit on while she ate.

"You're Anna von Murnau, right? I've seen you at the—at the…" I struggled to think of someplace I might have seen her before, but since I had been away from Regensburg for four years, nothing came to mind except the fish market, which didn't seem like a place that Anna would frequent. Finally, a stroke of genius: "At Adler's Apothecary on Goliathstrasse!" Adler's sold a variety of soaps and pomades that could not be found elsewhere in town, and I suspected that Anna would hardly send a servant to purchase such personal items for her.

Anna looked at me sharply for a moment, as if preparing some withering rebuke, then her eyes softened and she said, "You're Lisl's older brother, aren't you? You've been off studying at some foreign university?"

Ecstatic at having been recognized, I grinned broadly and nodded. "Yes, I've just graduated from Leeds in England!"

---

[72] Sausage made from veal and bacon.

She gave me the faintest of smiles, the tiniest suggestion of an upturned corner of her mouth, and I felt my inner organs dissolving. "Good, then you can fetch me a fork so I can eat my cake."

No soldier ever received an order more gratefully, and I reeled off into the crowd to search for cutlery. When I returned she was gone, of course, as the girls had decided to take Lisl to the park to play some silly game that involved ribbons.

Still I did not abandon my pursuit of Anna von Murnau. I took advantage of her friendship with Lisl and whenever they were together at church or shopping downtown or on their way to a tea-party, I would materialize as if by coincidence, greeting them fondly in hopes of being invited to accompany them. Anna was equally at pains to ignore me or to brush me off with frigid impatience. She would look everywhere except at me, would hear everything except my greetings and my compliments. She was less inviting than a swim in the Danube in January, although my fervent imagination never failed to interpret her behavior as subdued passion.

This went on for several weeks until winter came, and as Christmas approached I began to realize that Anna had no interest in me at all, and in fact seemed to dislike me intensely. About the same time, my father began to indicate that I might think about pursuing some profession or other. He tried not to grumble but he suggested that my life of idleness was hardly appropriate for his son and heir and that it reflected badly on my upbringing. I was aware of this, but indeed finding work in crystallography would have been impossible outside of a university or possibly one of the great chemical factories in Frankfurt or Berlin, concocting soap, cloth dye or rat poison. As a career it had little to offer, and it now occurred to me that my academic life had been useless in preparing me to make a living.

These thoughts weighed heavily on me on Christmas Eve, when after supper my father chose to open a bottle of brandy in celebration. I had not had anything to drink since leaving Rolf in Sweden, and downing a snifter of Sechsämtertropfen put me into a stew of self-pity, which prompted me to don my coat and wander off into the dusk, looking for companionship at a local pub.

Not far from our home was a *Kneipe* known as *Der Tanzende Bär*,[73] with a rather evil sign over its door depicting a snarling grizzly being taunted by two men with spears. Inside, the air was dense with tobacco smoke and the reek of alcohol emitted by a boisterous crowd of Regensburger men who had chosen to celebrate Christmas Eve with lager and ale rather than with their families. I spotted Ulrich and Dieter, two old chums from high school, slurping steins of beer, froth clinging to their upper lips where downy new moustaches had started to appear. Soon we were exchanging jokes and reminiscences, and they told me of the enlistment of our mutual friend Werner Einecke into the newly-formed Air Corps, where he hoped to become a pilot. When I had finished my second beer and was looking around to order a third, Ulrich said, "My brother Bertrand's broken off his engagement, you know. We'd been counting on a May wedding, but it won't happen now. He's miserable about it too."

"What happened?" asked Dieter.

"Well, he had enlisted in the cavalry, but his eyesight is rather poor—he's managed to hide it until now, but they found out somehow and told him it wouldn't do; I gather that cavalrymen don't wear spectacles. Neither the infantry nor the artillery will have him either, and he refuses to consider the navy, even though he could serve on a submarine where spectacles are hardly an issue. There's nothing left except the Army Service Corps." This last was the national guard which was generally held in low esteem. We all laughed at Bertrand's wounded pride.

"So his fiancée suddenly called off their engagement," Ulrich continued. "She was quite taken with him when he was wearing his uniform, before they found out about his eyes, and now she can't seem to stand the thought of marrying a nearsighted civilian. Arrogant girl, that Anna von Murnau."

I caught my breath—could it be? She had been taken, unbeknownst to me, and now she was free again, and

---

[73] The Dancing Bear

what stupendous luck—I had the secret to her heart! So runs the mind after an excess of beer, but it was love and youth that corrupted my judgment.

"Gentlemen," I said, raising my newly-refilled stein. "I've a mind to join the army." My comrades laughed and toasted my sudden bellicosity, and the following week I was off to the recruiting station.

And so on a warm Sunday morning in early May I found myself dressed in the smart gray uniform of an *unteroffizer*[74] escorting Lisl to the Regensburg Cathedral. Anna was going up the steps just as we arrived, and she turned her head to see who this handsome young soldier might be, with Lisl at his elbow. When she recognized me, her look of astonishment was a gift from heaven—her smile was genuine and her eyes gazed directly into mine. I felt a powerful charge of electricity surging through me. That fine moment was almost worth the twenty months on the Western Front that I spent dodging artillery shells.

"Melchior, isn't it? How dashing you look in your new uniform. Infantry?" Her eyes traveled down my brass-buttoned coat and I imagined her sizing up my character, my family history, and my physique, all favorably.

"Eleventh Infantry Regiment," I replied, adopting a self-satisfied drawl. "I'm applying for an officer's commission."

"Goodness! I *am* impressed." She blessed me with the full force of her magnificent smile, and I would not have felt more honored if God Himself had kissed my brow.

"Would you be kind enough to dine at our home this evening?" In disbelief I heard my own voice utter these words. Lisl gaped at me in astonishment, and Anna smiled even more broadly as she accepted. During the mass that followed I thanked the Almighty a thousand times.

It was, on the whole, a happy occasion for our family. My father was overjoyed because marriage to a wealthy von Murnau daughter offered numerous advantages, including an old Bavarian tradition that the bride's family would assume the groom's family's debts, and my mother was delighted at the thought of an invitation to dinner at the von Murnaus' stately mansion.

Anna and I made ourselves public, attending a variety of balls, *abends*,[75] and afternoon social events with me in uniform and she in all her radiant glory. But although she was beautiful and eternally charming in public, as a person she was vain and inconsiderate, obsessed with her family's high social position, and enchanted with her own beauty, insisting petulantly that I shower her with praise and expensive gifts. She had a cruel streak as well, and enjoyed nothing more than an opportunity to denigrate and despise other people, including her former fiancé, whom she referred to as "blind-as-a-bat Bertrand." The euphoria I had felt upon winning her heart soon began to fade. I could hardly confess this to anyone, however, least of all my family, who were busy planning an elaborate wedding even though I had yet to propose.

On weekends I would visit Anna for the obligatory round of teas and garden-parties, naively hoping that our relationship would somehow blossom with time, that she would grow kinder and more mature—and indeed, more affectionate—but our conversation was stiff and irritating. I realized that I had become nothing more than an ornament on Anna's elbow, for her to display to her friends along with her diamond earrings and emerald necklace. I was at a loss as to how I could thaw this chilly woman.

Matters were taken out of my hands in August, 1914 when the Archduke Ferdinand of Austria was brutally murdered on a bridge in Sarajevo. Austria declared war on Serbia and Germany declared war on Russia, France and Belgium. To longtime political observers this was no surprise, but since I had been blithely absorbed in my own affairs, it came as a thunderclap realization that I was about to be sent to war. Although I had just begun my officer's training and knew absolutely nothing, I was offered a second lieutenant's commission—a promotion that ordinarily took years to obtain but which became necessary as the regiment reorganized itself in preparation

---

[74] Non-commissioned officer
[75] Soirees

for battle. The following day we were ordered to prepare for transfer to the Lorraine border under the command of the Bavarian Crown Prince Rupprecht.

On the eve of our departure I had only an hour to visit my parents at home. They were both in a frenzy of worry—not that I would die in battle, as everyone was saying that this war would be brief and victorious—but rather that I had not yet asked Anna to marry me.

"We need to reserve the cathedral, Melchior," said my father gravely. "It's expensive and it must be scheduled weeks in advance. We won't be able to change it easily."

"That's exactly why I haven't asked her yet, Father!" I was madly pulling clothes out of a chest in my old room, trying to decide which socks and undershirts I should bring in case it got cold. "I don't know if I'll be home again in September or October, or whether I can ask for leave, or many other hundreds of things! Please, let me fight this war first, *then* I'll think about my wedding day!" What else could I say? He never would have accepted the truth, that Anna was just an unpleasant person, a poor choice for a bride except that she was breathtakingly lovely.

I was sorry later that I had spoken harshly to him, but of course I was violently nervous myself and since I was young and impetuous the words blurted out of their own accord. At the door I kissed my tearful mother and shook hands with my stone-faced father, threw my duffle over my shoulder and headed off down the street to find a cab. It was a sad and shameful departure that left us all feeling miserable, and which affected my father's health, I'm sure.

Two weeks later I received a letter from my mother telling me of my father's untimely death. He had passed an uncomfortable weekend coughing noisily and after supper on a Sunday, had retired to his study to read the papers. My mother heard a thud and had opened the door to find him slumped on the floor unconscious. By the time the doctor arrived he was dead—only a month before his forty-fifth birthday. I thought back to his grim expression on that summer night, the strength of his grip and the glisten in his eyes as my mother wept buckets. It was too sad that he would not be there upon my return, nor to see me marry Anna. I still believe he would have lived longer had I chosen gentler, kinder words.

When I returned to Regensburg on leave in 1916, I knew I would have to make a decision about Anna, who continued to represent a bitter conflict for me. We had exchanged a few letters, highly dispassionate ones, but the question of marriage was still in the air and I knew that on my return home I would have to answer it. Did it even matter? Would I live long enough to watch Anna's hair turn gray? Why not just marry her for one blissful night, then return to the front to accept my inevitable death? But I knew I couldn't go through with it.

Seeing Anna again awakened all those adolescent feelings—that giddy affection and a powerful craving to touch her, embrace her, and kiss her mouth long and forcefully. There were worse things than being married to an arrogant woman, I decided, especially if she is entrancingly lovely, enough to make your head spin when you look at her. Anna's parents were still disdainful at the thought of having me for a son-in-law, although they admitted that it was impressive that I had survived twenty months under fire and that I had attained the rank of captain, implying that if I became a general they might consider me worthy of their daughter.

On my fourth day home I invited Anna to walk in the park and we found ourselves at a loss for conversation. It was usually all Anna's conversation, anyway, but today she seemed a bit sad. This intrigued me: the only emotions I had seen her express so far were joy, scorn, and a kind of vicious rage in which she clenched her teeth, threw things and slammed doors. Now she was drooping like a flower on the hearth, and her hand seemed to clutch my elbow with more fervor than usual.

"Anna, we need to talk about something important," I began, not really knowing what I was going to say.

"Yes, my dear?" She had taken to using this term in a patronizing way, but now it almost seemed to have acquired a tone of sincerity.

I took a deep breath. "You know that it is possible that I won't return from the war, like so many other men." I turned and took her gloved hand in mine, and looked her in the eyes. She blinked for a moment, taken aback at the seriousness of my tone. I had grown a lot during those past two years, and I realized suddenly that Anna was no longer a fatuous girl who was beyond my control: I could make her listen to me now.

"Yes, I suppose that had occurred to me," she answered quietly.

"Well, I have a fairly strong premonition, Anna, that I am going to die on the Western Front, and…" I paused, not sure what to say next. Was I telling her that we were never going to be married?

"And…what? Should I purchase a cemetery plot for you, then?" She was all seriousness, but the incongruity of this remark made me laugh, and she laughed too. For the first time since I had met her, I felt a warmth of affection between us, and I saw now that Anna was growing up too.

"You may do so, Anna, if you wish. But it may be better if you…find someone else who can marry you." I had trouble finishing this sentence because quite unexpectedly I saw the face of my cousin Fritz, in the last few seconds of his life, terrified and yet looking to me to save him. I mused for an instant on what it would be like to be blown to shreds by an artillery shell.

"Dear Melchior," Anna replied, and to my astonishment she put her gloved fingers lightly on my cheek. "You're a strange and funny young man. You forget that you have not yet asked me to marry you, so I have every right to look for another man if I choose to. But I am quite certain that the Lord God will see you through this awful war and bring you back to me. And I will be happy if you come back. Fiddlesticks to your silly premonition!"

I regretted now that I had not returned home earlier, that I did not have more time to spend with Anna. I looked deeply into her eyes for a long minute. "Thank you, Anna, but I still can't ask you to marry me until the war is over. I hope you'll understand." She nodded and looked away, and I thought I saw her blinking back tears. Without another word we turned and walked back to her house.

But since our last encounter five months before, I had begun to hope that we could grow to love one another, and was anxious to see her during my holiday leave. Infuriating that Stutz had to meddle in this part of my life too! I had started to think about my future, which I fervently hoped would be peaceful enough that I could forget about the war. Was Anna having the same thoughts? I tore the envelope open with shaking hands.

"Dear Melchior,

I write this letter in anticipation of your Christmas leave, and I wanted you to be aware of something before you arrive in Regensburg.

After much careful consideration, I have decided to end our "understanding" as I will call it, although it has been treated as an engagement by everyone we know. My reasons for this are complex, but suffice it to say that I have recently re-acquainted myself with Bertrand Huffnagle, my former fiancé, and have realized that I am still in love with him. I do not try to defend my decision, but I do want you to know that I am fond of you still and that I very much regret that we have been separated by this atrocious war, as I would have enjoyed spending more time with you.

Bertrand has proven himself kind and patient, and I am certain that he will be a loyal husband. Our wedding will be on Christmas Eve, and if by any chance you are in Regensburg I hope you will be able to attend.

I certainly wish you the best of luck in your military career.

Yours,

Anna von Murnau

I was overcome with a sense of loss and humiliation, such a profound pain that I had to collapse on my bunk, crumpling her letter in my fist and fighting back tears. I felt bereft of my hopes for the future—even such tiny and childish hopes mean a great deal to a soldier away at the front. Anna had come to represent a distant star towards which I navigated my way through this long and unpredictable war. I felt wounded and betrayed; I spent the rest of that day in mourning.

Swiss border guards at the Hotel Dreisprachenspitze.

X. The Fall of a Leader

The next day at dawn Erich and I headed down the mountain by telpher, first to Trafoi, where we drove through the town in a supply truck just as people were clearing the night's snowfall off their front steps. The snow had obscured the dirt and trash accumulated by the army and returned Trafoi to an idyllic Alpine village where people came to ski and admire the scenery. We continued by dogsled up to the Naglerspitz, where we took the newly-completed telpher to Hohe Schneide, passing directly over the glacier under which we had tunneled so vigorously a month before. Looking down into blue shadows of the crevasses I thought I could make out our rope bridges, like a soul in Heaven peering into the reaches of Hell.

At Hohe Schneide the outpost had been enlarged and a pair of 75mm field guns brought up to harass the Italians in the valley below. We borrowed a dogsled and, the weather being calm, set out at early light the following day, obscured from Italian observation by tenebrous clouds that turned everything on the glacier to various shades of charcoal.

Surveying the ice-fields was dull and mechanical work, and I was distracted by noisome thoughts. Having finished our last reading, I told Erich to make a dash due west out over the open névé.[76] Erich had now become a competent sled-driver, though a cautious one.

When we reached it, we were in the midst of the largest glacier field between the Braulio and the Zebrù valleys. It is, in fact, one field, but here the conflict between the languages has divided it into the eastern Madatsch-ferner, the central Eben-ferner, and the westernmost Vedretta di Monte Cristallo, bordered by a ridge which overlooks the city of Bormio. We halted the sled and climbed part way up the crag, leaving the dogs curled up in the snow, where they waited patiently. Even in the bleak light, we could view the whole, eight-kilometer-long body of the triple glacier. By this time, the morning had begun to brighten and we could look north and see the winding road of the Stilfser Pass. With my field glasses, I could make out the curious confrontation that existed there. The Italian lines were on the western side of the old national border; in the center was a peninsula of Switzerland crowned by the Dreisprachenspitz Hotel (the name refers to the three languages—Italian, German and Romansch—spoken in the vicinity) which was occupied by Swiss border guards. To the east, behind the hotel, were our lines, lightly fortified positions guarding the pass, the westernmost limit of the Austro-Hungarian Empire.

I could see some of the heavily-cloaked Swiss standing on the verandah of the hotel, smoking their pipes. Not far from the hotel, on our side of the border, the Austrians had built some barracks, shoddy huts languishing in the snow at the foot of the regal Dreisprachenspitz.

"What a perfect war," I mused to Erich. "We cannot fire and the Italians cannot fire for fear of hitting the Swiss. The Swiss, meanwhile, enjoy two of their natural habitats—the mountains and a decent hotel. Can you imagine the white tablecloths in the dining rooms, the attentive waiters, the good cellar—*eh bien, garcon, je essayerai le vin du glacier, s'il vous plait*[77]—and the fragrant fondue? The Austrians and Italians live in the mud and cold. But it's only just, eh? Because they are the bloody-minded fools who started the war. Yet, thanks to the Swiss, nobody is getting hurt."

"It would seem that way, sir," said Erich in his best serving-man voice. He must have listened to more than one boring monologue from an employer.

"It is a fifteen-minute run on the sled to the edge of the gorge. We take our chances on the slope. Then across the pass to the Swiss border is no more than one kilometer. We can move fast and the cloudy day will obscure us. What do you say? Tonight we dine in that hotel. Tomorrow, we are on our way to Zurich."

"Both sides would enjoy shooting us as we came down the slope," Erich said.

"Well, I suppose you have something there," I said. I turned my fieldglasses south-westward and I could see

---

[76] Young, granular snow which has been partially melted, refrozen and compacted.

[77] Very well, waiter, I'll try the glacier wine, if you please

where the ice field ended at a ridge called Dosso Reit. There began the downward slope to Bormio—which the Austrians call Worms. From the ridge to the town, the distance is no more than four kilometers.

"Now, on the other hand, if we should strike for that ridge, we should arrive in about twenty minutes. The climb is graded 'easy' by the Alpine Club and the path was much used by tourists before the war, I'm told. We could be in Bormio before noon—think of it: *Saltimbocca alla Romana!* Smoking hot *bistecca alla Fiorentina!* Erich, do you know the land where the citron blooms? *Di Italia, il mar, il suol, chi dal cor ti cancellò?*"[78]

Erich was looking alarmed. No doubt, he had never had a master—even the very rich ones—quite as demented as this. I, on the other hand, was feeling both light-headed and charged with energy. I was indeed tempted by the sight of the Swiss border sign through my binoculars. If it had not been Erich with me, I might have made a try for it. But Erich was one of those completely honorable young men who would shoot me sorrowfully in the back if I attempted it. Why hadn't I found a scoundrel, a willing deserter instead?

I sighed in abnegation and began to climb down the peak toward the waiting sled. Following behind me, Erich said, "I'm glad you decided to stay, sir." There was relief in his voice.

"It would have been inhumane to abandon the dogs out here."

"To say nothing of the Fatherland."

"Ah, of course. That, too."

As if there were some enormous sheep-shearing in the sky, white fleece began to come drifting down, denser and denser. As we clambered down the last few meters, we watched the ice-world and its rebel peaks of stone move into darkness. Strangely, the biting wind of the Ortler had died away, leaving the flakes to cover us in relentless calm. The only sound was a vast rustle of the descending whiteness, accumulating rapidly on the already snow-enveloped ridges and peaks.

When we stood again on the level, I watched one of the broad white flakes, a miniature work of art in Austrian lace, dissolve on the back of my glove. When I was a child, my English grandmother told me that snowflakes were the tears of the angels at the passing of summer. Even at five, I knew better, though I refrained from disillusioning her.

We arranged ourselves in the sled, and Erich called to the dogs as he cracked his whip. We started off in a flurry. Before we were halfway home, I guessed that we were about to have one of the great snowfalls of the season. Already, through the white curtain, I found it hard to make out our first landmark, the Hintere Madatschspitz. I was enjoying a warm feeling of naturalness. Instead of making a rough and risky climb down to Switzerland, or to Italy, I was, like a good householder and patriot, going home in my dogsled. No sting on the tongue of cold *vin blanc* awaited me, but honest *schnapps* and *schinken*.[79] I sighed again.

Until I went to sleep that night, I carried an irritating thought like a sliver under my skin: Myself, there on the crag, staring with longing at Switzerland. Never to my knowledge had a von Fuchsheim led the charge, but, on the other hand, neither did a von Fuchsheim desert the ranks—unless the cause had turned out to be hopeless. I blamed my fragile state of mind on a coincidence of harm: Stutz with his sneers and threats and Anna with her offhand dismissal. My immediate response was a desire to escape it all for a nice meal and a warm bed.

But I had survived the worst of the war by building shelters: that is what I intended to do now.

When Erich and I returned to the Payerhütte, I was informed that the finishing touches on the Ice Citadel had been completed. Cornelius and the other sappers insisted that I ride to the inspection in style. As I came into the grotto, they were drawn up like a mock honor-guard, with crossed ice axes and a bit of red and white

---

[78] From Verdi's *La Traviata,* act 2, scene 1: "Who erased the sea, the sun, the land of [Italy] from your heart?" The original line referred to Provence.

[79] Ham

bunting overhead. I walked to the place where the U-Bahn[80] sledge stood ready to depart and found more of the joke. They had fixed a little overhang of shuttered roof, a theatre poster on the ice wall, and painted signs. One sign read "*Rathaus platz*"[81] and the second, with an arrow, "*Nach dem Wienerwald.*"[82] I seated myself in less-than-great dignity among the ration boxes and, while the men tramped alongside, I was drawn smoothly forward by the cable.

I felt much heartened. The *eisfestung*, that we had worked so long and hard to make, was complete and I was moving down its main railway line. The file of soldiers, boots crunching on the ice floor, lit by the electric bulbs we had strung from the arched ceiling, moved freely beneath the windswept no-man's-land. Franz's cold-madness was a relic of an uncomfortable past, and hypothermia and frostbite were rare occurrences of late, according to Dr. Schaller. We had reliable daily intelligence on the movements of the enemy, who still struggled over the tundra while we observed him from our periscope-niches. All told, we had excavated over twelve kilometers of tunnels under the ice. A man could ride the sledge from the Payerhütte to the base of the Königspitz, wearing only a light jacket, in under an hour. Best of all, the tunnels were impervious to even the heaviest artillery.

We came to a relay station, where the sledge was hooked to a new cable. Here there was a sort of bypass track where one sledge could be shunted aside to allow passage of the sledge going in the opposite direction. In several places farther on, the tunnel sloped at such an angle that I got out and walked up or down a flight of ice steps. We came into the abrupt, dazzling light of the crevasse and crossed over a plank bridge. More ascents, then a smaller crevasse traversed by a bridge strong enough to hold the sledge. Finally, the mysterious blue radiance in the ice walls began to increase as the final leg of the gallery angled upward toward the adit. I stepped out into a world of blinding-white diamond dust.

Once I had put my snow goggles on, I saw a Breughel snowscape scene with many figures—men clearing the approach-paths, others erecting snow barriers, others carrying cases of supplies or billets of wood up the steep path.

This was the Kristallspitzen, stage for the famous *poltergeist* trick on the Italian brasshats. In the first emplacement, I found insulated walls, a wooden floor, an iron stove, two benches, and a table. On the wall was a painted sign that read "Villa Brandauer". There was also an accommodating artillery subaltern who took me to the gun port overlooking the Zebrù valley and gave me his field glasses to view a column of Italian mules and muleteers on the narrow road. Now I looked into the face of our enemy: he was tired and he needed a shave. He was not at all monstrous. I said something to that effect.

"Yes, sir," said the subaltern. "Up here, it's not like other wars, I'd guess. We play a very human game."

I said that I'd heard that the Italians were ferocious and did not take prisoners.

"Once or twice, perhaps," he answered, "but it's a war of tolerances—narrow ones. You see, if we should hear that the Macaronis had shelled our dugouts at the Hallesche *Hütte* in the Eissee Pass, we should have to kill some of those poor mules and so starve the Capanna di Milano for a week."

"I was attacked not long ago and my sled-driver was killed."

"That happens, sir. One can always tell when a new commander with fire in his eye has come. They bleed us and then we bleed them for a while until he learns. It's the same on both sides."

I nodded at the guns, shrouded in their canvas coats. "Do you intend to fire at sleds or enemy ski patrols?" I asked.

"To speak the truth, Captain, I don't. Too little profit in hitting theirs and too much danger of mistaking ours for theirs. Nobody carries a flag, you know. Besides, patrols aren't of any real concern. It's the Alpini scaling parties that are dangerous. If they should decide to go up the Königspitz, we would need to lob a few shells in

[80] Underground railroad
[81] City Hall square
[82] To the Vienna Woods

their way to discourage them. Of course, they would only attempt such a thing at night, when we wouldn't be able to see them from here anyway."

"And if a scaling party tried to come up here?" I asked, looking down the slope.

"Ah, for that we have the *rollbomben*," replied the gunner. He picked up an iron sphere and hefted it in one hand. "Light the fuse and toss it over the side, then look out below! Crude but effective."

It was late in the afternoon when we started back. I was on foot this time because the sledges had brought up the quota of supplies and were no longer in operation. Our footsteps echoed down the long corridor. Because I was off duty the next day, I was anticipating a sound sleep and a lazy day of reading and writing before the fire.

As we neared the great crevasse bridge, we heard the voices of men coming from the other direction, and so we waited on the bridgehead platform to let them pass. I saw that it was a party of four or five signals men.

"Have you heard the news?" the leading soldier called out when he saw us. We said we had heard none.

"The Emperor is dead," he announced in a solemn voice. I thought of poor Willy[83] as I had seen him once, with his ox-horn moustaches, his eagle helmet, his golden cuirass, and his withered arm. Then I suddenly realized that they meant, of course, Franz Josef—the old man at Schönbrunn,[84] nearly 87, and I was no longer surprised.

"It happened a few days ago, but we've just had the news. It may be that Prince Karl has been crowned already," he said as he passed us. There were murmurs behind me but no remarks of lamentation, and we went our way.

When we emerged from the tunnel in front of the Payerhütte, a great commotion was taking place. Coatless men were emerging from the main door. Someone was shouting something unintelligible to a group standing by to await the approach of the telpher car. It was late afternoon by now and the sun was low and glaring in the west and I could make out a black oblong floating in the bright welter. In the bodily attitudes of the waiting men, I could see a strange expectancy.

I saw Franz among them. "What's this about? "What's wrong?" I called, but no one answered. As soon as the gondola came within reach, eight pairs of hands seized it and the men bent forward, almost as if they expected to see something in this empty car where nothing could be concealed. Franz and Viktor at once threw themselves into the car and, still rocking on its cable, it started off again. The others watched silently.

"What happened?" I asked again.

Then I heard Erich's voice behind me. "It's the Colonel."

I took him by the arm and looked curiously into his face. His good-servant serenity was gone and he had a troubled frown. He suddenly turned away so that I could not see his emotion, and I remembered how young he was.

I pushed through the crowd of men who seemed still stunned and silent. With narrowed eyes, they peered and pointed at something below, obscured by the rays of the setting sun. As I gazed into the valley, I saw a man suspended from the cable, perhaps a hundred and fifty meters below us.

Erich explained that the Colonel had been riding a telpher car up the mountain alone and had arrived at the last leg of ascent before the line leveled off to cross the glacial field. Nothing seemed to be amiss until he was three quarters of the way to the top when, in an instant, the hauling-cable broke. The two men in the winch-station—a sergeant and a corporal—watched in horror as the broken cable leapt like a long whip in the air and the two telpher cars careened downwards and finally tumbled end over end toward the valley.

The Colonel, however, had managed to reach up and to seize the main cable with his gloved hands and there he hung as the vibrations slowly lessened. His back was toward us and we could not see his face; we could not tell if he heard our shouts. The only expression was in the death-grip of the Colonel's hands on the cable.

The two winch attendants were not fools and, in the tedious hours one spends on duty in a telpher station,

---

[83] Emperor Wilhelm II of Prussia
[84] Emperor Franz Joseph I of Austria

they had no doubt talked of disasters and the ways of meeting them. They acted quickly to rig a double loop of cable, tied this to a climber's line, and paid it down the main cable. When it reached the Colonel, he could grasp it and be hauled to safety.

That famous moment betwixt the saddle and the ground. I have lived through it so many times since then that it has become a part of my inner life, of my mind's routine. A horrible messenger visits me at night and commands me to watch. Through the fieldglasses, I see the Colonel's body beginning to shudder slightly. It is the vanishing point of the future when only history remains to us. He still did not seem to hear the shouting of the men as the improvised rig neared his back and, finally, touched him. If death is the final tax we pay for life, the Colonel must have owed peculiarly to die in such a grotesque way. I can see his hands, often so frantic in conversation, now black knots on the cable. To die of trust misplaced is the bitterest death of all—as Mme. de Tourneville perhaps realized while she spun toward the rocky floor.

Waking we ignored it and forgot it, this living on a high wire. Daily men climbed ascents like the Königspitze or the Ortler that were the triumphs of famous Alpinists only fifty years before. They walked on ledges no wider than their boots and swung on ropes over chasms that fell forever. All this with an insolence of poise and a daring so commonplace that it had become a habit. But we all dreamed. And in our dreams we fell.

The Colonel must have felt or sensed something behind his shoulder. Even if he had not heard the shouts, he must have understood that some form of help had arrived just behind his back. He bent his head for a few seconds, then shook it.

When he unclasped his hands, he was loosing himself from debts that had become too heavy. I do not suggest that he ever thought of it in grander terms, but he was also, in fact, bidding farewell to a falling empire, its emperor dead and its armies frozen in the ice.

He fell like a shot, his body at attention and his arms held high over his head, not like a bankrupt committing suicide, but as if he were a hero, poor chap. Our eyes followed his diminishing form as it vanished into the vast whiteness of infinity, straining to see it long after it had disappeared. We stood clustered there in stunned disbelief, and below us a destitute wind hummed mournfully.

It snowed all the next day, in a gentle, elegiac fall. Everyone went about his duties in a kind of sobered silence. It was not that any of them had loved him, had been inspired by him, had pictured him leading them to great victories. It was rather as if their schoolmaster had left them—a fussy, pettifogging, nagging, inglorious *dominie* whose sole virtue was this: he had worried about them. He did not want them to die.

They could not find his body and after a few weeks the search was ended. A funeral service was held, an oddly silent one, and Father Weiss scattered some paper flowers to the wind. Later when I had occasion to ride the telpher, I would scan the surface of the snow continuously in hopes of locating where he had fallen. For decades the steady creep of the glacier bore him down into the warm valley where wildflowers bloom at the edge of the ice, until he was exhumed on Austrian television one day in June, forty-nine years later.

XI. White Thunder

In the coffee-houses and beer-halls of Regensburg I run into other old veterans from time to time, but we usually do not speak of the war. There is too much grief to justify fondling those old scars on a whim. It is only at the funeral of a comrade, or on Christmas when the schnapps is flowing, that we are tempted to relive the past for a short time. And even then, there are dark places that we do not open.

I have occasionally recounted the story of the capture of St. Mihiel, and of our defense of the heights against the French assault, and the tale of the attack on Hohe Schneide. These are easy anecdotes of facile triumphs; I did not feel the closeness of death in those brief fights, so I can talk about them with my friends and their children, who sometimes clamor for war stories.

But there are stories that I could not try to describe before an audience because to this day, they fill me with horror and anguish. Those stories must be written out so that the pen and ink and paper will shield me from my fear. They tell of times when I knew that I might be living my final moments, after which my heart would shudder to a halt, my eyes would close, and my insignificant life would be over. The story I am about to write is one of those stories.

This time it was no human enemy that threatened me but rather, the Ortler itself.

The weather continued mild through the end of November, giving us occasional sunshine and a gentle breeze, then in early December we experienced a steep drop in temperature and the arrival of hostile clouds that lay across the mountaintops like a crumpled sheet of lead. On December 7th it began to snow heavily, fat clumps of white dropping down to cover everything in a weighty quilt, softening the edges of the rocks and obscuring the world around us in an undulating netherworld mist. There was no wind, only the incessant whisper of flakes accumulating, obliterating the pathways and signs around Payerhütte and bearing down on the roofs of our rickety outbuildings.

I had come out of the Ice Citadel to send headquarters a report of my surveying journey, along with a list of supplies and equipment we would need to build new positions under the Vedretta di Monte Cristallo, according to Colonel Buchholz's plan. After delivering it to the courier, I lingered to watch the snowfall, still feeling a morose lethargy in the wake of the Colonel's death. I decided to sleep in the Payerhütte and return the next day down the long ice tunnel to the Citadel.

But in the morning the door of the Payerhütte was firmly blocked by a massive snowdrift, and Lieutenant Pauli, who was in command, ordered all of us to start shoveling. The enlisted men's barracks was barely visible under a smooth white shroud, and the entrance into the glacier had vanished behind a billowy mound. At least two meters of snow had fallen since the day before and it was still coming down.

Pauli sighed and shook his head. The courier would be unable to get to Trafoi in this weather and our weekly supply of firewood and canned sausage would have to stay in the valley. There was nothing to be done except order a detail to keep the paths clear, go indoors and wait for it to stop.

I wrote a letter to my mother, played chess with Karl, the warrant-officer who was waiting to go on holiday leave, then dozed in front of the fire until dinner. A glance out the door revealed that it was, if anything, snowing harder now. Pauli reported that the weight of the snow was causing the roof of the barracks to sag dangerously, and sent up a team of shovelers to clear it off.

By the next day I calculated that we had received four meters of snow in three days, and Lieutenant Pauli corroborated this figure. "It's heavy stuff, too," he said looking anxiously up the slope at the Tabarettaspitz and beyond it, to the broad shoulders of the Ortler, a dim specter in the flurries. "This is avalanche weather." Pauli had been raised in the Tyrol and although he looked young and innocent, he had seen plenty of avalanches in his time. We went together to the telephone office to call Major Stutz and request permission to move the men into the Ice Citadel, where they would be protected from an avalanche that could easily come from the mountain's north face.

I could hear Stutz's raspy voice through the telephone, asking Pauli if he was mad. "Abandon the Payerhütte? It's the center of our communications and our supply lines! You will hold your position, Lieutenant—I don't expect you to retreat just because it's snowing!" All Pauli could do was to hang up and watch through the window as the endless cloud of white settled on top of us. We heard that evening that an artillery post farther up the mountain at Pleisshorn had been buried by a small avalanche, but that no one had been hurt. The guns, however, were lost under a monstrous heap of snow.

It continued for a third night, and now the shovel teams had no place to put the snow—the paths had become canals between high walls, and men had to push the snow off the edge of the cliff to get rid of it. The barracks entrance went through a snow cave and slabs of snow slid off the pitched roof of the Payerhütte with a whoosh and a thump that startled us all.

The following day sunshine peeked through the clouds at last, and the cook reported that there was just enough firewood left to make coffee, but breakfast would be cold. Pauli immediately went to the telephone room to call Trafoi and ask for a team to clear the road up to the telpher station at Heilige drei Brünnen so that we could get supplies. In the bright morning I congratulated him on having stuck it out. He gave me a woeful look.

"This is the most dangerous time, sir. Once the temperature starts to rise, that snow will be ready to slide down the mountain at 200 kilometers per hour. If the Italians dropped a single shell on us, they could start an avalanche that would wipe the Payerhütte off the map. For God's sake, don't make any loud noises—even a resounding fart could bring down ten tons of snow!"

Slowly and with great effort the shovel teams began to dig out the trail leading down the mountain. Trafoi informed us that they were sending thirty Russian prisoners of war to clear the road and that they would probably reach Payerhütte within four days.

I joined a team of men to dig out the entrance to the Citadel. The wind had swept snow up against the ice wall and in the sunlight a hard crust formed on it, making the work laborious, but after days of doing nothing, it was exhilarating to be working outside. After we had cleared part of the entrance, a sheet of snow slid off the glacier and undid all our progress.

The following afternoon brought a gray drizzle that coated the landscape with a glistening sheen and made the paths treacherous. In this miserable weather the thirty Russian prisoners tromped wearily up the mountainside to the Payerhütte, breaking through the wet drifts to meet the shovelers a few hundred meters from our winch station. They brought food and firewood and a welcome supply of tobacco.

They were sodden and wretched in their worn greatcoats and shredded boots, which were tied up in rags to ward off frostbite. To a man they wore scraggly, matted beards which barely concealed their hunger and hopelessness. Over their shoulders they carried long-handled shovels and upon reaching the *Hütte*, they stood obediently in the rain while a corporal reported to Pauli.

"The road is clear, sir. Where shall they camp? I believe it is too late for us to try to return to Trafoi."

"Ah, but you must," answered Pauli. "They can't stay here. There's no place for them to camp with all this snow, and the barracks are occupied by my men."

I stepped forward. "Lieutenant, have them dig out the entrance into the glacier. The Russians can sleep in the tunnel. It won't be comfortable, but they'll be out of the rain." The prisoners had won my pity.

Pauli shook his head. "We don't want them to know we have an installation under the ice, Captain—it's highly sensitive information. The Major would be furious. Let's put them in the storage shed with the firewood. But they must leave at dawn."

The storage shed was largely empty since our supply of firewood had not been replenished, so the prisoners were able to bed down on a dry floor of wood chips. I gave them my own ration of tobacco, as I didn't smoke in those days, and they thanked me gratefully in their language. One of them, a short, barrel-chested fellow, stood up and grasped my hand. "God is blessed you," he told me in broken German. "We thank you for kindness. You good man." I had to smile at these simple words. Solemnly, the men stood in a circle, joined hands and sang a hymn there in that dim room, redolent of pine-boughs. It was a song of terrible sorrow and longing, of desperate petition to a higher power (so I assumed) to let them live and not to decimate their numbers any further through starvation and dysentery. Humbled, I stood quietly and bowed my head, listening to those deep warbling harmonies penetrate into the very mountain. If there is a God, I thought, He could not ignore such a heartfelt appeal. I felt tears in my eyes. Why did such cruelty need to continue? Was any victory worth so much suffering? The prisoners began to divide my little packet of tobacco into 30 equally small cigarettes, which they rolled using the pages from a Russian-French dictionary. I turned and went out the door.

Outside, night was spreading along the horizon and the drizzle had become a steady downpour. Fog was rising from the hissing snow like a battalion of phantoms, and through the rain I could hear Pauli ordering his men to put away their shovels and report to the mess for a cold dinner. I gazed up through the mist at the mountaintop, thinking disjointedly about God and war and the scarcity of human kindness.

Above me, on the Ortler, I heard a series of sharp reports, almost like gunshots, but less discrete, followed by a *sotto voce* rumbling—and I thought again of the *brontidi*. Before me I could make out a thick cloud descending the mountain, and I realized that it was approaching much faster than any fog. A white wall of flying froth came galloping across the slopes, pushing before it a fierce gust of wind. In the next instant I was struck by a powerful blow and found myself helplessly in motion, tumbling inside a violent maelstrom that roared and crackled, yanked my limbs roughly and punched me like some maniacal demon. Then I came to an abrupt halt, packed in frigid darkness, unable to breathe, struggling to move my arms and legs against the crushing weight of the snow. In a panic I realized that I had been buried in an avalanche.

After a long interval in which I nearly suffocated, I managed to get one hand to my face to push the snow away from my mouth and lay there gasping, trying to comprehend what had just happened. I was completely blind it seemed, and deafened by the sound of my own labored breathing. My arms, legs, back and head ached from the cold, but I did not perceive any serious injury.

I cried out, as much in terror as to summon help, and wondered if the force of the snow had swept me down the mountainside, far from any possibility of help. With a strength born of fear, I managed to free my other arm and pushed against the cold, densely-packed wall in front of my face, to try to create a breathing space. By some good fortune, I had a small pocket of air around my head, and in a moment my fingers encountered a hard, smooth surface, apparently wood, that I guessed was part of the woodshed that I had been standing in front of.

This had undoubtedly saved my life, creating a pouch in which the snow was loose enough to allow me to move. Running my hand over it, I found that the wood had been shattered as if by the hammer of a Norse god, and with some effort I was able to pull a piece from the edge, a shard no more than a hand's length, but enough to enable me to chisel at the frozen wall that was pressing down on my chest.

I paused to yell again, and heard a muffled cry in response. Rescuers! Pauli's men must have seen the snow-slide and were already digging me out! I yelled again, "Help! I'm down here! Help me!" Full of hope, I began to dig away at the snow with my tiny tool.

To my right I could hear digging sounds, and the faint babble of voices. Then I felt a movement underneath my left leg, and the most welcome sensation of a hand gripping my calf. "I'm up here!" I shouted now, thinking that somehow my rescuers had dug into the snow-bank and encountered my legs first. Then I heard a sound that for a minute, I could not understand: it was a deep voice speaking Russian.

Immediately I realized that I was not the only one trapped—that I had been buried along with the Russians. With that discovery, I again wondered if there was anyone looking for us, or if it was possible that all of Payerhütte had been obliterated. My desperation mounted, and I struggled to open the pocket around me further.

"Who's there? Who is it?"

"Russians! We are caught under! You help, please God!" I recognized the imperfect German of the stout, barrel-chested prisoner. I could feel his fingers clutching my leg, as if I had the power to free him.

With trembling hands I used my wood scrap to chop through the snow towards him. Although we were enveloped in darkness, I was able to reach out and grasp his hand, cold and wet, calloused from his unforgiving life, but it was the touch of another man, another living creature. He smelled strongly of tobacco.

"Look for something to dig with!" I told him. Beyond his hoarse breathing I could hear the sounds of other voices and someone crying in pain. The wreckage of the shed must have provided another air pocket which saved their lives. They were scrabbling furiously in their dark little space.

We worked in our separate burrows, grunting and groaning with the effort. I decided to concentrate on digging upwards and evidently the Russians had the same idea because shortly I heard the man below me push himself up to my side. I took his hand and put it on the wood surface from which I had pried my digging tool.

"Here—try to break off a piece," I said. Together we pushed until another large splinter came away with a crunching groan. Then followed more long minutes of digging. This brought a continuous shower of wet snow onto my face and neck and my head ached; my hands and feet were completely numb from the cold.

After some time I had managed only to create a tunnel the length of my own body, but at least now I could stretch my legs and keep my blood moving. Below me, one of the Russians had found a candle and matches in his pocket. The flame was weak and I knew it would not be long before we would be unable to breathe, but for the first time I got a look at the other survivors: The fellow who spoke a little German peered at me from behind his snow-caked beard, and introduced himself as Pyotr. The man with the candle was Ivan, and he had a severe injury to one eye: the snow around him was stained red with blood. He pressed a handful of snow to his wound and gave me a weak grin. There were several others whom I could not see, but I could hear them talking as they dug. We were by now close to exhaustion, but there was no choice but to continue.

After several hours of painfully slow progress, I found a man's hand buried in the snow. On its arm I recognized the sleeve of an Austrian Standschütze officer. At length I managed to uncover his head, and found that it was Lieutenant Pauli, quite dead. I tried warming his face and hand with my own breath, but his features were purplish gray from suffocation. Cradled in the packed snow, his boyish looks were even more apparent, as if he were a child sleeping on white silk sheets.

Then something occurred to me, and I dug down to Pauli's belt and found his pistol in its holster—one of the new Lugers that were being issued to commissioned officers (I had left my revolver under my bunk in the Citadel). Cocking it, I fired a shot upwards into the snow. The noise was deafening and I was immediately choked by the stench of cordite, but I imagined that this would get the attention of anyone who might be looking for us. The Russians set up a chorus of yells, a dissonance of distress. After a few moments they tired and fell into an uneasy silence. There was no sound of rescue.

"No one come," said Pyotr in a low voice. "We lost here. We die."

"Dig for your life!" I said. "We aren't dead yet. Or pray, if you think it will help." I went back to chopping at the merciless snow with my scrap of wood. Under his breath, Pyotr began reciting a prayer: "*Ótče nas, súščij na nebesách…*"[85]

I concentrated on the snow around the wood wall, thinking that it was part of the shed structure and that possibly the other end of it was still protruding above the surface. At length my wooden tool punched through into another air pocket under the door—for that's what it was, judging by its hinges. There I found two more Russians, both dead, lying in twisted unnatural positions. I called to Pyotr, and he was able to slide into the opening above me, holding the candle. He cried out at the sight of the two corpses, calling out their names to his comrades and then lapsing into long sobs. I continued digging, and after a time I heard him chiseling away above me.

An unknown period passed before I had to rest, wet and numb with cold, frustrated and increasingly fearful that we would never succeed in finding our way out. The Russians continued digging with their hands and

---

[85] Our father, who art in heaven…

whatever tools they had; I could hear them murmuring prayers intermittently. At one point we heard noises from above—what sounded like voices and footsteps—and I fired another four shots from Pauli's Luger into the snow. Together we cried out with all the strength we could muster. When we paused again, there was only silence.

The air was growing fetid and I felt myself weakening from lack of oxygen. Our brave little candle flame was now dwindling, which would leave us once again in total darkness—perhaps of no practical significance, but one which I knew would affect our morale. My fears increased that we would never reach the surface—we had been working for what seemed like hours with no discernible progress. With a sob of despair I dropped my little scrap of wood. I must have dozed until the pain in my feet woke me—I knew the signs of frostbite and realized that we would eventually freeze to death if we stayed buried much longer.

As the candle finally sputtered out, I managed to uncover the edge of a wooden beam, one of those which undoubtedly had formed the roof of the shed. Pushing against it with my shoulder, I felt it move slightly. I called to Pyotr to follow my little tunnel and help me—regrettably there was only space for the two of us, but our combined strength shifted the beam a bit and opened broad cracks in the snow around us. Either we would force our way out or we would collapse our tiny burrow and suffocate. Pyotr and I put our backs against the beam and pushed with all our remaining strength. There was a crumbling sound above us and a sudden rush of cold air: we were free.

Above us a splendor of stars stretched out like the jewels of the universe on a mantle of black velvet, and a fresh, sweet-smelling breeze was welcomed into our exhausted lungs. We were lying on a vast mound of snow, well-trodden and pierced by the splintered shards of the woodshed and the barracks. Above us the Ortler's silhouette loomed in the moonlight, and to one side posed the unscathed Payerhütte, its windows dark. Had everyone else been annihilated by the avalanche? But if so, what were the sounds we had heard? A few survivors, incapable of looking for us? Italian soldiers, indifferent to our plight?

I found a board and widened our opening to let the other Russians emerge, which they did with sounds of grateful adulation. There were seven survivors out of thirty, stiff with fatigue and cold. Ivan's face was swollen and purple with bruises; another man named Vlad had a broken arm from which the bloody bone protruded. On feet that felt like lumps of stone, I staggered up to the Payerhütte and burst through the door. The Russians stumbled after me into the sitting-room, where we collapsed in front of the embers of the fire.

Lights went on and Austrian soldiers appeared: Baldur von Obersdorf and Dr. Schaller descended the stairs, rubbing their eyes in disbelief. "Where have you come from?" asked Baldur.

"We were underneath," I said, "We dug ourselves out. We shouted and fired a gun—why didn't you hear us?"

I soon discovered a phenomenon often reported by avalanche survivors: that sounds from the surface can be easily heard by those buried under it, while noises from within the snow—even gunshots—are inaudible to rescuers. The dozen or so men who had not been swept away by the avalanche had been hampered by lack of tools, as all the shovels had been buried too, but with ski poles and hatchets from the kitchen they dug valiantly for twenty-four hours before concluding that there were no survivors; we had been buried for a day and a half. Reports from across the front told of numerous avalanches which had killed several thousand men on both sides. Austrian rescuers had even gone to extract Italian survivors, and vice-versa. At the Gran Poz five hundred Austrians had been buried all at once.

Baldur said, "Where shall we put these Russians? They can't stay here, for God's sake." Pyotr looked at me: his hands were bloody from scraping through the snow.

"Leave them be—they are men just like us," I said. Baldur shook his head and opened his mouth to object. I sat up. "That is an order from a superior officer, Subaltern. Doctor—please attend to these men first. I am not injured." I tossed more wood into the fire to bring it to a crackling blaze. The Austrians muttered but began removing the prisoners' wet clothing.

However, once my boots came off, my feet were both deep blue. "Early stages of frostbite," Schaller told me. "We won't know for a few days if it's gangrene. If you're lucky you'll only lose a few toes." A decision was made to transport me by telpher to the main road where I would go by truck to the military hospital in Trafoi. The long-suffering Russians were to make the same journey back down the mountain on foot.

They filed sadly out of the Hütte, Ivan with his head bandaged up and Vlad with his arm in a sling, to begin their weary march, as it was now sunrise. I hobbled over to Pyotr on my still-numb legs and took his hand. "Good luck to you," I said, "And *spasibo*." 'Thanks' was the only word I knew in Russian—I remembered it from when they had received the tobacco. He grinned at me and squeezed my hand, then shuffled outside with his comrades.

The hospital at Trafoi was a convent behind the church, its sisters pressed into service as nurses. Its narrow halls were full of other avalanche survivors, lying on the floor against the whitewashed walls, many of them barely alive. It was fortunate that, due to the snow, there had been little fighting on the front since October, so that the hospital had been nearly empty when these men arrived. I was housed in a ward with a dozen other officers where I was able to hear about conditions at other points on the front.

"I was on a ski-patrol: the doctor says I'll lose half of my right foot," said one thick-set captain, his legs wrapped in gauze. "Still I'm luckier than the other nine men, they're all still buried. You've been digging trenches in the ice, we hear, and bunkers too?"

"No trenches. We've relocated our rear supply lines under the glacier," I replied.

"Ha! It's logical, isn't it? I hear they've done the same over on the Marmolata. They have this engineer, Leo Handl. Very savvy fellow; he's set up barracks and storerooms in the ice. They would have been wiped out by avalanches otherwise."

While I was waiting for a verdict on my discolored feet, I was able to enjoy a few decent hot meals and some rest in a real bed. Once they had been properly warmed up and dried, my feet became extraordinarily painful, and I required assistance from a nurse to hobble to the bathroom like some crippled dotard. At first I found this humiliating: the nurses on our ward were stern and unsympathetic, and in spite of the fact that I hadn't laid eyes on a woman of any description since I had left Regensburg in 1916, I found them repulsive. There was Berta, a diminutive Slovenian nun with a moustache and a steel-vise grip; there was Murielle, a bulky Tyrolean farm girl with bad teeth who manhandled patients like sheep on shearing-day; and there was Karlotta, a gray-haired Viennese matron who took evil satisfaction in the suffering of those under her care. And then there was the charming and lovely Hildegard.

The Red Cross had been sending nurses to bolster the staff of hospitals that were overwhelmed with the sick and injured, and by her uniform and the red cross on her cap, I knew she was one of these. She spoke German with a Scandinavian accent, and indeed it was her voice that first drew my attention to her, as it was the most musical and tantalizing feminine voice I had ever heard. It was a voice that implied laughter even when she was serious, a voice that spoke of gentleness and succor. She would have been a magnet of male attention anywhere, but Hilda was kind and attentive and sincerely concerned about the men in her care, and without exception they all fell in love with her. In a place where army humor included plenty of ribald sentiment, Hilda brought out the gentleman in each of us, from Colonel von Guckenschlacker down to the lowliest, most illiterate private.

To describe her is difficult because the magic she worked on my senses made her seem saintly and not at all of this world: she was slender as a spring sapling with the finest, most delicate hands, but strong enough to help a legless man into his wheelchair or to calm an epileptic in the midst of a seizure. Her yellow hair was a rich sunset hue that mimicked the grain of polished maple wood and the color of ripened wheat woven together. She had porcelain-blue eyes that smiled even when she was lost in thought or frowning over some noisome task such has changing the dressing on a gangrenous limb—plainly she could see through life's horrors and filth to the grand joy of being alive, of having a purpose. He was indeed a lucky man who called Hilda his wife and held her in his arms at night.

On a fine sun-dappled afternoon a few days before Christmas she offered to take me on a stroll through the gardens that lay between the hospital and the convent. Snow was piled here too, and seeing it gave me an unpleasant shiver as I remembered the suffocating hours spent digging out of the avalanche. Birds frolicked in a fountain under a statuette of the Virgin, and even in the dead of winter the place seemed brimming with life. Hilda parked my wheelchair in the sun and sat on a low brick wall facing me.

"Do you know anything about the Russian prisoners that came down from Payerhütte?" I asked.

"They are reported to have escaped," Hilda said. I was staring at her heavenly-blue eyes and for a moment, I did not comprehend her reply.

"Escaped? But how?"

"They were accompanied by two guards, but one of them slipped on the ice and the Russians overpowered them both, then took their weapons and fled. The guards walked into town this morning. They'll surely never survive out there, those poor wretches."

"Perhaps not, but they are resourceful men." I went on to tell her about my hours with them under the snow. "I never thought of them as enemy prisoners of war. To me they were comrades. Without them, I'd still be buried. I'm glad to hear that they got away. Even if they die, they will die free."

She gave me a puzzled smile. "You're a kind man, Melchior. There's so much hatred among men these days, and it's pleasant to know someone who is not hateful. In my country there are many Russians and most people don't care for them much." She was from Sweden and had gone to nursing school in Vienna, where a rich uncle had offered to pay her tuition. Then the war broke out and her entire class had volunteered to join the Red Cross. "Some of my classmates are dead now," she added quietly. "What kills a man can kill a woman just as easily, even an innocent who is just trying to help."

"Are you afraid of death?" I asked.

"I don't know," she replied, looking up at the sky. "I've never been in danger of dying, myself, although I've seen many men die here these past few months. Most of them were frightened, when the time came. We all fear the unknown. I think I won't know if I fear death until my last hour. And what about you? You have been nearly killed several times, I would guess."

"I am terrified of death," I said, laughing, "But I am not a coward. I am just intelligent about risking my life. I would be frightened of losing my life foolishly, I think, but willing to sacrifice myself to save a friend."

We both laughed and exchanged that warm, intimate look that bonds two kindred souls. If I hadn't been in a wheelchair, I would have kissed her. She took me in my chair back to the ward, walking slowly and gently, as if something in our lives had just become immensely beautiful and joyous.

XII. The Assault

The next day Hilda debrided some dead skin from my feet. Bright red blood leaked out of the wounds but now I could wriggle my toes. They had started to regain their normal color, and Hilda shook her head in admiration. "Two days ago I was thinking that you would lose both feet, they seemed so lifeless. You've recovered quickly."

"Frostbite destroys the tissues by forming crystals which rupture the cells. Ice crystals are larger than water molecules, so they burst the cells with their increased volume," I said. The very glacier was forming within my body, it seemed. I was becoming a part of the Ice Citadel.

Hilda looked at me with her eyebrows raised in a question. "Do you have some training in medicine?" she asked.

"No, but I have extensive knowledge of ice. That's why I'm here."

An hour later, a beak-nosed doctor with horn-rimmed spectacles declared that my feet had both returned to life and pronounced me fit to return to duty. Soon I was dressing and preparing to run up to the telpher station, to return to the glacier. As I limped quickly down the corridor I saw Hilda carrying a load of clean sheets up the stairs.

"I'm on my way," I called out. She turned, and when our eyes met I felt a twinge inside me. Then she looked away.

"Be safe, Melchior."

I hesitated for a moment, then I ran up the stairs and stood in front of her with my forage cap in my hand. "May I write to you?" I asked. She smiled suddenly as if a question in her mind had been answered.

"You may and you must. I will expect a letter from you tomorrow." She tucked the sheets under one arm and took my hand in hers. "And visit me too, when you can." Her fingers were warm and soft, unlike Anna's cold hands, which had never caressed me. I was afflicted by a moment of vertigo. Her eyes searched mine sadly and with longing, and I could almost hear her heart beating. I gripped her hand and smiled.

"Yes, I will see you again soon, Hilda. And next time, not as a patient."

* * *

I hopped onto a supply truck carrying firewood up to the winch-station. It was snowing lightly and the air was exquisitely cold under a tarnished silver sky. As the gondola glided slowly uphill, I searched the slopes in vain for signs of my Russian friends.

Austrian troops in front of the Payerhütte.

At the Payerhütte they had already rebuilt the woodshed and were putting up the skeleton of a new barracks. The snow had been cleared away but the glacier sprawled lazily over the mountainside like a freshly-fed polar bear. Looking across the Alps from this point, one could see the sugar-cake coating of snow that blanketed the peaks was interrupted in those spots where an avalanche had torn itself from the snow-pack and fallen. The wind rose in a phantasmal wail as I walked into the entrance grotto in the ice and down the long stairway towards the officers' quarters.

I reported immediately to Major Stutz in his office. His desk was piled high with papers, and I noticed that he wore a new uniform with blue embroidery on the collar and three gold stars.

"I am *Colonel* Stutz now, for your information," he said, without looking at me. On the wall I noticed a plan of the Sulden-ferner tunnels and another one sketching out plans for the Monte Cristallo *eisfestung*.

I wanted to say something snide about a battlefield commission, but his manner warned me that all was not well. At length he put his pen into its little wooden box, folded his hands in front of his chest and gave me a cold glare.

"I am told that you nearly died in the Payerhütte avalanche, along with the sixteen soldiers and one officer who were killed." He spoke wistfully, as if he faulted the avalanche for not having done the job properly.

"Yes, sir, this is true."

"But it is my understanding—and please correct me if I am mistaken—that you were billeting Russian prisoners of war in the Payerhütte barracks, contravening orders I had given to Lieutenant Pauli."

"I was not informed of any such orders, sir. The prisoners were to spend one night in the storage shed. It was raining and too dark for them to descend safely."

Stutz stood up and began to pace slowly with his hands behind his back, like a professor about to reprimand a disobedient freshman. "You say 'safely' without recognizing the fact that if they had descended to Trafoi, they would still be alive."

I opened my mouth to reply, but he cut me off.

"And for what? To save *Russian prisoners of war* from getting wet in the rain? That shows a blatant disregard for military discipline. The Russians were to be kept ignorant of the *eisfestung*, Captain, however they probably observed the entrance into the glacier, and now those who survived the avalanche *have escaped!* Very likely to the Italian lines, where they will surely report what they have seen. Your carelessness has compromised this entire operation, Captain. I am grossly disappointed—even though I had not held you in high esteem before this, your incompetence is abundantly clear to me now."

All this seemed quite improbable to me—particularly in that the Russians could not speak Italian, and I knew that the entrance to the Ice Citadel had been covered with snow. But I did not want to argue with Stutz. Whatever action he was going to take had already been determined.

"It is your good fortune that I still need you here to work on the Sulden-ferner tunnels. However I have sent a requisition to High Command to send us a real engineer, an Austrian who will be respectful of military discipline and perform competently. After he arrives you may stay or return to your unit, as you please."

"Sir." I stood at attention in the manner of a soldier receiving the judgment of a court-martial. Stutz was using this opportunity to get rid of me and I felt a mixture of relief and devastating sorrow. The Ice Citadel was my creation, my palace, my wonder of the world. But I knew that Stutz would only seek to make me suffer, so leaving was my best choice. Perhaps there was another glacier nearby that needed to be hollowed out before this bloody madness of a war ever ended.

"So, about the Sulden-ferner." Seeing that I would not put up a fight, Stutz seemed to relax. He turned to the map on the wall that showed the stretch of tunnels we had dug south towards the base of the Königspitz.

"In spite of our best efforts, the Italians still hold Mount Zebrù," he said, tapping firmly on the obstinate peak. "But given our success in retaking Hohe Schneide, I have decided to attempt a similar tunnel assault here."

"What about the Monte Cristallo project?"

"Mount Zebrù is a more urgent and less complex objective," Stutz replied. "If we are successful in capturing Zebrù, division headquarters in Meran will be easily persuaded that Bormio can be taken using similar tactics. You must understand the psychology of the military, Captain," he added, eyeing me critically. "Success breeds confidence. With confidence comes autonomy. Do you see?"

I nodded and he returned to the wall map. "The base of the mountain is entirely covered with thick ice, which will be to our advantage. Our Sulden-ferner tunnels can be extended up the north face of the mountain and on also the southeast face, which is still technically no-man's-land. Once we reach the rock face, we can organize a nighttime assault on the summit. Our artillery on the Eiskögele will bombard them from the northwest and that on the Königspitz will hit them from the southeast. When they least expect it our men will climb to the top and claim the summit." I could see Stutz imagining this scene, probably with himself in the lead, planting a flag on the peak. Well, I would make sure to be far away, not at the forefront as I had been at Hohe Schneide.

"Your job, Fuchsheim, is to prepare broad tunnels, as deep as possible, as far as you can under the ice, up to where the glacier ends. The passageways will need to accommodate men carrying climbing equipment, and it will be a steep uphill grade, so steps will be needed. You will also build galleries where the men can assemble before the assault, and a dressing-station. I'll make an infantry company available to you as diggers. How long will it take?"

I examined the map for a moment. "I believe we'll need over a kilometer of wide tunnels, plus four galleries. In deep ice we normally can't do more than eight meters a day under optimal circumstances, but with several teams working simultaneously we may double that. And you must take into account the crevasses—there are several large ones in this area."

Stutz glowered at me impatiently. "Well, how long?"

"I would guess at least eight weeks of digging. Add a few days to move supplies from the Oberer Ortler-ferner to the Sulden-ferner, once storage space is available. And have you considered the fact that many men are on holiday leave, sir?"

"The 60th Company is made up of Jews from Salzburg. They are replacing the others who have gone on leave. You have nothing against Jews digging your tunnels, I hope? I'm not fond of them myself."

I nodded, since this did not seem to merit a reply. Jews from Salzburg would be mainly watchmakers, tailors, goldsmiths and accountants—men with no experience wielding a pick. Well, they would just have to learn, I thought.

"Very well, then, Captain. You have forty days and forty nights to complete the preparations for this assault. I will be inspecting your work regularly. By the end of January I expect sufficient progress that we can start preparing assault units and bringing up artillery shells."

"Of course, sir."

"And Fuchsheim—do not disappoint me in this. If I detect the slightest breach of discipline, insubordination or negligence of duty, I will crucify you. Do you understand, Captain?"

"Yes sir, I do."

"Very well, get started. Time is passing and you have a lot to do."

I left Stutz's office with a sensation of dread piled onto a faint euphoria at having been assigned another opportunity to extend the Ice Citadel. It would not be the elaborate warren of barracks and storerooms that we had built under the Ortler, but the upper Sulden-ferner was firm, dense ice that would be safe to work in. The crevasses would be problematic, however. To make matters worse, we had received close to six meters of snow so far this winter, meaning that nearly all the crevasses were now covered over and would only be discovered as we tunneled into them. This could be very dangerous for our teams.

In the officers' mess I dined with Franz Pichler and Gianni Lizzola. They already knew about the plans for the Sulden-ferner and like me, they were both excited and anxious.

Lizzola said, "The tunnels under the Sulden-ferner are Stutz's new baby." Apparently none of us could bear to call him 'Colonel'.

"But it won't be an easy job," said Franz, who had been in charge of excavating the Oberer Ortler-ferner. "He's asking you to go deep and then build two upward passages to the rock face. That might take longer than forty days, Melchior."

"I'll do the hard parts first," I said. "The easy things like the assembly-points can wait until the end. We'll build narrow tunnels to start with, then widen them. We'll use that harpoon-gun to make temporary bridges, then put in planks. When you get back from your holiday leave, you can help me."

"*Naturlich*,"[86] said Franz, smiling. "Who do you think Stutz has assigned to lead the assault?"

A current of change ran through our garrison as Christmas approached. Officers and men kept departing on the telpher for their holiday leave. "So, Melchior," one of them would say as he prepared to go out the barracks door, "*Grüss Gott und Fröhliche Weihnachten*.[87] When do you leave, by the way?"

I would reply that someone had to keep the war going; someone had to be on hand to protect our treasured half of the glacier. They would laugh and offer to bring me back some real coffee from Vienna.

Mindful of my promise to Hilda, I sat down one evening to write a short letter to her and found myself without words. Writing to Anna had been easy because our letters were so perfunctory, but to Hilda I wanted to express my feelings in a way that was uniquely sincere. After several false starts I was left with only one sheet of stationery and decided that inspired brevity would have to do:

Dearest Hilda,

You are the sweetest young woman I have ever known, and I long for the hour in which we meet again. Your eyes tell me what is in your heart, and you should know that the same feeling exists in my heart as well. With deepest affection, I wish you a merry Christmas.

Melchior

The coming of Our Lord Jesus Christ, or rather, the day of His mass, had a strangely dissipating effect on our front. Once again I reflected that this was a neighborhood more than anything else and that the Austrians fully expected that while they were attending mass in their onion-domed village churches, their Italian counterparts across the range would be doing just the same. And the priests would pray for victory in very much the same words on either side.

We attended mass in Father Weiss's glacier chapel, which was adorned by an enormous ice cross hewn directly from the glacier wall. A shaft drilled all the way to the surface brought the sunlight in to shine on it, and I admired the workmanship, which was Franz's doing. A devout Catholic, Franz never spoke of his faith, but in the chapel he became humbly reverent, engulfed in a piety that seemed alien to this beer-drinking, coarse-humored Goth. The cross was his offering to the honor of Christ, and although it was built after hours, in time that ordinarily would have been spent resting, the men willingly devoted themselves to the effort. Father Weiss himself spent days smoothing the cross with a small chisel and a warm cloth, to make it as perfect as humanly possible. The sight of it gave me goose-bumps even though, by this time, I had lost my allegiance to the Almighty. I was, as they say,

---

[86] Of course
[87] God bless you and merry Christmas

unentschieden,[88] meaning that I did not deny the existence of God, but I was not convinced of it either. I came to this state of confusion after seeing Fritz killed at St. Mihiel, and somehow the Russian prisoners reinforced my doubts, although I was still too superstitious to articulate them clearly. It seemed to me that no god would create man and then allow him to suffer so profoundly. Indeed, the Russians had just finished praying for mercy when the avalanche struck.

So I stood inside this elegant and incomparably graceful chapel, admiring the sheen of the sunlight on the lovingly-crafted cross, and listened to Father Weiss's soft voice exhorting us to be kind to our fellow man.

"Gentleness and generosity embody God's love in our everyday lives. We are compelled to protect the vulnerable and assist the weak because love and kindness are the very soul of Christ. When we commit an act of selflessness, we cleanse our souls of baser desires and grow closer to heavenly grace.

"And for this very reason, we must vanquish the enemy on these slopes and drive them from the Fatherland. We must confront the evil and cruelty of these unjust people and demonstrate to them that the just will not be struck down—that when they challenge us, they challenge the Lord's will! Therefore raise your weapons with pride and assuredness that you are fighting in God's name!" He thumped his fist on the wooden pulpit.

God is love, they tell us, but we are encouraged to kill. We will all go to Heaven and the Italians will burn forever in Hell. It seemed impossible to me that anyone could believe this foolishness. And yet anyone who questions this doctrine is also condemned to the inferno. I can't deny the existence of Hell—I lived there when I was on the Western Front, and I saw many good Christians suffering in it. I was compelled to help them find shelter from danger—not to please God, but because it's in my nature.

After church I went down to the second barracks to meet the Jews.

I don't know what I had expected, but I was stunned by the level of taut military discipline these men practiced. I had wandered rather casually into the barracks, looking for a sergeant to whom I could introduce myself, but as soon as I was noticed someone shouted *Achtung!* The men, who had been engaged in polishing their boots and folding their clothes as though preparing to go on parade, snapped to rigid attention in front of their bunks. It reminded me that while the Standschützen lacked the trappings of the regular army, these men—though not Tyrolers—were trained to follow orders. Again I felt like an imposter: since I had arrived in the Tyrol very few soldiers had honored me with a salute. Now I was being treated like a general.

They were trim and fit, many of them still boyish but with an air of military experience. I gazed down the line of men, examining their faces: they looked like all the other Austrians I had met; there was nothing that seemed particularly Jewish about them. In Regensburg there was a small Jewish population, and though the city had expelled them at various times, they had built a new synagogue in 1912 and in many respects were treated as equals. My father had Jewish clients—a fact he kept to himself—but he once decried the bullying of a Jewish boy at my school, telling me: "Be kind to all those that are kind to you, Melchior. You never know when you might need their help." This was a rule I took to heart.

A man wearing a sergeant's insigne stepped forward and saluted. He was tall and slim with lanky arms and bony hands, but his bearing was professional. "Sergeant Reinhardt, Sixtieth Company, Third Battalion, presenting for inspection *sir!*"

I had to think for a moment how to answer this. "At ease, Sergeant. This isn't a formal inspection. I'm just here to, uh, to meet the troops. Where is your commanding officer?" The sergeant's eyes flicked quickly in my direction and I caught a glimpse of his bewilderment.

"Begging the Captain's pardon sir. We will be prepared for inspection at nineteen hundred hours, sir. Would the Captain be so kind as to return then, sir?"

They seemed bound to protocol. "Very well, Sergeant, carry on. I'll return at seven—at nineteen hundred hours. For inspection." I could barely conceal a smile.

---

[88] Undecided

I went back to my quarters in the officers' barracks to allow them their time. There I found Lizzola seated by the pot-bellied stove, smoking his long-stemmed pipe and reading Dante in Italian. When I entered he slipped the book under his chair.

"I've just been to meet the 60th," I told him. "Tight discipline in that unit. Do you know them?"

"I do," said Lizzola, puffing. "They've seen the worst of this war, the poor beggars. And they've never been in combat."

"What are you talking about, the worst? What's worse than combat?"

"Hatred. Prejudice." Lizzola gazed at me with a seriousness that was quite uncharacteristic. "Being distrusted because of your parentage and your name, rather than being judged by your actions."

"I thought everyone was equal under Franz Josef." Lizzola gave me a smirk. "The military is a law unto itself, Captain. These men are under the command of Lieutenant Spielmann, a man who hates Jews more than he hates Italians."

"Spielmann who won the Merit Cross at the First Battle of the Isonzo?"

"One and the same: he captured an Italian machine-gun nest single-handed, then turned the gun on the enemy. He has been an outspoken anti-Semite for years, so the Austrians decided to put him in charge of the first company in the Royal and Imperial Army to be composed entirely of Jews. He decided that it was his calling from God to make these men's lives miserable. It was one of the few units to suffer fatalities during training, if you can believe it. The generals felt that Jews couldn't be trusted under fire, so they've been guarding supply trains and building fortifications on the Eastern front since 1915. Spielmann favors corporal punishment, half-rations and the firing squad to maintain discipline. He has even performed some executions himself, with his pistol. Did you say discipline is tight? It's a stranglehold."

A wave of nausea passed over me. "So how did they end up here?"

Lizzola sucked on his pipe. "Rumor has it that the cold, the avalanches and exhaustion have decimated the troops on this front. No doubt Speilmann volunteered his men as replacements."

I was amazed at this. This was jolly, lighthearted Lizzola who had cheered me up on several occasions. Now he chewed on his pipe with a bitterness born of deep disappointment. I wondered how I should ask him about it.

"It's no different being a *Welsch-Österreicher*,"[89] he said before I could open my mouth. "My mother was a Schmidt, born in Vienna, but my father was Tyrolean from Vadena. I am a product of two worlds, but my heart is Austrian. I would rather die than see the House of Savoy ruling the Tyrol! And yet, I am considered a potential traitor, untrustworthy and duplicitous, told to dig storerooms while Pichler is sent to lead the assault." He chewed moodily on his pipe.

Around us the glacier groaned in its sleep. "I'm sorry, Gianni, I don't know what to say. This kind of thing is painful for me, too. No one deserves to be humiliated." We sat in silence in the empty barracks. "I'll need your help in the Sulden-ferner," I said at last. "It's far too much for one officer, and Franz will be occupied with the assault team. These Salzburgers—" I was loath to call them Jews now— "They'll need some instruction on digging in ice. And I'll need help bridging the crevasses. It requires the kind of experience you have. Let's make the best of this one, Lieutenant."

Lizzola looked up at me with a half-smile. "You make it sound entertaining, Captain."

Lieutenant Speilmann was standing by the door at attention when I returned to the enlisted men's barracks at seven. He was a short, muscular fellow with a split chin and eyes as gray as ashes. He saluted with such vigor that I thought he might injure himself. On his tunic I noted two small holes where his Merit Cross had been

---

[89] A slang term for an Italian Austrian.

pinned. On his hip he wore a long-barreled army revolver, an American-made Colt .45—odd, I thought for an Austrian infantryman. I wondered where he obtained ammunition for it.

"Lieutenant Kristof Speilmann, 60th Company, Third Battalion, presenting the unit for inspection *sir!*" In the barracks the men were rigid in front of their immaculate bunks. I would not have found a speck of dust on any man's kit, even with a microscope. Their boots were polished obsidian, their hair was glued into place, their equipment seemed to have been manufactured an hour ago. I found it all inhumanly perfect.

I picked up a bayonet and drew it out, testing the blade on my thumb. It was sharp enough to shave a gnat's backside. "Lieutenant," I said lazily, feigning indifference, "How many of your men have worked in a tunnel underground?" I was afraid the answer would be none.

"About half of them, sir. Perhaps more."

I found this hard to believe. "Did you hear my question Lieutenant?" Speilmann stared into space and swallowed nervously. "Sir, I did, sir. Many of these men were employed at the Hallein Salt Mine, sir."

I was incredulous. "*Half* of them, Lieutenant? *Guter Gott im Himmel!*[90] What about the others?"

Speilmann took a deep breath and said, "We have a butcher, a gunsmith and a man who makes violins. I don't know about the rest, sir."

I sheathed the bayonet and strolled between the statuesque rows of men. There was something missing, and at first I couldn't think what. Then I realized that the men had no firearms.

"Where are their guns, Lieutenant?"

"Sir, this is not a combat unit. These men build fortifications or handle supplies. They have no need for rifles." Speilmann looked straight ahead at the wall as he spoke. I couldn't tell what his feelings were about this; no doubt for a combat hero it was a dull existence.

"Nevertheless, Lieutenant, you are now on the front lines. Are their rifles in the weapons storage room?"

"Sir, they have no rifles. In the event of an enemy intrusion they will not fight, sir."

I strode across the room and confronted him. "What will they do, Lieutenant—surrender? These men are soldiers, are they not?"

Speilmann stared at the wall for a long moment without any expression. I realized that he did not have an answer to this particular question, much as though I had asked whether his men were human beings. At last he gave a short sigh and said, "Sir, most of them are salt miners, sir. They have not been required to fight, therefore they do not have rifles. Sir."

"Salt miners," I said, almost to myself. It seemed highly irregular for an entire company to be without rifles, but then I doubted they would ever have to shoot any Italians here in the Citadel. I put my hands behind my back and in my best professorial voice, asked: "Lieutenant, are you aware that rock salt, otherwise known as halite, normally crystallizes into a perfect isometric hexoctahedron?"

"Sir?" The expression of confusion was plain on his face.

"Never mind, Lieutenant." I wanted to puzzle him, to portray myself as the mysterious and unpredictable Bavarian. He was looking for a promotion, no doubt, and as long as he was unsure of how to please me, he would be easy to work with—if he kept his sadistic tendencies under control.

The next morning I stopped in at Stutz's office to deliver a supply report. He was bent over his desk, working on a requisition for a new generator, and barely glanced at me when I entered. I stood at attention for a long moment, waiting for him to look up.

"Yes, Captain, what is it?"

---

[90] Good God in Heaven!

"Sir, I've been to inspect the 60ᵗʰ Company and I discovered that they have no rifles, sir."

Stutz glanced irritably at my boots. "Why does that concern you, Captain?"

"It just seems a bit irregular, sir. We *are* on the front lines."

"Obviously they are not a combat unit, Captain Fuchsheim. If we come under attack there are fifteen hundred other men here to defend our position. Is that all, Captain?"

"Sir, the 60ᵗʰ works in the tunnels that are closest to the enemy. It would seem prudent to give them some means of defending themselves until reinforcements arrive." Anticipating Stutz's anger, I added: "Just planning for contingencies, sir."

Stutz dropped his pen and stood up. "Captain, you continually astonish me. First you want to find comfortable lodgings for Russian prisoners of war, now you want the Jews to be able to defend themselves. You have a soft spot for the offal of mankind, don't you?"

I could not think of a reply to this other than, "Sir."

Stutz grimaced and leaned forward. "Please don't waste my time with requests of this nature, Captain. I am not interested in your petty sense of justice. In Bavaria you can occupy your time aiding Jews, Russians, Negroes, or Anabaptists, but right now I need you to attend to the preparations for this assault. Is that clear? Now get out."

Our Sulden-ferner *eisfestung* was a series of long, straight corridors heading southeast through the central portion of the glacier, running close to the surface with half a dozen observation posts using periscopes that poked up through the snow to keep a watchful eye on the Italians' position on the ridge atop Mount Zebrù, which was well fortified with artillery pieces and Fiat-Revelli machine-guns. Our ski patrols had also reported a sniper, although not a very accurate one.

We were to construct two new corridors leading west, one passing to the north of the Zebrù and the other to the south, through a *cirque* known as the Payer-ferner, an ice pocket that flowed downhill into the main glacier. We would penetrate the deep ice and then dig upwards along the slope of the mountain, using ice stairs covered with wood to keep them from wearing down. To dispose of debris from our tunneling, I planned to construct two shafts through which the ice chips would slide downhill into a nearby crevasse.

We started by hollowing out two spacious galleries in which we would store equipment, food and water, and where teams could rest during their off-shifts. The Salzburg Jews were marvelously efficient and well-suited to the work, being much smaller men than their Tyrolean counterparts. They worked quietly, with little conversation, but they knew how to construct tunnels with arched ceilings and neat, symmetrical steps. Since they were used to tunneling through solid rock, they found the ice easy to work on, and soon we were progressing much faster than I had predicted.

I put Lizzola in charge of the south tunnel while I supervised Speilmann at the north tunnel. On the first day a man slipped while carrying a heavy ladder—a common occurrence in this work, since most of the workers were not wearing crampons. Speilmann stepped forward angrily and produced a leather strap from under his coat. He had raised his arm to beat the prostrate man when I seized his hand. In a rage he wheeled to see who was restraining him, only to come face to face with me, his superior officer. Slowly and with great reluctance he came to attention, with my hand still gripping his.

"Lieutenant, you will not beat your men while you are under my command."

"Sir." He acknowledged my order but did not affirm it. Around us the men had paused, their faces expressionless. The man on the floor had covered his face with his arm, but now he peeked past it to see what was happening. Struggling to control my temper, I extracted the whip from Speilmann's grasp. It was a leather thong about a meter long with a short braided handle, the kind used on mules or oxen. The end of it was knotted and well-worn from use. I folded it up and put it in my pocket. Speilmann gazed at the wall, stone-faced.

"Back to work, everyone. We're on a schedule!" To Speilmann I said quietly, "At ease Lieutenant. Behave professionally from now on." He turned and strode quickly down the corridor, his hands quivering at his sides. The soldier on the ground stood up and as he retrieved his fallen ladder, his eyes met mine for a split second. I couldn't tell if he was thanking me or warning me.

The north tunnel broke through a wall the next morning and we found ourselves gazing into an immense crevasse, its upper reaches covered by snow, its lower depths enveloped in shadows. I estimated it to be about twenty meters across but in the light of our carbide lamps it was difficult to see the opposite wall. At first I thought it was the largest crevasse I had yet seen, but when I peered upwards towards the snow-capped opening, I thought I recognized the gargoyles that I had climbed past on that day long ago when the Italians had shelled our sled.

I knew it could only be bridged using the harpoon gun. I had Lizzola bring the device down from the storeroom. The barrel was dull with tarnish.

At this distance the harpoons would not stick firmly into the ice, so we had to fire several times before we had two lines that would support a man's weight. I elected to be the first one across, since I was unwilling to risk the life of anyone else if the harpoons didn't hold. Although I had lost much of my fear of heights since arriving in the Alps, I felt a thrill of terror as my feet left the ground and I slid on my chest-harness out over the void. Before my eyes a fine ice-down floated dreamily in the glare of my headlamp; on the walls around me danced weird shadows of ice-goblins and ice-gnomes. Over the noise of my breathing I could hear the faint rush of water far below and in the distance the glacier grumbled and snored. Far overhead a razor-sharp January wind whistled as it caressed the firn.

Once I had reached the opposite wall, I pounded pitons into the ice, disturbing the ethereal music of the crevasse with my tiresome hammer. Then I anchored a pair of stout ropes to start the bridge. I failed to notice, however, that the harpoons from which I was hanging were pulling loose, and without warning I found myself falling amidst a great crackling of broken ice, down into the darkness. Fortunately, I had a grip on one of the bridge-ropes, so I ended up swinging from it on one side and my harpoon-ropes on the other like a human pendulum. I felt a moment of panic which subsided into annoyance at the interruption of our work. Above me I could see Lizzola's anxious face peering over the edge.

"I'm fine, just pull me up!" I cried. But around me I sensed the eternity of cold darkness that was the inner soul of the glacier. Slowly, in halting stages, I was hoisted back up to the tunnel.

After constructing our bridge, we began boring into the glacier again and found ourselves at the point on the map where our tunnel would need to veer upwards. Here we would start building our *Himmelsleiter*[91] which would take us out of the glacier and onto the rocky slope at the foot of Mount Zebrù. It would mean that debris could be shunted into the crevasse, but it also meant that if anyone slipped and fell here, they too would slide over the edge into the murky depths. I ordered the men to don crampons and use safety ropes hooked to pitons in the wall.

Our progress was now much slower, even though we were digging through the more porous white ice, because it took longer to build stair-steps. I put Speilmann in charge of hauling supplies to the storerooms, to his obvious disgust, and made Sergeant Reinhardt the *de facto* foreman. The 60th Company was divided into two groups of one hundred men each, laboring away in teams of 25. Everywhere at the pithead picks were flying and ice chips filled the air. The noise was so dreadful that I feared the Italians would think a volcano was about to erupt, but our sentries reported no unusual activity on the Zebrù summit.

We spent the next week building a sturdy wooden bridge over the crevasse, not an easy task with only short beams, however in the end it was part suspension-bridge, part plank-and-rope, firm enough to cross if you were burdened with an ice-axe, a bag of grenades and a rifle. The whole area was illuminated now by electric lights hooked up to our generator back on the Ortler, a real feat of engineering but one which simplified our work

---

[91] Stairway to heaven

considerably. With the lights blazing it was possible to peer down into the crevasse and see where our ice shards were falling out of the debris chute to tiny heaps on the distant canyon floor.

The south tunnel posed a more complex challenge, and one which I should have predicted. The upper edge of the glacier was separated from the rock face, creating a peculiar type of crevasse called a *bergschrund*, with ice on one side and the mountain itself on the other. Bridging it was impossible because our harpoons would not penetrate the rock wall. Our only choice was to descend into the crevasse on ropes until we encountered the slope of the mountain, and from there chop a series of "buckets" into the rock, large hand- and footholds on which the assault team could scale the mountain.

Reinhardt secured the line while I abseiled into the fissure between rock and ice. Sliding down the rope, I eventually planted my feet on the ground, which was covered with loose scree and lit from above by an anemic winter sun. The ice here seemed older, mixed with soil and gravel, displaying its wood-grain striations. The mountainside was rutted and worn from the pressure of the glacier as it shouldered its way past. Far above me, I imagined the Italians standing guard on the ridge. Our men would need to be stealthy to catch the enemy unawares.

I jerked the signal line and the Salzburg miners pulled me back up into the ice-tunnel. Sergeant Reinhardt coiled the rope expertly between his hand and his elbow, awaiting my orders. He had adopted a lighter poise and a trace of a smile since Speilman had been sent away. Behind him a dozen men labored on a gallery in which the assault team would assemble.

"Who is working the mine now that all of you are in the army?" I asked him.

He frowned and shook his head. "Poles. Croats. A few Bavarians. But they use a new technique to get the salt out now, one that doesn't require much manpower. They flood the mines with water, wait for the salt to dissolve, then pump the saltwater out into pools which dry in the sun, leaving the salt. When the war is over, they won't need these men at Hallein."

"Well, I don't suppose you'll miss it much, anyway."

Reinhardt laughed. "Me, sir? I make violins. There will always be work for me, sir." He dropped the coiled rope on the ground and watched the men working on the gallery. Then he turned to me with an odd gleam in his eyes.

"May I ask you a question, sir?"

"You may."

"Do you pray, sir?"

I was astonished at this, and touched. This man who had suffered abuse and derision had the courage to strike up a conversation about religion, of all things. I smiled and looked him in the eye. He seemed relaxed, even friendly.

"In a word—no, I don't. May I ask why you want to know?"

"Sir, the reason is simple. All of us in the 60th pray, sir. But we have no rabbi and we have no place down here where a man can spend a moment of peace with God. There is a chapel, but—" Reinhardt paused. "Sir, I have seen the way you deal with Speilmann. I thought I might just ask, on behalf of the men, if you would allow them to create a space for religious observance."

"Where would one find a rabbi in the Alps, Sergeant?"

"There are two attached to the Third Battalion, sir, which is based in Trient. Perhaps you could ask Colonel Stutz for permission for one of them to visit? It would mean a great deal to the men, sir."

I frowned and kicked a chunk of ice over the edge. "I'm afraid, Sergeant, that Stutz owes me no favors. I'm far out of his good graces. As for creating a prayer room, you're welcome to do so, but you must invent another explanation for it if someone asks. A guard room or a tool nook or something."

Reinhardt nodded and gave me a careful salute. "Thank you, sir."

I was turning to leave when a question popped into my mind.

"Sergeant, tell me—why don't your men have rifles?"

Reinhardt winced. "We should have them sir, but Speilmann was concerned that it might interfere with his style of discipline if the men had guns, sir. He likes to think that men without rifles are helpless."

"I see. Well, this is a war, so I think soldiers should be armed, don't you?"

The sergeant shrugged and glanced down the corridor. "The 60th Company can fight sir, even without rifles." Odd, I thought, he's concerned about prayer but not about rifles. Prayer might be the only alternative, if one is unarmed and must face an enemy. Prayer offers a strength of mind and spirit from which courage blossoms in the belief that the Almighty will protect us and lead us to victory. Isn't that more useful in some ways than a rifle? Or is either one useless without the other? They are both tools with which we try to control our destiny, and perhaps we deceive ourselves—perhaps we can never control what happens. We are either victims of a callous God, or helpless denizens of an insensitive universe.

I walked back up to the main tunnel to get hammers and chisels that the miners could use to make bucket-holds in the rock. I could have sent a soldier to do this, but my real purpose was to find Speilmann and make sure he was not up to mischief. As I approached I spotted him chatting amiably with Stutz in front of the storeroom.

"Captain Fuchsheim," said Stutz, "I want to introduce you to a specialist who has arrived to attend to some security precautions." At this a man who had been crouched against the wall straightened up and saluted. "This is Lieutenant Friedrich Pockengruber, our explosives expert."

Uncomfortably, I eyed the infamous Pockengruber, whose services we had long ago dismissed as irrelevant. Stutz smiled at him. "Lieutenant Pockengruber will place explosives along the corridor so that it can be closed in the event of an enemy infiltration."

I had forgotten about this particular precaution. It was a tactical measure that I had once recommended to Colonel Buchholz, but which we had never had occasion to use. Now I was reluctant to leave explosive charges lying around for fear of accidents. It seemed improbable to me that the Italians would descend from their perch on Mount Zebrù to infest our tunnels. At the same time, I knew I could not argue with Stutz.

Pockengruber was a stout young man who spoke German with a Bohemian accent. His eyes stared off in two different directions so that even when he was looking at you, he seemed to be thinking about something else. He had a quick grin and a somewhat uncanny giggle that would sound off in response to nothing. I asked him how he was planning to set up the charges.

"I'll dig little pockets up high where the corridor walls meet the ceiling, see, and pack a few charges in there with an electric cable attached to a crank-box at the bridge. It won't be hooked up unless we hear an alarm, and even then we can set off the charges separately in case we still have men in the tunnels, you know. I'll place charges all along the south corridor, since that's where we'll want to close down fast and hard if the Macaronis get in." He giggled and fidgeted carelessly with a stick of dynamite in his hand. I found him intensely irritating.

"Well, make sure you mark each lead carefully so we know what we're blowing up," I said, without much confidence. I was not overjoyed at the thought of pulverizing all our hard work. Pockengruber took his stepladder and, climbing up on it, began chopping a little cubbyhole in the ice in which to place explosives.

"Sir, if I might make a suggestion?" I turned to address Stutz.

"Yes, Fuchsheim, what is it?" Stutz was clearly not interested in my suggestion.

"Instead of destroying the tunnels with explosives, what if we were to use gas instead? Nobody uses gas in the Alps, so the Italians won't be carrying masks. And because the ice doesn't absorb gases, we can use gas to effectively block off a tunnel and then clear it by opening the ventilation ducts. A few canisters can be sent up from Meran and stored at key points in the Citadel. It would be preferable to blowing up our *eisfestung*."

"I'll take it under consideration, Captain. Thank you."

Everything was nearing readiness far ahead of schedule, and so a few days later Lizzola and I took Stutz down to the south tunnel and showed him where a team of Salzburg miners was completing our doorway from the ice onto the rock wall, with neatly placed holes cut into the limestone wall so that the assault team could ascend to the Italian position. Franz was hoping to capture a machine-gun there and make use of it. Silence, surprise and hand grenades would be our main strategy, though, and this time (hopefully) there would be no pissing sentry to alert them to our presence.

The miners had built a sturdy ladder down into the *bergschrund*, and it seemed strange to exit the ice and descend to the solid earth, with a breeze blowing and sunlight making our eyes hurt. Above us the rock wall extended upwards into the sky and the sun painted the Zebrù the gentle rose tint of a church window. In spite of the warm colors, the wind was starting to pick up and the temperature was dropping. Stutz, Lizzola and I climbed back into the tunnel and went up the corridor towards the *Himmelsleiter*.

"We're preparing the artillery now," said Stutz as we walked back. "Tomorrow night they'll start showering the summit with high explosives. After four hours of that, Captain Pichler and his men will attack. This is sure to be a successful mission, and I know headquarters will be pleased. You may yet expiate some of your sins, Captain." Behind him, Lizzola gave me a clownish wink.

We reached the bridge over the crevasse, where Pockengruber was fussing with the crank-box detonator. "Leave it," I told him. "We don't need it now: the Italians will all be dead or captured in two days." Pockengruber shook his head sadly. "It's a lot of work for nothing, sir." I could have kicked him into the crevasse, but instead I returned to the south tunnel to see if Reinhardt's men had finished the last assembly point.

After a hundred meters the corridor split; the south tunnel led to Mount Zebrù, and the other part was the main passageway which had been dug several months ago towards the Eissee Pass, where we had been planning to create a periscope post but had never done so. We had not even extended the electric cable this far, and the corridor was pitch black and quiet, echoing faintly with the sounds of our workmen a hundred meters to the north. It was a moment of peace for me, deep in the heart of the frozen mountain.

I paused and closed my eyes to listen to the deep creaking of the ice around me, imagining its infinitesimal motion beneath my feet. What would it be like to make a home here, I thought, a comfortable Swiss chalet in the womb of the glacier, that would ride slowly down into the valley over the course of decades. Then there would be time to learn about this great crystal beast, to truly understand its mysteries.

My thoughts were interrupted by an odd noise, a chopping sound coming from behind me. I turned, and as I peered into the darkness of the unlit tunnel there was the faintest suggestion of a light. For an instant I was disoriented: had someone ordered work on this section of the tunnel? It seemed unlikely that they would have been digging here without my permission. Then I thought: the prayer room! Reinhardt has sent someone down here to start it, in this secluded section of the Citadel. It seemed logical, but I was curious nonetheless. I followed the corridor for a few meters. There was definitely someone there: a light bobbled up and down and I could hear the sound of an axe chopping through the ice. I was just about to call out when I noticed something that made my blood freeze.

The tunnel ended in a blank wall, where construction had stopped months ago. But the light was coming from the *other* side, through the ice.

Whoever was digging was not one of us.

I stood paralyzed, staring at the fractured light wavering behind the translucent wall. I could make out a man's figure, distorted by refraction and the shadows, but as I watched he swung his axe and the ice wall crumbled into shards. In the lantern light that flooded through the hole, I could see other dim figures behind him, holding rifles.

A sensation of panic gripped me with such violence that I couldn't breathe. I stumbled back against the wall of the passageway, my mind blank with terror. This was the enemy—this was doom. What could I do? I struggled to catch my breath and think.

Austrian soldiers in a tunnel inside the glacier.

The shadowy figure enlarged the hole, punching out the ice with the head of his axe. Behind him there were murmurs, the shuffling of boots, the sound of a bolt expressing a bullet into a chamber. He motioned with his hand up and down, a signal for the others to be quiet, and cautiously he stepped into the corridor. I realized that I was invisible to him where I stood, and with trembling hands I removed my Reichsrevolver from its holster. I hadn't fired it since St. Mihiel, and I could only hope that it was still loaded. With trepidation, I cocked the hammer.

The man with the axe picked up his lantern and moved forward, peering ahead into the shadows. Wary of the light, I stepped backwards and my boot came down on a pebble of ice. It slid a few centimeters; I staggered and caught myself quickly, but it was too late: the axe-man heard me and stopped short, then crouched in a defensive movement that all soldiers learn. Behind him, the others raised their weapons, short carbines as I could see now, designed for cavalry but ideal for fighting in closed spaces. I had a vision of myself tied to a post in front of a firing squad.

I raised my revolver and fired three shots in rapid succession, and the man grunted, dropped his axe and his lantern and pitched forward onto his face. In all these long years of war, it was the first and only time that I killed a man, but I barely had time to consider that. Behind him, the others began shouting and took aim at me with their rifles.

I stumbled backwards, lost my balance and fell onto my back, which surely saved my life as the Alpini opened fire. The noise was deafening; bullets gouged out holes in the ice walls and somebody roared, *"Avanti!"*[92] I scrambled to my feet, revolver still in hand, and sprinted up the tunnel towards the bridge. Behind me I heard boots clapping against the ice floor, and a rabble of voices drawing near. I turned and fired three more shots to make them hesitate, then my gun clicked on an empty chamber. I turned and ran on into the darkness.

I reached the intersection with the south tunnel and almost slammed headlong into Speilmann. He had heard the shots and had drawn his long-barreled revolver; in the gloom he looked like Old Shatterhand from a Karl May novel.

"Italians!" I shouted, skittering on the ice in panic. "They've broken into the Citadel—they're in the tunnel!" Speilmann squinted into the shadows behind me, then wheeled and ran down the south tunnel. Surprised, I mistook this for an act of cowardice until I heard him shout Reinhardt's name. I followed and as I reached them, he was giving the sergeant orders and gesturing with his gun.

"Bring your men up here, Sergeant—the Citadel has been infiltrated!" Reinhardt began organizing the miners into a column of pairs, each man armed with a pick-axe, a shovel or a hammer.

Speilmann turned to me, his features taut in the dim light. "Run—warn the others at the bridge!" he said, without any military formalities. The Salzburgers came trotting up the passageway, picks in hand, and filed past me.

"What? What are you doing, Lieutenant?"

"We'll hold the passageway," he replied. "You get Captain Pichler down here with his assault team. If we aren't outnumbered we can push them back into their own tunnel!"

"You can't! Your men are unarmed, Lieutenant!" I gripped his arm, trying to make him see reason. His men would all be killed. "Pull back to the bridge until—"

Speilmann shoved me hard against the wall of the corridor. "These are *my* men, this is *my* command! There isn't time to do anything else!" His eyes were like silver bullets in the flickering light. After a few seconds he stepped back and, cocking his pistol, he jogged off alongside his men.

Sergeant Reinhardt paused in front of me. "Sir, you should alert the Colonel. We'll keep the Macaronis pinned down."

"Without guns? Are you mad?"

Reinhardt grinned. "We will, sir. The Lord of Hosts is with us!" With that, he followed the last of the miners into the darkness.

This is suicide, I thought as I watched them go. Then it occurred to me: Speilmann *wants* them to die, but I

[92] Advance!

pushed the thought away. If Speilmann had some nefarious plan, would he be leading the charge? Whatever his feelings about Jews, he understood his duty. As for the miners, they were soldiers after all, even without guns.

Immediately I heard the first noises of battle—shouts, then an explosion of gunfire and the incongruous sound of picks and shovels hitting flesh. In spite of myself I ran towards the noise, confused and frightened but also fascinated. Ahead of me I could make out a struggling mass of bodies, illuminated in yellow half-light by their carbide headlamps and brightened intermittently by the muzzle-flash of a gun. Over the heads of the miners I saw Speilmann empty his pistol, firing point-blank into the knot of attackers; Reinhardt was wielding a captured carbine like a club as beside him, two of the Salzburg miners stepped over a pile of the fallen, their ice-axes raised like the Sicarii defenders of Masada battling Roman legionaries. The Italians were clustered too tightly to defend themselves and the first ones fell back against their comrades as the axes cut them open: the close air was filled with smoke, shrieks of agony and the sour smell of blood. The miners pressed forward, grimly methodical, and a note of panic rose from the Italian voices. Then a bullet ricocheted off the wall behind me, reminding me of the urgency of my message, and I took off down the corridor as fast as I could run.

After an eternity which was in reality only minutes, I reached the bridge over the crevasse. Ahead of me in the glare of the overhead lights, I could see Stutz and Lizzola approaching, their sidearms drawn.

"The Alpini have breached one of our tunnels!" I shouted, gasping for breath.

"We surmised as much, Captain," snapped Stutz, "Why aren't you assisting in the defense?"

I gobbled incoherently at this, trying to justify my role as message-bearer, but Stutz didn't care. He turned quickly to where Pockengruber was squatting next to the crank-box. "Attach the leads! Blow the south tunnel! They can't be permitted to enter!"

"We can push them out!" I retorted, furious. "Let me get to a telephone and call Franz!"

Stutz thrust his face at me. "What for? It's too late, anyway—the enemy has uncovered our secret. Secrecy was the Citadel's primary asset. Now stand back—"

"Wait!" I yelled, "Speilmann's miners are there—they're holding the tunnel!"

Stutz wheeled angrily at this. "Will you shut up, Fuchsheim! The miners are unimportant—they're Jews! Blow them up, Pockengruber! That's an order!"

I raised my empty revolver and pointed it at Stutz's face. I don't know what insane idea I had concocted—probably a wild gesture meant to buy a little time—but he snarled at me, "Surely you don't value the lives of some Jews over the security of the Ortler? You're suffering from cold-madness, Fuchsheim! Drop your weapon!"

My hand was trembling so violently I could hear the cylinder of my pistol rattling, but I held it steady, pointing it at Stutz's forehead. "Pockengruber! Disconnect those leads!" I croaked, in a voice hoarse with fear. I didn't dare remove my eyes from Stutz to see if the lieutenant was obeying.

Stutz's face screwed itself into a grimace of fury and he shouted: "You insubordinate *bastard!*" With astonishing strength, he swung his arm and struck my wrist with his own gun, knocking my revolver out of my hand and sending it spinning into the crevasse. He tried to bring his pistol around to use it on me, but I seized his arm with both hands. At the same instant Lizzola plunged forward onto Pockengruber, thinking, I suppose, that he was preparing to destroy everything, as indeed he was.

There was a blurred moment of struggle with the four of us swearing and bellowing, while behind us the clamor of battle echoed throughout the maze of tunnels. It lingers in my memory like an endless nightmare of rage and panic, with Stutz's twisted face an inch from mine, his hand striving to regain control of his gun, while I punched at his hateful visage with my free hand. My first blow bloodied his nose, and he gave me a hard shove in the direction of the crevasse. My wrist blazed with the pain of torn ligaments and my feet were sliding on the ice. In the midst of all this commotion, I heard Pockengruber giggle, and Lizzola let out a weary groan. And in the next instant the cavern around us erupted with a thunderous blast.

The explosion struck me like an invisible hammer coupled with an unearthly crackling roar, so overwhelming and vast that it might have been the very earth splitting open beneath our feet. The ice wall disintegrated into a shower of splinters and jagged boulders, while great dark fissures spread along the ledge as it, too, fell apart. All four of us were flung abruptly into space, tumbling into sudden darkness as the electric lights failed. I fell and fell for hours, it seemed, pitching head over heels, anticipating an impact that would smash my body into shards of diamond ice. All around there was a chaos of shattered wreckage striking me and filling the air with a hellish rattle, drowning out the cries of the other men as they too spun into the depths.

This nightmare haunts me even today—the helplessness of hurtling down towards an inevitable fate enveloped in blackness. I flail, I thrash, I writhe, but it does nothing to change my trajectory. In my recurring dream I realize with horror that my life is about to end, and then I awake with a stuttering gasp knowing that, had I slept one second longer, I would be dead.

XIII. The Way Out

I woke with an intense pain in my legs and for a moment I believed that I was back under the avalanche again, trying to dig my way back to the Payerhütte. Opening my eyes produced no result: the darkness was full and perfect. Only a few scattered sounds gave me a clue that I was lying at the very bottom of the crevasse: the occasional clink of something falling from above, and the faint but clear noise of rushing water.

I sat up to see what had happened to my legs and found that I was pinned down by a pile of broken ice chunks which were forcing my legs against a substrate of sharp chips that cut into my flesh. By wriggling, I gradually inched my legs out from underneath the rubble, and after an agonizing struggle I was free.

My body ached and tingled, but in the utter blackness I was unable to see the extent of my wounds. One of the things they had taught us in training back in Regensburg was to run your hands over your body to see what cuts or fractures you might have. Doing this revealed that my uniform was in shreds and that I was bleeding from a dozen small lacerations on my torso and face. I could taste blood from having bitten my tongue and my hair was sticky from a wound over my left ear. My wrist throbbed from Stutz's blow, but it seemed fully functional. Nothing life-threatening, and having determined that, I began to explore my surroundings.

I was lying on a pile of broken ice composed of small chunks and large jagged blocks, debris from our tunneling that we had tossed into the crevasse. Moving forward on my hands and knees I encountered the crevasse wall, smooth and impenetrable. Bracing myself against it, I stood up and began to feel my way along, until I stumbled over something and fell.

I felt cloth and then hair and realized that it was the body of a man. I ran my fingers over his face to see if I could identify him. All I could discover was that he had a moustache, so I felt his collar, which is where Austrian uniforms bear the insigne of rank. Here I encountered a quantity of something warm and sticky, which I presumed was blood, and I decided that the man was dead. I felt for pockets hoping to find matches, but his uniform was also torn and all I could locate was a metallic disc that felt like a watch.

At this point I heard the sound of someone coughing, far off to my right. In a hoarse whisper and spitting blood, I asked: "Lizzola? Pockengruber? Is that you?"

The coughing continued and then a voice said, "Help me get this thing off my chest." It was Lizzola.

I stumbled blindly along the wall until I touched him. He was lying under a massive ice boulder, far too heavy for me to lift, but under his back I could feel a space. Thrusting my hands underneath his arms, I was able to drag him out. He groaned and gasped beneath me.

"Are you injured?" I asked.

"What the hell do you think?" he replied irritably. "I feel like I've broken my back—it hurts like the devil. And I've torn my trousers, to boot. Good thing it's dark."

Good old Lizzola—he managed to make me laugh even in this desperate situation. I patted him on the shoulder, wishing that I could see his face. For a moment we sat quietly in the darkness.

"Where's Stutz and Pockengruber?" Lizzola asked.

"There's a dead man over there—I can't tell who it is." I raised my voice: "Stutz! Pockengruber! If you can hear me, answer!" My voice echoed eerily into the space above us, then there was only silence.

"How the hell are we going to get out of here?" Lizzola wondered.

"The bridge—it might still be fixed to the wall, with part of it hanging down. If so, then we can climb up. I can't think of any other way out." I strained my eyes, trying to see through the blackness, but it was complete. My head throbbed. Around me I could feel the cold of the ice walls closing in on us. I shivered in my ragged uniform.

"Well, I don't know about you, but…" Lizzola paused. "What's that sound?" The tremolo of splashing water was louder now; it was close by.

"It's ice melt from the glacier. It forms streams and lakes inside the ice. It must be underneath us."

"Ice melt in January?"

I was not in the mood to deliver a lecture on glaciology, but conversation was comforting. It reminded me suddenly of my Danish friend Rolf. "Most of the time the interior of a glacier hovers near its melting point. The pressure of tons of ice bearing down creates just enough heat to melt the lowest ice, and the water collects in rivulets, which follow gravity until it…" At that moment I had an epiphany. "That's it, Gianni! If we can find our way into the water, there may be a way out—going *under* the glacier!" Carefully I began stepping along the floor of the crevasse, listening for the water, hoping to locate an opening of some kind.

"Gianni, can you walk? Can you follow me this way? If there's a *moulin*…"

"A what?"

"A *moulin* is an opening that drains meltwater so that it empties out under the glacier. We must follow the sound of the water…"

"Go ahead, I'll wait here." Lizzola's voice sounded weak. I turned back and shuffled along the wall until I could feel his legs.

"You have to get up, Gianni."

At first he didn't reply, and when he spoke, I could hear the worry in his voice. "I can't move my legs, Captain." He gave a long sigh. "We'll die down here, won't we," he said quietly, as if talking to himself. I heard him stifle a sob.

"Let me explore the crevasse," I said, trying to think of some way to maintain hope. There had to be a way out—I just needed to look around. I had been trapped in the same kind of darkness after the avalanche and had managed to escape. "There may even be some way to climb up again. Don't despair," I said, patting him on the shoulder. "We're not here to die. We'll both live to fight again."

"Ha!" said Lizzola, and I guessed that he had managed to gain control over his fear. Then, after a pause he said, "*Welche lust, soldat zu sein!*"[93]

Overhead there was an abrupt noise, like someone's footsteps on gravel. I thought I heard a voice, then another. Looking up I could see a faint beam of light playing on the walls high above us—a carbide lamp. Lizzola must have seen it too, and began to shout.

"Who's there? Help us! We're trapped!"

The footsteps quickened and to our delight, the carbide lamp appeared over the edge of the crevasse. A few chunks of ice rained down on us.

"*Attenzione! Soldati nemici!*"[94] said a voice.

A second voice replied, "*Sono intrappolate, che buona fortuna!*"[95]

Lizzola bellowed : "*Vi preghiamo di aiutarci ad uscire da qui!*"[96]

There was a hurried consultation far above in the shadows. The blessed carbide lamp swung back and forth, causing shadows to dance among the echoes.

"They think we're Italians," whispered Lizzola hopefully. "They're trying to decide how to get us out."

"They won't be fooled once they get us up there," I said.

"Better to be a prisoner up there than a corpse down here."

The light reappeared and with it several faces peered down at us. The first voice said, "*Molto bene, questo è per voi, bastardi austriaci!*"[97]

From out of the shifting stripes of gray and blue an object came dropping towards us. I had only a few seconds

---

[93] What joy to be a soldier!

[94] Look! Enemy soldiers!

[95] They're trapped, what good luck!

[96] Please help us get out of here!

[97] Very well, this is for you, Austrian bastards!

to guess what it might be—food? Medicine? A hook attached to a rope? The object clattered at my feet and to my horror I saw it was an Italian hand grenade.

This time the explosion was in no way metaphysical—it blinded and deafened me even as I threw myself backwards, shielding my face and crying out in despair. I heard Lizzola scream, then the floor of the crevasse sank down beneath me and I dropped into another realm of utter darkness, plunging into a frigid, fast-moving current.

Numbed by the icewater, I fell, somersaulted, and was pushed and buffeted blindly down a long series of smooth slopes and curves before I finally reached a pool and was able to get a breath of air. Already I felt the cold entering deep into my soul, its icy fingers squeezing my tired heart, compressing my weary lungs. I knew there was no escape now: no matter where this under-ice stream would carry me, I no longer had the will or the strength to fight it. As my consciousness began to fade, I opened my eyes and found myself looking up at a rock wall weakly lit by the sun. Even as I raised my numb hands towards it, I felt my mind dissolve into oblivion.

I was dreaming about the Payerhütte, its grand sitting room with ancient oil-paintings on the walls where climbers and glacier-hikers would gather at the end of the day before a roaring fire to exchange stories of the Alps and the arctic. In front of the fire stood the seven Russians, their hands joined, singing a soft and magnificently loving hymn to the Creator, thanking Him for the beauty of the world and for the gift of life. The sweet-sour scent of pine logs filled the room, mixed with the odor of wet, unwashed clothing. I opened my eyes.

I was in a cave next to a crackling campfire, my hair and clothes drying in its friendly heat. On the other side of it stood Pyotr, Ivan, Vlad, and the other four whose names I never learned. Vlad's arm was tied to a splint made from a tree-branch, and Ivan wore a rag around his head to hide his missing eye. Seeing that I was conscious, they stopped singing and applauded.

"You don't die yet, good! God is good," said Pyotr.

They were shaggier and filthier than when I had seen them last, but they were free men now. We were in a spacious cavern lit by the leaping flames; behind me I could hear the splash of a waterfall. Two Mannlicher rifles leaned against a boulder. I sat up and rubbed my face: the skin had been scraped off my right cheek and it burned wickedly. My whole body ached. The Russians stood watching me, grinning through their scraggly beards. Pyotr made some remark and they all chuckled.

"Where is this place?" I asked, but Pyotr just shook his head. He had no map, and then it occurred to me that they must be heading south, towards the Italian lines. It had taken them over a month to make their way around the Ortler to the edge of the Sulden-ferner, where they must have seen me wash out from under the glacier, probably into their drinking-water. I was unable to guess what they had been eating here in the dead of winter.

I stood shakily up and limped to the edge of the cave. It was morning and the day was clear; a shy sun peeked at me from between two mountains. From where I stood I could see the tree line a hundred meters down, snow-covered pines like stalwart guardsmen. The Russians had obviously decided to camp here because it was easy to see if anyone was approaching. Far below in the valley I could make out a smudge of chimney-smoke from the village of Sulden. If I walked quickly, I would be there by late afternoon.

I turned and gazed at my Russian comrades who had rescued me. They were no doubt cold and hungry, but being free had restored their dignity: they stood facing me with calm fortitude. I regretted that I could not bring them with me to a warm house, to eat a good meal and sleep in a clean bed. But I was powerless; I didn't even have anything to give them. Then I felt in my pockets and found the mysterious metal disc that I had taken from the corpse at the bottom of the crevasse. It was a compass of very fine workmanship, with different colors for each of the four quarters and a silver needle. On the back, underneath a crust of dried blood, were engraved the initials "K. S."

I pressed it into Pyotr's hand. "Head south," I said, indicating the "S" on the face of the compass. "Then trade it for food."

"*Udáchi vam, moi droog*,"[98] said Pyotr. "God bless to you." I embraced him and stepped out into the snow. As I strode down the hill I turned to see the seven ragged, long-haired men standing together like neglected saint-icons in the mouth of the cave. Together they sadly waved good-bye.

[98] Good luck, my friend

XIV. Sunshine

I staggered into the village expecting no more than a change of clothes, a hot meal, and transport up to the telpher station so that I could return to my duties. But a medical orderly thought I should visit the hospital first, and since they were still treating hundreds of avalanche survivors, the doctor ordered me transferred to Trafoi. There the doctors felt that, in addition to dozens of scrapes, cuts and bruises, I may also have internal bleeding, so I was given a bunk in the outpatient barracks and told to report to the hospital the next day.

I found a military intelligence adjutant and reported that the Italians had entered the Citadel. "The situation's under control," he told me. "We're awaiting a report from Colonel Stutz." I considered telling him that Stutz was probably buried under a pile of ice chips at the bottom of a crevasse, but he was in a hurry so I kept mum.

When Hilda heard that I had arrived she came running into the barracks (where women were not permitted), took my face in her hands and kissed me. She clucked and cooed over every wound and insisted on taking me to the clinic for a thorough dressing change. I was both embarrassed and secretly pleased by all this attention, as it gave me ample opportunity to gaze into her sweet blue eyes and feel her soft hands on my skin.

Under this special care I should have recovered quickly, but that night I developed a cough and a fever and by morning I was deathly ill with pneumonia. I lingered at death's door for a week, then spent the rest of February in recovery. I joked to Hilda that Herr Death and I were becoming old friends, we had spent so much quality time together.

After a few days Franz came to visit me in the hospital. He told me that Speilmann and his men had managed to drive the Italians out of the Ice Citadel, but that much of the fortress had been destroyed by Pockengruber's explosions. The Jews had fought their way into the Italian tunnels where Speilmann was shot and killed. Sergeant Reinhardt led the surviving miners to the glacier surface and eventually to the Königspitz, where they were rescued the next day. At first I was astonished that they had not been slaughtered, but they probably knew how to fight in a tunnel better than the Alpini, who were mountain troops used to open spaces.

Rumor had it that Speilmann would receive a posthumous award. He was a cruel and unjust man, but he died like a soldier, and I am willing to honor him for that.

The bodies of Stutz, Pockengruber and Lizzola were never recovered, and I took on the task of writing to Lizzola's mother, describing his death as a valiant hero in combat, omitting to mention that he and I had been fighting our own men. Indeed, the full and complete story of what happened there in the Citadel has never been told to anyone except my darling Hilda, who was my patient audience for many decades and coaxed me through countless nightmares in which I fell repeatedly into that hellish maw.

Franz was promoted to Major, and he would have brought me back to rebuild the Citadel, but Stutz's request for an authentic engineer to take over the work on the Ortler was honored at headquarters, and once I had recovered my health I was ordered to return to my regiment in France. In any case, by mid-1917 the focus of action on the Italian front was at Görz on the Adriatic coast and the Austrians could spare no resources to refortify the Ortler. Franz himself was sent off in October to fight in the Battle of Caporetto, where he was wounded and died later in a field hospital, far from his mountain home. Most of our positions, including the Payerhütte, were abandoned in November of 1917.

As for my replacement, it was Leo Handl himself, although he didn't arrive on the Ortler until the fall of 1918, when what remained of the Citadel was being manned by starving men in rags. Handl did start designing a new installation, but it was never built, as by then the exhausted, heartsick nations of Europe had begun suing for peace.

Many years later I ran into him at some veterans' club in Innsbruck, but by then the Ice Citadel was a trivial event lost in history and we didn't have much to say about it. To tell the truth, I was a bit shy about my work, which was invention born of necessity and had none of the finesse that Handl employed under the Marmolata.

Had we been given an opportunity to exchange ideas during the war, I'm sure I would not have made the mistakes that nearly cost me my life.

It is one of my lifelong regrets that we never had an opportunity to build an *eisfestung* under the Vedretta di Monte Cristallo, to launch an attack on Bormio as Colonel Buchholz had envisioned. It was deep, pure ice with few crevasses in a slow-moving glacier; we would have been very snug and the Italians would have been genuinely startled. They were formidable opponents, and as much as we mocked them I believe the Austrians did in fact respect them. Certainly their vigilance kept us from catching them unawares as we had planned.

The rest of my story is unremarkable. I returned to Regensburg for two weeks of leave, visited my aging mother and was saddened by the deprivations forced on the German people by the war: everyone was hungry and the basic necessities of life were scarce.

I was sent back to my old unit, the 11th Infantry, which was bogged down under heavy fire in a trench near Arras, but I had the good fortune never to reach the front because in late April 1917, a troop train carrying me through Belgium was bombed and derailed, and I broke both my legs. I spent the next few months in hospital and then was reassigned when it became clear that I was no longer fit to charge across no-man's-land into enemy machine-gun fire. With mixed feelings of sorrow and relief I returned to Regensburg to oversee shipments of munitions until the end of the war.

All the young men I had grown up with were either dead or crippled: Dieter had lost his eyesight and both hands to a grenade and Ulrich had drowned when his submarine sank. Poor sweet Werner Einecke had gone to his death in a flaming Zeppelin during a bombing raid on London, leaving my sister Lisl a widow at twenty. She was a resilient young woman, however, and after the war she made a fortune investing in chemical cloth dyes, one of which was accidentally discovered to cure malaria. She never remarried and donated great sums to charity until her death a few years ago.

Anna von Murnau-Huffnagle's family's fortune was wiped out by the war, and Bertrand's failing eyesight created additional hardships for them, however he became an accomplished pianist and acquired some renown as an author of church music. He turned out to be, as Anna had predicted, a loyal husband and a devoted father. Anna herself shed her lofty airs and became a charming and very heavy middle-class matron who greeted me warmly whenever we chanced to meet at Adler's Apothecary. She had eleven children and died giving birth to the twelfth in 1935.

Hilda completed her volunteer service and in the early weeks of 1919 she arrived in Regensburg to become my wife. The war had disrupted Europe so much that I had to abandon any hope of finding work as a crystallographer, although I toyed with the notion of becoming a glaciologist. Instead I found an apprenticeship as a sculptor of wood and stone, an occupation which suited me much better and has brought me enormous satisfaction over the years. In the winter I have even attempted some ice sculptures, and have perfected the spring-operated dentist's drill that I observed the Gypsy using so many years ago in Munich. Alas, I have never yet been so bold as to attempt a rendition of Neuschwanstein Castle, but now that I have completed this memoir, it may become my next project.

Hilda and I became the proud parents of Georg and Stefan, two remarkably handsome and athletic boys who honored their father by visiting the Payerhütte in 1938, and reported that although the glacier had swallowed the Citadel long ago, many signs of our struggle remained: rusty strings of barbed wire, crumbling artillery pieces, and gun emplacements carved into the rock. During the last months of the Second World War my sons both gave their lives in the Ruhr Pocket. I would have preferred that they stay away from war, but it was an inevitable part of German life in those years and I know they were proud to die for their country.

So what was the legacy of the Ice Citadel? Did it bring us any closer to winning the war? No, although it undoubtedly delayed our defeat by giving us a safe and clandestine position to defend. But in the grand tapestry of the war the Ortler glacier was an insignificant corner, a skirmish compared to the Somme, Verdun and for that matter, the Isonzo. I take pride in the recollection that for one winter at least, over a thousand men were sheltered from the weather and from enemy fire, which allowed them to go home to their families. If God has any pity on soldiers, then perhaps I was His instrument.

Is there a God? It is no longer a question that concerns me very much, just as I am no longer afraid of death. Whether or not we understand our existence is irrelevant. What counts is to feel satisfied that our lives have been meaningful and just, and I am pleased with what I have done.

It has now been several months since I saw Colonel Buchholz extracted from the Ortler Glacier on television, and I believe I may be seeing the autumn leaves change color for the last time. The Colonel rests peacefully in his grave, and the glacier is still guarded by Gianni Lizzola and Friedrich Pockengruber, as well as Klaus Stutz. No doubt they will be uncovered by future generations when the sun melts the glaciers away entirely, or perhaps no one that cares will be left on our sweltering earth to put them in their graves.

That's enough. The story of the Ice Citadel is complete. I think tonight I will be able to sleep without nightmares or dreams of any kind, the kind of sleep that calms and soothes the soul, and puts the mind at peace.

Afterword: Truth, falsehood, and exaggeration in *Citadel of Ice*

This novel is based on events that occurred during the First World War, but as in all good historical fiction, the authors took a number of liberties with the facts. To start with the truths: The construction of the citadel closely models the true story of Leo Handl, an Austrian engineer who constructed an actual glacier fortress under the Marmolada Glacier, at about the same time, the winter of 1916-17, about 100 miles east of the Ortler.

In April, 1916, Italian troops captured the crest of the Adamello Glacier. Lieutenant Leo Handl, commander of the 9th Company of the 2nd Tyrolean Kaiserjäger Regiment, was attempting to reach an outpost with a group of men when they came under enemy machine-gun fire. Spotting a crevasse in the snow, Handl anchored a rope and led his men down into the silent underworld of the glacier. By luck, they landed on a sturdy ice bridge and made their way beneath the surface, beyond the Italian position to a spot where they could tunnel up through the firn and reach their destination. Handl was elated, and having been trained as an engineer he immediately began developing plans for exploiting the glacier. His brief venture into the crevasse demonstrated to him what glaciologists already knew—that the ice was not solid but, in the lower depths, where immense pressures cause melting and motion, there were fissures and caverns in the ice.

The construction of the Marmolada Ice Fortress took two years and created an installation over five miles long, housing over 1,500 men. In 1918, following the battle for the Marmolada, Handl was transferred to the Ortler where he began to design a new "city of ice". However, Germany's surrender in November canceled the project.

At the end of the war, Handl continued to study glaciers and their structure. During World War II he was sent to Norway, but due to his anti-Nazi convictions he was dismissed. Following the war, he spent almost a year living inside a Norwegian glacier, studying its movements. He died at Innsbruck on May 13, 1966. This book's descriptions of the design and construction of the Citadel are closely based on Handl's own writings. The Italians built a smaller but very similar *Città di Ghiaccio* under the Punta Serauta Glacier. They augmented their ice fortress with tunnels through the soft limestone of the mountain, many of which can be visited today.

Citadel of Ice opens with a reference to Colonel Buchholz's body being exhumed from the ice in 1966. In fact, a number of fairly well-preserved corpses of World War I soldiers have been removed from the ice, including three Austrian stretcher-bearers who were uncovered in 2004. Moreover, the Colonel's fall from a broken cable-car is based on an actual incident recounted in *Our Italian Front* by Martin Hardie and Warner Allen (1920):

"When the hauling wire breaks, the cars start headlong downhill and soon run off the cable into nothingness. On one occasion an officer managed to catch hold of the cable above his head before the car fell, and he was left there suspended in mid-air. Nothing could be done for him, and the men on the mountain watched him hanging there for half an hour until his grasp failed and he was dashed to pieces." (p. 75)

In the same vein, the recovery of two mountain-climbers from the ice, who had died in an avalanche in 1875 and were found 41 years later some three kilometers from the site of their death, is based on an identical incident described in Mark Twain's *A Tramp Abroad* (1880).

Now for the fiction. Melchior styles himself the inventor of trench warfare, which is a long way from the truth. Trenches had been used in Europe for centuries prior to World War I, and in France even before the first Battle of St. Mihiel, which Melchior describes his part in. Trenches and other earthworks had been built around Nancy in the weeks preceding Melchior's arrival there. However, Melchior is accurate in his view that antiquated military notions of tactics and strategy died hard in the early months of the war, and digging in was regarded as cowardly and antithetical to overrunning the enemy with "infantry charging across grassy plains, [officers] waving their blades as they cried encouragement to the men." Melchior's innovative construction of deep trenches with firing-steps, duckboards and wicker retaining walls develops his motivations as a builder of a "safe and clandestine position to defend… [where], for one winter at least, over a thousand men were sheltered from the weather and from enemy fire."

In building the Citadel, Melchior devises a miniature railroad (based on the Berlin U-Bahn) which hauls men and materials on sledges using an electric pulley, so that "a man could ride the sledge from the Payerhütte to the base of the Königspitz, wearing only a light jacket, in under an hour." Although this is certainly a very practical idea, no such system was ever developed in the Marmolada Citadel.

The attack on Hohe Schneide did in fact take place in the spring of 1917, almost exactly as it was described in the book, using a tunnel from the Naglerspitz outpost. Indeed, the attack was prematurely launched when an Italian sentry fell through the ice and alerted the outpost with his cries. The two areas of fiction here both concern the tunnel used by the Austrians. Although Melchior uses "magnificent" sappers "with titan blood" to complete the two-kilometer tunnel in forty days, the actual tunnel took over five months to complete. Secondly, Melchior's harpoon device to create rope-bridges over crevasses was pure invention and, given the fragile nature of ice, probably would not have worked as well as it did in the book. One reason it took the Austrians five months to build the real tunnel was that they constructed sturdy wooden bridges over each crevasse they encountered along the way. Melchior's description of the battle being won by hurling hand grenades into the outpost is accurate.

Melchior's story of his near death in an avalanche relies on actual descriptions of several avalanches, which took place on "White Friday" after a heavy snowfall in early December, 1916. Up to two thousand men on both sides were killed and most of the bodies were not recovered until the following spring. The fiction here is that the avalanche occurred on the Ortler slope near the Payerhütte. The Payerhütte is built on an outcropping of rock that was deliberately chosen by Julius Payer because it is out of the path of any avalanches.

Melchior's escape after being buried alive is derived from a true story recounted in *Die Stadt im Eis: Der Erste Weltkrieg im Innern der Gletscher* (The Ice Fortress: The First World War in the Interior of a Glacier) by Michael Wachtler and Andrea de Bernardin (2009). Six Austrian soldiers survived an avalanche that destroyed their barracks on the Gran Poz:

"In a corner of the company barracks, a hollow space between boards and cliff remained. But inside were half a dozen people who had escaped the avalanche's murderous embrace. And there was a small, iron guy among them, loaded with courage and energy, who wanted anything but a miserable death. He had only his knife, and he began to dig, moving along the broken beams and boards. It was an eternal darkness to them; they did not know whether time stood still or ran rapidly, whether they were buried hours or months. But the little man, whose name was forgotten like that of so many silent heroes, dug and drilled and comforted the others who were then crammed up behind him, and on the fifth night he came through to the air of the mountain, seeing above him the stars as though for the first time. And he cried for help, not for himself but for his comrades down there. They had been trapped for one hundred five hours." (pp. 98-99)

As for the Russians and the Jews, they are fictitious but plausible. Russian prisoners of war were used to haul equipment up the slopes and might very well have been assigned to shovel snow. The conditions in which they lived were every bit as atrocious as those described by Melchior.

Jews volunteered and were conscripted into the Austro-Hungarian armed forces, and often bore the brunt of bigotry and hatred, although not always. Melchior was enlightened for a Bavarian of that era, but he was by no means unique. As for Jews working in the Hallein Salt Mine, there is no record that there were many, if any, Jews there—the mine was operated mainly by Bavarians—but the mine's modernization by using water pumped in and out is factual.

A bit of trivia: Melchior von Fuchsheim's namesake, referred to in the book as a soldier in the Thirty Years' War who was "disliked and envied by all", is the protagonist of the novel *Simplicius Simplicissimus* by Hans Jakob Christoffel von Grimmelshausen (1668).

Finally, although there was never any Ice Citadel on the Ortler, it was in fact the scene of combat at the highest elevation in recorded history, over 3,900 meters above sea level. Man may spread out into the farthest reaches of the universe, but by his very nature, he will bring his weapons and bloodshed with him.

The Meaning of War in *Citadel of Ice*

The story of the Ice Citadel expresses a basic conflict between what it is to be a soldier and what we are as human beings. Like many other people throughout history, Melchior von Fuchsheim becomes a soldier not because he wants to fight, to kill enemies, or to defend the Fatherland, but because he wants the social prestige attached to being in the army. He enlisted at a time when there was no war and none in the foreseeable future. Even when World War I started, few people foresaw that it would evolve into a protracted conflict, so Melchior was astonished to find himself on the Western Front in a nightmarish situation beyond anything he could have imagined.

War occupies a peculiar place in our cultural imagination: it can be thought of and discussed in abstract terms as conflict, battle, the fray, melee, and so on—terms which don't conjure up anything much more graphic than a child's toy soldiers do. But Melchior discovered soon that being a soldier means killing other people, often at close enough range that you can witness the end of another person's life as a result of your actions, with fear, pain and suffering as "the enemy" realizes that he will never see another sunrise. Many soldiers take this in stride or become accustomed to it, temporarily at least. Some do not.

Melchior is a humanist: he not only cares for his comrades but seeks to protect Russian prisoners of war and even spares the life of an Italian who falls through the ice into a tunnel just as the Austrians are about to attack: "*Strange to say, we were unarmed except that I still wore my little Reichsrevolver in a holster. Now was the moment for action, and the four other men were in the tunnel behind me, so it would have to be my action. The Italian was bellowing his head off as he drew his bayonet, no doubt alerting the entire outpost, so I simply picked up a shovel and clapped him over the head with it. His soft wool forage cap did nothing to save him, and he slumped over, still clutching his blade.*" Instead of shooting the man, Melchior knocks him unconscious, and thus saves his life.

As soldiers, we voluntarily suspend the moral compunction that inhibits us from killing and injuring each other, and society largely accepts this. The difficulty comes when we must distinguish between necessary killing and that which comes from thoughtless habit or arises from bitterness and hatred which must be satisfied somehow by murdering innocents. Melchior feels compelled to do whatever he can to preserve life, even the lives of "the offal of mankind" as Stutz refers to them, the Russians and the Jews.

We think of war as being psychologically traumatic because of the terrible injuries and deaths that soldiers witness on the battlefield. In fact, witnessing this physical violence is less traumatic than the moral violence that it is the result of, the moral violence we do to ourselves when we decide that killing and injuring people is acceptable—as long as they are "the enemy". This is because we can suspend our belief that killing is immoral—but only temporarily. Eventually we return to the belief that the act of killing is wrong.

The psychiatrist Jonathan Shay, who treated Vietnam Veterans suffering from PTSD, writes in his book *Achilles in Vietnam: Combat Trauma and the Undoing of Character* (1994) that the single most important factor in the development of psychological trauma was the violation of a moral code. Soldiers suffering the most severe forms of psychological trauma nearly always felt that a wrong had been committed—against them or someone else, often in an act perpetrated by the soldiers themselves. This was far more traumatic to them than the horrifying violence of war. It was the cruelty and inhumanity that affected them most deeply.

Dr. Shay points out that soldiers feel an overwhelming loyalty to their comrades-in-arms, the men who fight alongside them, and often describe their fellow warriors as closer and more important to them than their own family members. In Melchior's words, "*What was the legacy of the Ice Citadel? Did it bring us any closer to winning the war? No, although it undoubtedly delayed our defeat by giving us a safe and clandestine position to defend. I take pride in the recollection that for one winter at least, over a thousand men were sheltered from the weather and from enemy fire, which allowed them to go home to their families. If God has any pity on soldiers, then perhaps I was His instrument.*"

Author's Note

This book was based on an incomplete manuscript that my father Robie Macauley was working on when he died on November 20th, 1995. He had planned to devote the last years of his life to writing a series of novels which he had been elaborating in his mind over the course of several decades. Unfortunately he was diagnosed with Non-Hodgkin's Lymphoma in February, 1995 and wrote much of this book while undergoing chemotherapy and radiation therapy. I accompanied him to the hospital on one occasion and watched him scribbling in a notebook in the time-honored ritual of pen and paper performed by so many other novelists throughout history.

He spoke to me lovingly of the concept for this book which I thought bizarre at the time; I dismissed the story of a citadel in the ice as rather implausible science fiction.

In 2010 my stepmother Pamela Painter graciously gave me the unfinished 112-page manuscript along with my father's research notes. Upon reading it for the first time I realized that this story was not pure invention, and a brief investigation revealed that during World War I, both the Austro-Hungarian Army and the Italians built extensive and sophisticated installations under the alpine glaciers, including the Ortler, and that much information about these works is available. Virtually everything in his manuscript was based on historical facts that my father carefully researched at the Athenaeum Library in Boston.

I decided to finish the book, adhering as closely as possible to my father's original conception and leaving most of his prose unchanged. I hope it approximates what he himself would have written.

--Cameron Macauley

About The Authors

Robie Macauley's career spanned 50 years during which he published fiction, *The Disguises of Love* (1952), *The End of pity and Other Stories* (1957), *A Secret History of Time to Come* (1979) and a popular textbook on writing (*Technique in Fiction,* 1966), plus over a hundred short stories.

He taught literature and writing at Bard College, The University of Iowa Writer's Workshop, The University of North Carolina, Kenyon College, The University of Illinois, Emerson College, and the Harvard Extension. During the final years of his career he was a Senior Editor at Houghton Mifflin Publishing Company.

Cameron Macauley has worked in humanitarian aid and international development since 1984. He was the Trauma Rehabilitation Specialist at James Madison University's Center for International Stabilization and Recovery, and now works in a hospital emergency room. He has published short fiction in *The North American Review, The Sonora Review, Prism International,* and *Quick Fiction.*

Printed in the United States
by Baker & Taylor Publisher Services